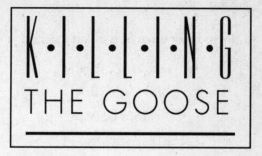

KILLING
THE GOOSE

K·I·L·L·I·N·G
THE GOOSE

FRANCES & RICHARD

LOCKRIDGE

M
Lockr

HarperPerennial
A Division of HarperCollinsPublishers

This book was originally published in 1944 by J. B. Lippincott Company.

HarperCollins books may be purchased for educational, business, or sales promotional use. For information please write: Special Markets Department, Harper-Collins Publishers, Inc., 10 East 53rd Street, New York, NY 10022.

First HarperPerennial edition published 1994.

Designed by R. Caitlin Daniels

Library of Congress Cataloging-in-Publication Data
Lockridge, Frances Louise Davis.
    Killing the goose / Frances & Richard Lockridge.
      p. cm.
    "A Mr. and Mrs. North mystery"
    ISBN 0-06-092515-9
    1. North, Jerry (Fictitious character)—Fiction. 2. North, Pam (Fictitious character)—Fiction. 3. Private investigators—New York (State)—Fiction. 4. Women detectives—New York (State)—Fiction. I. Lockridge, Richard, 1898– . II. Title.
PS3523.O243K5 1994
813'.54—dc20   93-510657

94 95 96 97 98 ❖/CW 10 9 8 7 6 5 4 3 2 1

• CONTENTS •

• 1 •

TUESDAY, MARCH 9, 7:30 P.M. TO 8:10 P.M.

AFTER almost two years of marriage you ought to be able to watch your wife across a room and experience no emotion whatever. William Weigand told himself this firmly, watching Dorian leave the table and walk half a dozen steps and sit down in a chair. That, obviously, was essentially unexciting; it was not even difficult. Thousands of women could do it without falling over anything. Hundreds of women, having accomplished this maneuver, would sit with their feet flat on the floor and their knees together. Assuming that Dorian Weigand was exceptional, as he unhesitatingly assumed she was, it remained ridiculous to believe that she had proved it by walking across the Norths' living room without falling flat and sitting in one of the Norths' chairs without falling apart.

And yet, Weigand realized, his face was rather fatuously decorated with what could only be called a beaming smile. The smile reflected his continued glad surprise that Dorian Weigand lived and moved; that she moved with the unconsidered grace of a first-rate athlete or a medium-rate cat; that, watching her, one realized suddenly what the human animal could do if it put its mind to it. Not, certainly, that Dorian was consciously putting her mind to it. Her grace came, presumably, from some special sense of balance which she possessed without willing it, as

1

some people possessed unusual hearing and others the ability to see to uncommon distances.

After two years of marriage, or almost two years, you should grow accustomed to these minor superiorities in the woman you had married, and grow able to look at her reddish brown hair with only matter-of-fact approval and not any longer fall to speculating in the middle of even your own conversation as to whether there was really a just perceptible tint of green in her eyes. From all he had ever heard of marriage, and from a good deal he had seen, people very quickly got over these small, gratifying surprises and learned to take other people comfortably for granted. It was supposed to take about six months. The supposition evidently was wrong.

"Flagrant," Pamela North said, out of the small silence in which Bill Weigand had been living. "Isn't it, Jerry?"

"I don't know," Jerry said. "I think he's sort of cute, Pam. So round-eyed and everything."

Weigand looked at them, smiling slightly.

"Hey," Jerry North said. "Hey, *Bill!* We're here."

Weigand looked at them. He said he was afraid of that.

"I felt all along there was something," he said. "An influence or something. I was just thinking—"

"Don't tell us," Pam commanded. "I don't think—"

Dorian rested her head against the back of the chair and looked up at them, her eyes not more than half open.

"I hope you're all having fun," she said. "Lots of fun, darlings. Don't you, Bill?"

"Right," Bill Weigand said. "Why not?"

Probably, he thought, he should feel embarrassed. But the Norths were not really embarrassing. And he was too comfortable, in any case, to achieve embarrassment. And they would drop it in a moment, anyway.

Pam North sat in the chair by the fire and tucked one foot under her. She moved well too, when you thought of it. But her mind always seemed to be moving faster than her body. Probably that was why she sometimes picked things up before she had hold of them. Bill Weigand looked away from Pam, who seemed almost laughing, and found Jerry looking at him. Jerry was smiling faintly and he nodded slowly. But there were no words to go with the nod. Jerry merely said, "Coffee, everybody?"

Everybody had coffee in small, white cups. Jerry looked at his cup and sighed.

"Remember brandy?" he said. "Cognac? Armagnac? Way back?"

"That reminds me," Pam said. "News. It must be time for news."

Jerry put his cup down and reached out to the radio at the end of the sofa. He turned a knob and pressed a button. The radio said nothing for almost thirty seconds. Then it said—

"—to own those small things which have always been man's life. The little house and the grass in front of it and earth to dig in. The little store. A farm. To hold these things in the old way and—"

"Darlings," Dorian said, sitting up, "not Dan Beck. Do we have to have Dan Beck?"

The anxiety in her voice was exaggerated. But it was not simulated.

But almost before she spoke, Gerald North's long fingers had twitched at the radio's dial.

"Here is a summary of the headline news," the radio told them. "On the Eastern Front—"

They listened to the summary of the headline news and were silent a moment thinking about it. Jerry turned the radio off.

"I'm sorry," Jerry said. "It was set on the dial instead of the button. So we got dangerous Dan and little houses for all mankind. *And* every man a delver. *And* the old country store at the crossroads."

"Is he?" Pam North said. She looked from one to the other. "Because I think yes," she said.

"Well," Weigand said, slowly. "There's something in it."

"There's *something* in everything," Pam said. "Jerry likes to grow corn. I like to keep house." She paused and considered herself. "In theory," she added. "With somebody to wash the dishes, except very good glasses with a very clean, dry towel and very hot water. Of course there's something in it."

"And it's dangerous," Dorian said. "Isn't it, Jerry."

"Yes," Jerry said. "I think it's dangerous. I think the great Dan Beck is—well, dangerous. Because he promises things people will never get. Most people. Because he makes them believe—really believe—that we can go back."

"However," Weigand said, "we've got to go somewhere. And the world is full of promises—and beliefs. Some of the things—the things we're promised—sound worse than Beck's things."

Jerry nodded and said most of them did. And that there was no harm in remembering other ways, and thinking they had been good ways. But it was dangerous to promise people we could go back to them, when in fact we could never go back. Even if it would be a good idea. Even if you saw quite clearly that there had been a wrong turn back there somewhere, so that now what we called "private property" was not really the old private ownership, but for the most part the possession of pieces of paper with printing on them—so that now we confused the word and the fact.

"But really," Jerry said, "it's what he does with the ideas—with Herbert Agar's ideas, and the ideas of the old liberalism, and what was good in laissez-faire. You can demagogue any good thing, and he does."

"You listen to him," Weigand said.

"I—" Jerry began.

He became conscious of Pam's voice, engaged, it was evident, in an entirely different conversation.

"—helps me," Pam said. "He loves to, really, but it drives the salesgirls mad. Because he just looks through them and—"

"—listen to him sometimes," Jerry said. "Enough to know that he doesn't mean to take everybody in. Enough to hear him talk about 'native American stock' and not mean the Indians and—"

"—Bill too," Dorian said. "But he won't. I can't get him into one—"

Jerry wrenched his attention back and came in on the middle of a sentence from Bill.

"—and so, eventually, 'protestant' and 'white' and finally something like 'Aryan' although of course—"

"—six of them," Pam said. "And he just shook his head. But the seventh—"

Jerry ran a hand through his hair. He found he had, now, come in on the middle of one of his own sentences.

"—so we build a wall around it," he heard himself saying. "And take care of the non-white, non-protestant, non-nat—"

"—with murders what they are," he heard Pam saying. "And no regular hours—"

Jerry stopped abruptly, partly because he had forgotten what he was saying; partly to hear more clearly what seemed to be the statement of Pam North that murderers did not keep regular hours, but built a wall around them. It occurred to Jerry that he was getting confused.

"By the way, Bill," Pam said, "speaking of murders. How are they?"

It occurred to Jerry that Bill had some minutes earlier abandoned the problems raised by the great Dan Beck. At any rate, Bill answered without seeming to come out of a fog.

"Routine," he said. "Very routine, I'm afraid, Pam."

"I don't see how it can be, ever," Pam said. "If I were going to murder somebody it would be—oh, tremendous—overwhelming. Or going to be murdered. You're getting professional, Bill."

"Getting?" Bill Weigand repeated. "I've always been professional. A professional murderer-catcher." He looked quickly at Dorian. There had been a time when the thought of him as a catcher, even of murderers, made her eyes go suddenly blank and far away. But now she smiled in reassurance. "I'm a policeman, with the outlook of a policeman. They're routine if they're easy, with a familiar cast. The boy whose girl ditches him and who kills her in a rage. The wife who gets tired of her husband and hits him with something heavy. The man who kills for insurance. And the mobsters, who just kill when they get annoyed. Things like that."

"Gangsters are dull," Pam agreed. "Or they always sound dull. Are they, really?"

"Yes," Bill said. "Boring—and dangerous as hell. You wouldn't like them, Pam."

"And nothing else?" Pam insisted. "No stories to tell?"

Bill Weigand, lieutenant of detectives, acting captain of the Homicide Squad, started to shake his head. He thought better of it. He said he would give them an example—Type A. From today's blotter. Emotionally interesting—possibly. If you went into it from that side, like a novelist. Routine, if you went into it like a policeman. A girl killed by a boy who was in love with her, after a quarrel, because he thought she was two-timing him. The last, a guess. But no other guesswork.

The girl had been a filing clerk, doing routine chores in a large investment house. She had been about nineteen—slight and dark-haired, pretty because she was young; talking, they said, with the suggestion of a Southern accent. The police had never heard her talk; when men from a radio patrol car pushed their way into a confused, excited crowd in the coffee shop of the Hotel Greystone on Madison Avenue, a block above Madison Square, Frances McCalley had been beyond talking. She had been a collapsed object in a corner of a booth, with blood around her and a gash in her throat; she had been dead only a matter of minutes, those who found her thought. She had died, they could guess, a few minutes after she had pushed back a plate which still, when the first policemen arrived, held the remnants of a bacon and tomato sandwich on toast. Whoever had eaten with her had had liver and bacon. The plate was near the other plate. Some blood had splattered on the green composition top of the table; there was a great deal of blood on the green composition floor under the girl's body. A cut throat bleeds.

"That was what they found," Weigand said. "That and girls who knew her and were ready to talk. A girl who had stood beside her at the counter—it's a cafeteria—and seen her put the bacon and tomato sandwich on her tray; seen her take a custard cup for dessert when she couldn't get a baked apple because they were out of baked apples; seen her talking to the boy who killed her."

"The boy—?" Pam repeated.

Weigand nodded. The boy who killed her—the boy who was in love with her and thought, they supposed, that she was two-timing him. Or was, for some other reason, emotionally disturbed to the point of murder.

There had been no problem about finding him; it was all routine.

Three or four girls knew him by sight; one knew him by name. She had bumped into him a few minutes before the girl's body was found. He was leaving the coffee shop—going out so rapidly that he left the revolving door spinning wildly. The girl—one Cleo Harper—had been exasperated and looked after him, ready to say what she thought of him if he stopped. He had not stopped; he had gone on violently, his face, as she subsequently remembered it, "terrible—all full of hate." She also recognized him as Franklin Martinelli, Frances McCalley's friend. She had wondered why he was so angry and had suspected a quarrel between the two. She had told her story to the police after Frances's body was found. It was found, she said, about ten minutes after she had seen the Martinelli boy, his dark face twisted, hurl himself out of the coffee shop.

That would have been enough—that and the suspicion held by the police that Italians are violent in emotional upheavals and apt with knives. It alone would have been enough to set them after young Martinelli. They did not need the statement of two girls in the next booth that they had heard angry voices through the partition and that the girl's voice stopped suddenly.

Mullins had it pretty much in hand by the time Weigand got to the cafeteria, late because he had been at lunch himself and there had been delay in reaching him. The boy had been sullen and stubborn—and he had seemed to be shocked and overcome with grief. Perhaps he was; murderers sometimes were, especially when they had killed violently, without thought. He had denied, of course, that he had killed at all. For a time he had denied the quarrel; then he had admitted it, but still insisted that they had made things up before he left and that then Frances was alive.

"She smiled at me," Franklin Martinelli had insisted. "I tell you she smiled at me."

He had left hurriedly because he was already late at the loft-factory where he worked as a shipping clerk. He had not wanted to be fired. Perhaps he had looked worried because he was late, and because he didn't want to lose the job. He was trying to save all the money he could before he went into the army, and he had to have the job. But anybody who said he looked scared or angry was making things up. Everything was all right between him and Frances.

"She smiled at me when I left," he said, over and over. "She looked happy and smiled. Everything was all right."

But nobody believed him. They made him tell it over and over again and shook their heads and said, "No, buddy, it wasn't that way." "Come on, son," they said. "Spill it. You may as well spill it."

They did not hit him, with fists or rubber hose. They kept him sitting on a straight chair with a strong light on him and they made him tell it over and over again. And over and over again he told them he had not killed the girl; that she was alive and smiled at him when he left the restaurant; that he ran out of the restaurant, with the door whirling behind him, because he was late back at his job.

"All right," they said. "Tell it over again, fella."

They looked at each other and let heavy disbelief show in their faces; they laughed a little, contemptuously. Weigand said that he had sat in on it for a while and decided the boy was going to hold out for a long time yet and left it to Mullins. When the boy broke and told it, Mullins would call him.

"It's horrible," Pam said. "If he didn't do it—it's horrible. Because if he didn't do it, it was bad enough without that."

"Right," Weigand said. "If he didn't do it. Only it's a hundred to one he did do it—two hundred to one. And it was horrible about the girl. She was—well, she was sort of a pretty girl. And very young, Pam."

He looked at her and then he looked at Dorian.

"Right," he said. "It's tough—it's too damned bad. And do you want us to let him get away with it? Is it all right he stuck a knife in the kid's throat?"

He spoke rather harshly, for him, and rather defensively. Dorian smiled, not happily.

"It's just the poor kids, Bill," she said. "The poor young kids. We know you can't do anything else."

Bill Weigand, who had been leaning forward, looked into her face and into Pam's, and then he sat back and for a moment said nothing. When he spoke, it was in his normal tone.

"So," he said. "There you have it. From the police point of view—routine. A poor fool kid kills a girl he's in love with because he gets mad at her. And we—"

He did not finish, because the telephone bell rang. Jerry crossed the room and dug under a table where the telephone lived. It seemed to be caught on something, and he jerked. There was an indignant yow and Toughy came out, his tail enlarged. He stopped, looked at Jerry reproachfully, scrambled suddenly on the carpet, ran headlong across the room, leaped to the windowsill, crashed into the venetian blinds, bounced, landed halfway across the room, leaped convulsively into the air, dashed furiously at the sofa, climbed the back of the sofa and suddenly sat down. He began to wash his back. Toughy had awakened.

"My," Pam said. "His tail must have been caught in the telephone wire, or something. Isn't he strange?"

Roughy came into the living-room at a dead run, evidently abandoning the bathtub in which, for days, she had decided to live. She leaped over the radio, put both forelegs around Toughy's neck in an embrace and rolled with him to the floor. Toughy landed underneath, flat on his back with a plunk. He lay there and began to eat one of Roughy's ears. She hissed at him.

"Children," Pamela North said. "Be good cats." She explained to Dorian. "They're showing off, now," she said.

"Please," Jerry said from the telephone. "I can't—Oh, Weigand. Yes, he's here."

He beckoned with the telephone and Bill took it. He said, "yes" and "yes."

"All right," he said, "we'll just have to keep after him. I'll be along after a while. Anything else?"

He listened.

"What difference can it possibly make," he said. "However—"

He listened again.

"We knew that," he said. He listened further.

"And that," he said. "But thank the good doctor. Tell him he's very thorough." He started to cradle the telephone. He thought better of it.

"Mullins!" he said. "Hold it. Don't tell him that last." He waited.

"Right," he said. "In a couple of hours. I'll be here, meanwhile."

He cradled the telephone this time and crossed back to his seat on the sofa. They looked at him, enquiringly.

"Mullins," he said. "The boy's still holding out. The M.E. says she died about an hour before his man saw her, which would make it about a quarter of one. He knew what she had to eat. But so did we. Bacon and tomato sandwich, coffee, a—"

Suddenly he broke off, with an odd expression in his eyes. And then, softly, he said that he would be damned. He said it slowly and with some surprise. Then he was back at the telephone and dialing; then he was speaking into the telephone with a new tone in his voice.

"Weigand," he said. "Get me Mullins." There was a moment's pause. Then Bill Weigand spoke again. "Mullins?" he said. "Read me that again." He waited. "Are they sure?" he asked. He did not wait to be answered. "Don't ask them that, Mullins. Of course they're sure." He held the telephone for a moment at a little distance from his ear and tapped on the table with the fingers of his free hand. Then he made up his mind.

"Mullins," he said. "Let up on the boy. Hold him; put him in storage somewhere. And give him a cigarette and something to eat." He listened. "Right," he said. "Screwy is the word for it, Sergeant. I'll be along."

He put the telephone down and turned and looked at the others, but not as if he saw them clearly.

They waited for him to speak and when he did not, Pam spoke.

"What's the matter, Bill?" she said. "Is it blowing up on you? Didn't the boy do it?"

Weigand shook his head, slowly.

"I don't know," he said. "Mullins says it's screwy. You see—she'd eaten a baked apple."

He looked at the others, who looked back at him, evidently unenlightened. He gave them time; then he explained.

"It's a catch," he said. "I told you we knew everything, even what she had to eat. Maybe we knew too damned much. You see, she didn't have any baked apple. She wanted one, and there weren't any. So she took a custard. And now the M.E.'s office finds out she had a baked apple. Where'd she get it?"

"Probably," Dorian said, reasonably, "she went back to the counter and had another try and got a baked apple. I don't see—"

"Right," Weigand said. "I don't either. Not certainly. Maybe she did just that. And maybe somebody else was there and brought her a baked apple. Because the kid—this Franklin Martinelli—swears she didn't leave the table while he was there, and he's confirmed—a dozen times, probably, that she had a sandwich and a cup of custard and coffee."

"But," Jerry said, "you didn't believe him before. Why believe him now?"

Weigand nodded, and said it was a point. Maybe the Martinelli boy was a very bright boy; maybe he'd figured something out. But he would have to be very bright to know that it would matter whether Frances McCalley had a baked apple with her lunch.

"It would take figuring," Bill said. "I doubt whether the kid figures that way—figures that if she didn't have a baked apple with her regular lunch, didn't leave the table during the time he was there, showed up with a baked apple in her stomach—that all this would mean maybe he didn't do it after all." He paused, considering. "It's funny," he said. "Where did she get the apple?"

"Somebody brought it to her," Pam said. "Maybe the person who killed her. Maybe somebody else. Or did she leave the table, but perhaps after the boy had gone, and get the apple herself. Could she see the counter? Where the things were, I mean? From where she sat?"

Weigand shook his head. He admitted he hadn't noticed.

"Because," Pam amplified, "maybe she saw somebody bring the apples in. And went and got one. Anyway, it isn't so routine as it was, is it? Perhaps it wasn't the Martinelli boy."

"Right," Weigand said. "So we're giving him a rest. And instead of sitting here, basking comfortably, telling sad stories of the death of gangsters, I've got to go around and get to work. Tracing a baked apple from—from the counter to the morgue."

"Bill!" Dorian said, firmly. "For heaven's sake, darling!"

Bill smiled.

"Nevertheless," he began. Then the telephone rang again. He looked quickly at Jerry, who waved a hand; he said, "Lieutenant Weigand speaking" into the telephone. He looked pained and held the receiving end a couple of inches from his ear.

He looked at the others and made the word "Inspector" with his lips. He said, "Yes, Inspector?"

He listened. He whistled softly. He said, "Right." He listened again.

"Right away, Inspector," he said. "But how about the McCalley case? In the Greystone's coffee shop." He listened. "No," he said, "I'm not sure it is. Something else has come up. A question of a baked apple."

Across the room they could hear the telephone splutter. Grinning slightly, Weigand held it farther from his ear.

"Right," he said. "But I'm not joking. I'm not sure it's the Martinelli boy, and the reason is a baked apple. However—"

He listened further, said, "Right" again, and replaced the telephone in its holder. He stood up.

"Inspector O'Malley," he said. "In person. From a house on Gramercy Park. They found Miss Ann Lawrence dead there. Somebody hit her with a poker. A brass poker, O'Malley says."

"Lawrence?" Pam said. "Ann Lawrence? Ought we—"

Weigand shrugged. He said the Inspector seemed to think so. Apparently she had been important, since the Inspector went around in person; apparently she had money, since she lived in a house—her own house—on Gramercy Park. And apparently the Inspector was now ready to turn it over to Weigand.

"To assist," Weigand explained, gravely. "To do the routine. And after I get there, our O'Malley will decide he has already done the important thinking, got everything well in hand, and had better leave detail to me. So he will go and play poker with the boys."

Weigand was amused, not aggrieved.

"He's got a right," Dorian said.

"Sure he's got a right," Bill told her and both of them smiled.

"And the other one—the girl in the cafeteria?" Pam asked. "What about her?"

Mullins, for the time being, Weigand said. After the time being they would see.

"And now," he said, "I've got to join the Inspector."

Pam said it was too bad. She said she had been thinking of a rubber of bridge. But she did not, and Weigand was a little surprised by this, suggest that they all go along and help. She said they would see Dorian got home and to come back right away if somebody confessed, or Inspector O'Malley had it all solved, and that it was nice that the department had let him come at all.

After he had gone, Pam stood for a moment with her back to the closed door, and found Jerry looking at her speculatively. He was, she decided, puzzled. She waited for him to mention it.

But after looking at her, he apparently decided to let sleeping issues lie, because when he spoke he seemed to be skirting murder rather elaborately, and to be about to return to the subject of Dan Beck, as if he had never left it. Pam waited, politely, until he reached what might be the end of a sentence. Then she spoke.

"I think," she said, "that we'd better all help Sergeant Mullins. About the baked apple. Because it's going to confuse him dreadfully, without Bill. And because—because the girl was just a baby, really. Don't you think?"

"No," Jerry said, firmly.

"I do," Pam said. "I think we ought to."

• 2 •

TUESDAY, 8:10 P.M. TO 8:55 P.M.

IT HAD begun to snow, which was discouraging, because already there had been enough snow; because, against all evidence, one persisted in thinking of March as one of the months of spring. It was not cold, which was something; you might think of the large, stolidly falling flakes as a spring snow. There were a great many of the flakes and they were falling heavily, but without hurry; it was a tired snow. It was forming slush on the sidewalks and streets; it had plastered on the top of Weigand's car, and on the cold hood and on the windshield. Weigand flicked snow from the windshield with heavy gloves and got into the car. The motor started, with no enthusiasm, and the snow on the hood almost at once began to melt.

From inside the car, looking out through the smeared glass, the snow seemed heavier than it had before. It was a soft, moving, implacable wall around the car. When Weigand switched on his dim lights, their faint radiance bounced off the snow. It seemed improbable that a car could move through the white wall. For a moment, Bill Weigand felt shut off from everything, in a new, strange world. Then he switched on the windshield wipers. They floundered against the snow, pushed it aside. They began to clear spaces on the glass, each space looking— Weigand decided—like the amount of the national income spent for the war effort.

14

Starting, the car skidded in the slush. Weigand coaxed it to a straight line and eased it through the half-melted snow, not hurrying. He turned up Fifth Avenue and, after a few blocks, crossed to Fourth. At Nineteenth he turned east and, when he reached the park, groped slowly around it. The snow was heavier than ever when the car moved; the soft white wall turned into a maelstrom, sweeping and twisting toward him, swirling up in front of the windshield and over the car. It was dizzying. Weigand did not look for street numbers, but watched for a small cluster of cars. On the north side of the square, east of Lexington, he found it and nosed the Buick in. A uniformed patrolman started forward, identified the car and made a gesture which was, in its fashion, a salute.

Weigand stopped on the sidewalk for a moment and looked up at the house. It was a small house, as New York houses went—narrow, three-stories, sedate. Brass rails, which probably glistened under more favorable conditions, curved on either side of the few steps which led up to the door, off-center in the façade. It was a pretty little house, Weigand thought, and went up the steps. He pushed against the door and it opened quietly, softly resisting against its pneumatic check. There was another uniformed man just inside, much drier and more contented. He saluted with more spirit and said, "Hello, Lieutenant. The inspector's upstairs."

The entrance hall was wider than he would have expected. Off it, on the left, was a small room which was, he decided, dedicated to the Capehart which seemed almost to fill it. Ahead, the entrance hall ended in a large room which occupied what remained of the first floor of the house. It was a comfortable room and there was a man in it, sitting in a chair and staring at the carpet. A third uniformed man stood beside him, watching him and not saying anything. Weigand's eyebrows went up slightly.

At his left, just inside the big room, Weigand found a stairway, curving delicately upward. He curved up with it, as delicately as seemed appropriate. It conducted him into a hall between two rooms and then he followed his ears. Deputy Chief Inspector Artemus O'Malley was in the larger of the rooms, which fronted on the street. He was supported, and attended, by several men. One was, Bill Weigand recognized, the precinct homicide man and another was a sergeant on his staff. There were two more men from the headquarters squad and Detective Stein was on the floor, measuring something with the folding rule. The distance from somewhere to the chalked outline which was, roughly, the outline of a human body. Not a large body, evidently. Stein was marking the spot.

"Well, Lieutenant, where the hell have you been?" O'Malley said. O'Malley was large in all dimensions and red-faced and emphatic. "Not," he added, "that it matters a damn. All cleaned up."

"Good," Bill said. "Congratulations, Inspector."

O'Malley looked at him and there was a momentary doubt in the inspector's unmelting blue eyes. He saw nothing in Weigand's face to support suspicion.

"Open and shut," Inspector O'Malley said, driving it home. "None of this fooling around. None of this fancy stuff. Routine, Lieutenant."

Weigand, involuntarily, said, "Oh." Inspector O'Malley said, "Huh?" with great emphasis.

"Nothing," Weigand said. "It was good work, Inspector."

"Nothing to it," the inspector said, his tone indicating that there had been, particularly, nothing to it for him. What Weigand would have done with it, the tone indicated, was another matter. "A set-up. Guy who was going to marry her did it. They had a quarrel and—slosh! Hit her with a poker. Brass poker, stuck in one of those gadgets."

He pointed at the gadget, a rack for fireplace tools. There was a shovel in it and a bellows dangling from a hook and what was, evidently, intended to be a hearth brush. There was no poker. That would be because the lab boys had it, checking the prints; setting them for photographs. There was no body, either. Dr. Francis, assistant medical examiner—or another—would have that.

"Well," Weigand said, "in that case, I'd better get back on the Greystone killing. There's a funny sort of thing about—"

Inspector O'Malley, interrupting, told Weigand not to be a fool. He'd fooled around enough with that already.

"Twice as long as you needed to," he said. "I got the reports. The kid did it. This—this—"

"Martinelli," Bill told him. "Franklin. But—"

O'Malley said there were no buts about it. It was as simple as this one. "This one right here," he specified. It was, further, small-time stuff. This wasn't.

"Decided I'd better handle this myself," O'Malley said. "Considering who she was, and everything. Thought it might be complicated. Screwy. Some of these—But as soon as I looked around and listened to the old gal downstairs I saw it was a set-up."

"Does he admit it?" Bill asked. "The man who was going to marry her. Whoever he is. The guy downstairs, I suppose."

O'Malley said, yeh, the guy downstairs. And no, he didn't admit it. "Yet." He would, though.

"I'll leave that to you," O'Malley said. "Nothing you can't handle, with the boys. He'll spill it, soon enough. I've got him softened up for you." He looked at Weigand and was pleased. "Shows you how to do it, don't it, Bill?" he said. "Couple of hours and it's cleaned up. None of this fancy stuff. When I think of the way you young fellows—"

Bill Weigand, resigned, listened to the way of young fellows, as contrasted with the superior way of experienced policemen, here represented by Deputy Chief Inspector Artemus O'Malley. It was not unfamiliar. He nodded at intervals, said "Right," once or twice, watched Stein measuring. He did not look at the faces of the other detectives from the precinct, and particularly not at Detective Lieutenant Armstrong of the precinct. He suspected that Armstrong would be grinning; he suspected that, if he saw it, his own face might reflect the grin.

"So," O'Malley finished, "there it is, Bill. In your lap." He looked at his watch and seemed surprised by it. "Got to be getting along," he said. "Can't spend the night here. Nothing you boys can't do now."

"Right," Weigand said. "If we need you, Inspector—?"

"You won't," O'Malley promised, and Bill Weigand thought it probable. "Got to see a man at the club."

"Right," Weigand said again. "At the club."

"Business," O'Malley said, severely, and for a third time Weigand said "right." Without inflection.

Inspector O'Malley went out; Lieutenant Armstrong and Bill Weigand considered his progress down the stairs, which creaked with it.

"Our only Artie," Armstrong said, with tenderness not to be taken at its face value. "Our only Artie. The miracle man."

"Right," Weigand said. "Our only Artie. And so he's cleaned it up?"

Lieutenant Armstrong of the precinct said it looked as if he had, at that. Except for a few details, like maybe a confession. Or some evidence. That part, Armstrong said, belonged to Bill Weigand. At the thought of what was left to Bill Weigand, Lieutenant Armstrong did not seem displeased. Weigand waited, and Armstrong said it was this way—

The body was found where the chalked outline near the fireplace showed. It was found at a little before four o'clock in the afternoon by the housekeeper, Mrs. Florence Pennock. It was clothed—

"Do you," Weigand said, "have to call it it?"

Armstrong was willing to start over. "It" was Miss Ann Lawrence, twenty-three, daughter of Mr. and Mrs. Frederic Lawrence, both of whom had been dead for several years. And both of whom had had money since man could remember. Money that the girl had had until— well, until twelve hours, perhaps, before her body was found. Hence the house, hence large property possessions and many stocks and bonds; hence the Social Register and membership on junior committees. A very lovely, lucky lady, she must have been.

"Not too lucky," Weigand said.

Armstrong shrugged. Obviously, in the end, not too lucky. In the end her luck had run out. Some time the previous morning. When a heavy poker hit the back of her head and crushed it, so that blood and brains ran out and soaked into the gay rose carpet of her sitting room, or whatever she had called it. This room.

Mrs. Pennock had found the body of the girl and had screamed and then had crossed the room and tried to awaken the girl. Because she looked, from a little distance, as if she were sleeping, lying on the floor on her back. She did not look that way when you got nearer; she was still lying that way when the police came, and the horrible wound in the back of her head was not easily visible as she lay. From the door she looked like a very lovely girl lying on her back and looking intently at the ceiling out of widely spaced brown eyes, with rather long, gently curling hair strewn out around her face.

"And matted together with blood and stuff," Armstrong said.

She had been, Armstrong added, quite a looker. She had been wearing an evening dress when she was killed; a two-tone dress with the bodice of light yellow silk and a broad sash and a swirling skirt of dark blue. The clothing was not disarranged particularly, except that on one side the bodice, cut in a deep, narrow V in front, had fallen aside so as to leave a shoulder bare. The body was quite stiff and cold when they found it; there had been a fire, but it had burned itself out hours before. As she lay, her head was near the fireplace, but there was some evidence that she had not first fallen where she was found, or in that position. She had fallen forward, or started to, been caught and lowered to the floor and left there on her back. The reason for this was not clear, unless the person who struck her had not realized the force of his blow immediately, or what it had done, and had perhaps had a moment's remorse and a moment, which must certainly have been very short, of thinking he might undo what he had done. If he had had any such idea, it could not have lasted long; one look at the wound would have made that clear to anyone.

"The poker had a crook, you know," Armstrong said. "The kind of dull-pointed hook most pokers have. Well—that went in first. Halfway through her head. It was—" he stopped a moment. "Sort of messy," he said.

Weigand nodded.

That was what they had to start with. A girl in evening clothes, lying on a gay rose carpet with her head bashed in. When the medical examiner arrived, and by the time the body was removed—and Inspector O'Malley was in charge—they had an approximate time of death. Somewhere between two and four o'clock that morning. About an hour after the end of the party.

"Party?" Weigand encouraged.

Ann Lawrence had given a party the evening before. She had had some people in for dinner and others after dinner and things had been gay. Or so Mrs. Pennock, the housekeeper, said. So far as they had discovered it had not been a party celebrating any particular occasion—just a party, eight at dinner, four or five after dinner; drinks and conversation and some dancing, but mostly drinks and conversation. The guests had left, or the last of them had left, about two. Ann had gone up to bed, presumably.

"The back room," Armstrong said, gesturing at it, was where she slept. "This room was just a room to live in, sort of. And sometimes a guest room."

The preceding evening it had been a place for the women to leave their wraps and to fix their hair. The men had put their things in the room near the door; the room with the big Capehart. There had been no overnight guest; Ann Lawrence had had the second floor to herself. After she had gone to it, Mrs. Pennock, who lived in the house, had gone to her own room, which was on the floor above. The maid who had been serving had gone home about the middle of the evening; Ann's personal maid had gone after she had helped Ann dress. So in the house after the party there had been only Ann herself, and Mrs. Pennnock—and someone else.

"The guy downstairs, if Artie's right," Armstrong said. "And I guess he's right. Name of Elliot—John Elliot. A writer or something."

Mrs. Pennock had told them that—that and enough more, it looked like, to send John Elliot to the electric chair.

Ann had been in her bedroom, with the door closed, when the housekeeper passed the second floor on her way to her own room. The front room had been dark. Ann was still up, and the housekeeper heard her moving about.

"And singing," Armstrong added. "Not knowing yet what had happened to her luck."

Mrs. Pennock had gone on upstairs, undressed and gone into the bathroom. And by that time, Ann was not alone. Elliot was with her, and to that the housekeeper would swear willingly—eagerly. "She's pretty sore about the whole thing," Armstrong said. "On account of liking the girl, and maybe being out of a job. And not much liking this guy Elliot. The girl was going to marry him, see?"

"Elliot?" Weigand said. "They were engaged?"

Armstrong pointed out, with reason, that that was what he had just said. John Elliott and Ann Lawrence were going to get married. Or had been going to get married.

"Right," Weigand said.

If he was sure that was clear, Armstrong said, he would get on with it. There was a ventilator in Mrs. Pennock's bathroom, on a shaft which also served the larger bathroom below—the bathroom which connected, with its adjoining dressing room, the two rooms used by Ann on the second floor. Even when the doors of the second floor bathroom were closed, you could hear a good deal of what went on on the second floor. With them, or one of them, open you could hear just about everything. One of them—the one leading, by way of the dressing room, into the front sitting room, apparently had been open the night before, since Mrs. Pennock had heard plenty.

Elliot must have come up the stairs almost immediately behind her, Mrs. Pennock thought, although there had been ten or fifteen minutes between the time she reached her own floor and the time she went into the bathroom. He had been there long enough, anyway, to have got well into a conversation with Ann. And they were quarreling.

Armstrong thought Weigand would want to talk to Mrs. Pennock himself, probably, but this was the gist. The girl was refusing to do something that Elliot wanted her to do. He was insisting, with growing excitement. She kept saying "No," and "No, John, I won't have it that way," and finally they had both got excited. Mrs. Pennock could not tell what they were arguing about, although she evidently listened carefully, but she did hear enough to decide that it was no ordinary argument—that it was emotional and violent. Particularly on Elliot's part.

The quarrel had gone on for several minutes, getting more and more violent until, Mrs. Pennock said, Elliot was shouting and the girl's voice was raised. And she heard sounds which made her think that at least one of the two was moving around violently. Elliot, she thought; it sounded as if he were striding back and forth and pushing things which got in his way. And then he had shouted some words of which she wasn't sure and after that, in a very loud voice—

"It's a showdown, then! You can't make—"

And then some more she wasn't sure of. Because then, she thought, one of them had closed the door leading into the dressing room; probably Ann herself, since she knew how voices carried up the airshaft. But even after the door was closed she heard voices, still raised and growing, she thought, angrier. And then one more phrase clearly. It was Ann speaking this time, and apparently near the door—perhaps with her back to it. She said—

"I've made up my mind too, Johnny. Unless you do, it's all—"

Then the girl had moved, apparently, and the rest of what she was saying was lost. Mrs. Pennock heard the man's heavier voice once more, and then a dull sound which she decided was a door slamming as he left the room, because after that she heard nothing more. But now she thought that perhaps it wasn't a slamming door.

"She couldn't hear a blow—I mean the poker," Weigand said. "Not if she couldn't hear the voices more clearly."

There could have been a scuffle, Armstrong pointed out. Perhaps the girl saw Elliot pick up the poker and come at her and perhaps she had time to try to run and—oh, knocked over a chair or something.

There wasn't, admittedly, a chair knocked over when the police got there, and Mrs. Pennock had denied anything was out of place—except the body of the girl itself—when she entered the room. But Elliot might have put the chair back on its feet for some reason. Or perhaps for no reason, abstractedly. People did funny things, Armstrong pointed out. Particularly after they had killed somebody. Weigand agreed. He also said that he would have to talk to Mrs. Pennock. For one thing, he would like to know why she had not discovered the body until late in the afternoon, twelve hours after the girl had died.

Armstrong could tell him that, or what Mrs. Pennock said about it. She had been waiting for the girl to ring and had not, because of the lateness of the party the night before, expected a ring much before two o'clock. She had been clearing up, which she had not tried to do after the party, and the two maids had been helping her, and she had not noticed the time. When she did notice it, it was already three o'clock and, although Ann usually slept most of the day after a party, Mrs. Pennock had thought it odd. But it took her the better part of another hour before she decided to risk waking the girl. Armstrong, after explaining this, thought it over and wondered, audibly, if it didn't sound a little fishy.

Bill thought not; or not necessarily. Probably Mrs. Pennock was glad enough to have her mistress asleep and out of the way, if there was much cleaning up to do; glad not to have to fix breakfast, or whatever you called a first meal taken in the middle of the afternoon. Probably Mrs. Pennock, letting her preference control her reason, had not allowed herself to notice how late it was really getting. Armstrong agreed that it was possible. At any rate, there was nothing against it.

Mrs. Pennock had been sent to her kitchen and Detective Sergeant Stein summoned her out of it. She was broad and substantial in a black dress which suggested, but was not, a uniform. She stood solidly in the room and did not look at the chalked outline by the fireplace and did not look as if she had ever screamed. When she spoke, her voice was flat and heavy.

The story she told was much the story Lieutenant Armstrong had told in her behalf. She said she had gone up, after turning out the lights on the lower floor, about two-thirty. She must, Bill Weigand thought, looking at her, have gone up heavily—a tired, heavy woman in her middle years, up too late. When she had reached her own room she had dropped into a chair and for a time "just sat there."

"I'm not as young as I used to be," she said, solidly and flatly. It was fifteen minutes perhaps—perhaps almost half an hour—before she was rested enough to begin undressing. It was perhaps five minutes later that she had gone to the bathroom and walked in on the conversation of Ann and John Elliot. Her account of that conversation—of the overheard fragments of that conversation—might have been an echo of Armstrong's account. The girl had said "no" to something; and John Elliot had said, in a loud, angry voice, that it was a showdown. Ann had said that she had made up her mind. "Too." She had said that, unless he did something, it was all—And then Mrs. Pennock had not heard the rest.

"All over, she was going to say," Mrs. Pennock told them. "If she'd known that sooner, she'd be alive. I told her."

"What did you tell her, Mrs. Pennock?" Weigand asked, his voice quiet and interested.

"Not to have anything more to do with him," Mrs. Pennock said. "He's—no good. I told her he was after her money."

What, Weigand wanted to know, had Ann Lawrence said to that?

"Told me not to meddle," Mrs. Pennock said. "Naturally. Told me I was a fool. But I wasn't. He killed her."

It was not an assertion. It was a routine statement of the obvious. In the same tone, after looking out the window, Mrs. Pennock might have remarked that it was snowing.

Why, Weigand asked, was she so sure? Mrs. Pennock looked at him without change of expression. She looked at him as if he, after watching the heavy flakes falling outside, had said it was not snowing.

"Why?" Weigand insisted. "You heard their voices raised, deduced a quarrel, heard a sound which may have been a door slamming. It needs more than that, Mrs. Pennock."

Mrs. Pennock said, flatly, that the other policeman hadn't thought so. The stout policeman. Lieutenant Armstrong made a muffled sound at the description of Inspector Artemus O'Malley. Weigand nodded and said probably the inspector was right. However—She spoke as if she had some other reason for her certainty.

"He's no good," she said. "That Mr. Elliot. After her money. Whining around her. He's crafty. He'll fool you if you let him."

"And kill you too?" Weigand said.

"Why not?" Mrs. Pennock asked. "He found out she was through with him and that he wasn't going to get her money. He got mad and killed her. He's no good."

It occurred to Bill Weigand that Mrs. Pennock and Inspector O'Malley must have enjoyed an almost perfect meeting of minds. Both liked it simple. "Sing something simple"—Weigand just stopped himself from humming it. And probably they were right, at that. In any case, there was nothing to be gained by discussion. He led her to the other point. Why had she waited until so late in the afternoon to go upstairs to waken Miss Lawrence?

"She liked to sleep late," Mrs. Pennock said. "She could, not like some people. And I had plenty to do as it was, with only the girls to help. And not much help."

"But you must have wondered," Weigand insisted. "After all, she had had more than twelve hours to sleep. That would have been a lot of sleep."

Mrs. Pennock repeated that she had been busy. She hadn't noticed. Miss Lawrence didn't like to be waked up before she was ready. And, finally, she *had* wondered in the end.

"Right there she was," Mrs. Pennock ended suddenly. "The poor, pretty thing. With her head all smashed in."

She pointed. But still she was not emotional. The woman was, in what was probably an unimportant fashion, baffling. It was hard to guess what her attitude had been toward Ann Lawrence.

"You were fond of her?" Weigand asked, almost out of curiosity.

"Fond?" the heavy woman repeated. "I don't know about fond. She was all right. She was fair, in her way. The job was all right."

Something didn't jibe, Bill Weigand thought. If it was no more than that, why had Mrs. Pennock tried to intervene against John Elliot?

"You tried to persuade her not to marry Mr. Elliot," Weigand reminded her. "Wasn't that because you were fond of her?"

Mrs. Pennock seemed to be thinking it over.

"Maybe it was that," she said, finally. "She was a pretty little thing and didn't know much. She couldn't see through your Mr. Elliot. But she didn't want my advice, it turned out. Might have saved my breath to cool my porridge."

She had, Weigand decided, a talent for the familiar. She was altogether an odd person. But perhaps she was a very good cook, or a superior housekeeper, or both. She had not, he decided, been employed for her charm.

"Well," she said. "Why don't you take him away? Now that you've arrested him."

She was talking, clearly, about John Elliot. Weigand said that they hadn't arrested him yet. Mrs. Pennock allowed herself a facial expression. It apparently was contempt.

"Where's the stout policeman?" she said. "He'd tell you to."

"Gone," Weigand said. "He did, practically, Mrs. Pennock. He agrees with you perfectly."

She nodded. That, her nod said, was foregone. It merely indicated that the stout policeman was in his right mind. Weigand watched her for a moment, half-amused. Then he thanked her and told her there was, for the moment, nothing more she could do. He sent Stein downstairs for John Elliot. Stein went down casually, in no hurry. Weigand was looking around the pleasant room, waiting without anxiety, when Stein yelled. The detective sergeant's voice was angry and surprised and excited all together. But all he yelled was, *"Hey! Lieutenant!"*

Weigand ran down the delicate, curving stairs. In the middle of the spreading living room, a uniformed policeman was sitting on the floor, his head in his hands. Stein was leaning over him, cursing steadily. There was nobody else in the room. Mr. John Elliot, presumptive murderer, had gone away.

• 3 •

TUESDAY, 8:10 P.M. TO 9 P.M.

MR. NORTH put his foot down. He did not think they had better help Sergeant Mullins. He was fond of Sergeant Mullins; he wished him well. But he did not wish him the assistance of Mrs. North. Mr. North ran a hand through his hair.

"For once, Pam," he pleaded. "Just for once—no. We aren't private detectives."

"Well—" Pam said, speculatively. "The baked apple is pretty subtle, Jerry. Isn't it, Dorian?"

Dorian was purposely noncommittal. She said it was an odd thing to call a baked apple.

"Well," Pam said, "obscure, then. Because there isn't, really, anything less subtle than a baked apple. Is there?"

"A boiled potato," Jerry suggested. "Or anything with whipped cream on it."

Pam said not on a boiled potato. She said Jerry had the oddest ideas. She looked at him with reproach. Nobody, he said, ever put whipped cream on boiled potatoes.

"Listen, Pam," Jerry said.

"Even tea shops," Pam said. "I don't think, anyway. Do they?"

"Probably," Jerry told her. "They put it on carrots."

27

"Jerry!" Pam said. "You're making it up."

"Salads," Jerry told her. "With shredded carrots *and* whipped cream. In tea shops. And women eat it."

"Really, Jerry," Dorian said. "Really. And how did we get here?"

Pam answered for her husband. She said because Jerry insisted on talking about whipped cream on boiled potatoes.

"Instead of Mullins," she said. "He's just trying to change the subject, of course."

Jerry tugged at his hair and looked around wildly. He looked at Pam, and, beseechingly, at Dorian.

"As a matter of fact, Jerry," Dorian told him. "You did."

"I—" Jerry said, a little desperately. "I—whipped cream on boiled *potatoes?*"

Both Dorian and Pam nodded contentedly.

"Because I wanted to help Sergeant Mullins," Pam said. "Because baked apples are subtle. And Mr. Mullins isn't."

"Never," Jerry said. "Never did I say anything about whipped cream on boiled potatoes. I couldn't have." He looked at them. "What *did* I say?" he demanded, urgently.

"That we shouldn't help Mr. Mullins," Pam told him. "But you didn't mean it. Because you're just as fond of him as I am. And he'll never solve the baked apple. Come on."

"Dorian!" Jerry said. "Do something!" It was evident that he was obscurely shaken. "Tell her Bill wouldn't want us to."

"I don't suppose he'd mind, really," Dorian said. "And it *is* sort of interesting. And it will confuse the sergeant, I'm afraid."

"I—" Jerry said. Pam smiled at him.

"Just this one point, Jerry," she said. "Bill didn't have time to explain, really. And if he has to leave it to Mr. Mullins, and gets all interested in this other one, everybody might forget all about it. And that nice boy would go to the chair."

"Listen," Jerry said. "I haven't the faintest idea whether he's a nice boy or not. Neither have you."

"Of course I have," Pam said. "He didn't commit the murder."

"Therefore," Jerry said, "he's a nice boy. Really, Pam." He thought of more to say, but did not say it because Pam had suddenly gone into the bedroom and from it was calling to Dorian to come on. Then, apparently, she looked out the window, because next she called:

"Darling. You'll have to wear rubbers."

Jerry went to the living-room windows and looked out. Lights from windows on the floor below fell across snow in the backyard. It looked like deep snow. It was fine-looking snow and it was coming down heavily. He would have to wear rubbers, he decided, and only then remembered that his foot was down and he wasn't going anywhere. Abstractedly, he looked at his foot. It would be fun to go out in the snow, and probably they wouldn't be able to find Mullins anyway. It would be fun to go out in the snow and perhaps walk in it, and turn in to some warm bright place and steam a little and have a drink. That was probably what it would come to, when they couldn't find Mullins.

And it was fun in the snow, when they got into it, slipping and clutching at each other and laughing and seeing the snow plaster on their coats. For a while, too, it appeared that they would never find Mullins, because they could not even find a taxicab. But then one skidded up to them, its windshield wipers churning madly, and they got in and at once began to drip. And Pam appeared to know precisely where Mullins would be, because she gave the address of the Homicide Squad offices.

"You see," she said, "he would have been at the precinct. But after Bill called him, he'd go back to the office to think about the baked apple. So that's where he is. That's where I'd be, anyway."

It startled Jerry, somewhat, to discover that Pam's thought processes had, in fact, coincided with those of Sergeant Mullins. For some reason this made him reel internally; it suggested that the whole world was about to come apart. It suggested that the human mind was, not only as exemplified in the mind of his wife but universally, more strange and wonderful than he had ever thought. Mullins was sitting in Bill Weigand's office, at Bill Weigand's desk. He looked at them.

"You're wet," he said. "It must be raining."

This, obscurely, made Jerry feel better. Here was simple, straight-forward reasoning, ending up solidly at the wrong conclusion. He smiled at Mullins and felt much better.

"We've come to help," Pam told Mullins. Sergeant Mullins looked at her with doubt. He looked at Dorian Weigand and said, "Hullo, Mrs. Weigand. The lieutenant ain't here."

"Of course not, Mr. Mullins," Pam said. "We know he isn't. That's why we are."

Mullins looked at Jerry North. Jerry disengaged himself with a shrug.

"Because," Pam North said, "of the baked apple. I mean—do you understand it?"

"Yes," Mullins said. "Sure. She didn't get a baked apple at first. Then she got a baked apple and it—showed up. So maybe she got the apple after this kid left. And maybe, just as easy, she didn't. Maybe she got it while he was still there, or he got it for her, and then maybe he stuck the knife in her after she ate it. Is that what you mean, Mrs. North?"

"Well," Pam said, "it's more complex than that."

"How?" Mullins said, with simplicity.

"Well," Pam said, "it just is. Are those her things?"

She was looking at things spread out on a table against one of the walls of the small, ancient office. There was a dress and other articles of clothing; there was a purse, and, beside it, all the little, odd things which had apparently come out of the purse. A small compact with an enameled cover, two keys and a worn coin purse, an unused kleenex, an envelope with something written on it—pathetic things.

"Yeh," Mullins said. "Those are her things. I was just—looking at them." He looked at them again. "She was a little kid, sort of," he said.

Pam North walked over and, without touching any of them, looked down at the things Frances McCalley had worn or carried when someone had thrust a knife in her throat, leaving her small and crumpled in a cafeteria booth. She had been a little kid, Pam noticed. It was a little dress. Then she looked again. It was a smaller dress than it had been once; the seams along the side had been taken up.

There were small, neat stitches which still had not come from a professional workshop.

"Can I look at it?" Pam said. Mullins nodded. She picked it up. It was a black silk dress and on the front—on a great deal of the front—there was something which had dried. It did not show red now, against the black; it showed only a different, duller black. Pam turned the dress in her slim hands and saw that her hands were trembling. But there was still something curious about the dress. Forcing herself not to drop the stained dress, Pam turned back the collar and nodded at what she saw. Then, still holding it, she shook her head.

"Look," she said. "This isn't her dress. It couldn't be. It's Bergdorf's."

Mullins looked at her, uncomprehending.

"McCalley," he said. "Frances McCalley. She was a filing clerk. Sure it's her dress. Who's Bergdorf?"

Pam looked at Dorian Weigand, who crossed and looked at the dress with her.

"She couldn't," Pam said. "Not if it came from Bergdorf. It might as well be Carnegie."

Mullins looked at them, and then anxiously at Jerry North.

"Bergdorf-Goodman's," Jerry said. "Hattie Carnegie." It was, he decided, wrong. He went over to look at the dress too. There was no doubt about what the label said.

"Look," he said, and now he was getting interested. This worried him a little, but the interest remained. "Maybe she just got the label somewhere—found it or something—and sewed it in. It seems to me I've heard—"

"So have I," Pam agreed. "But that isn't it. Is it, Dorian? You know about things like that."

"No," Dorian said, holding the dress away from her and looking at it. "It isn't that. This is the real thing—see the line, Pam?"

Pamela North nodded. Jerry looked at the dress. He thought he could see what they were talking about.

"And," Dorian said, "it cost plenty. About what—she was a filing clerk, wasn't she, Sergeant?"

"Yeh," Mullins said. He crossed to join in the examination, looking puzzled.

"Then," Dorian said, "this dress cost what she'd make in two months. Maybe three, depending on the mark-up."

"Well," Mullins said, "some girls are crazy about clothes. Some of these poor kids—"

Pam and Dorian both shook their heads. They looked at each other, and Pam told Mullins how it was. A girl might spend two or three times what she made in a month on something to wear. She might go hungry for something to wear. But that would be for a fur coat at so much a week. Or for a dress to wear to parties, perhaps. But most likely a fur coat. But not for a black dress, however artfully cut, however good in material, to wear to an office.

"This can't be her dress," Pam said. "Or else she can't be who we think she is—a little filing clerk. Dorian will tell you that too, Mr. Mullins."

Mullins looked at Dorian Weigand. He looked at her hopefully. She shook her head.

"She's right, Sergeant," she said. "No little filing clerk ever bought this dress."

Jerry watched the hope die out of Sergeant Aloysius Mullins's face; he watched with sympathy and understanding. He watched another expression take its place and waited, with anticipation, for the certainly to be anticipated remark.

"Jeeze," said Sergeant Mullins, and he spoke in sorrow. "Jeeze. It's going to be another screwy one."

He looked at Pam North and shook his head slowly. His tone was not accusing, but it was resigned.

"Another screwy one, Mrs. North," he said.

Pamela North looked at Sergeant Mullins, and there was only one thing for her to say.

"I'm sorry, Mr. Mullins," she said. "Really I am."

"O.K.," Mullins said. "O.K., Mrs. North. It ain't your fault."

But Sergeant Mullins, Mr. North was interested to note, did not make this last remark with any real assurance.

But, Pam North thought, dropping the dress back on the table, it has really been a screwy one since the baked apple and I didn't have anything to do with that. She thought of saying as much and then noticed something about the dress, now sprawled on the table, which she had not noticed before. Clipped to a seam near the bottom of the dress was a cleaner's tag. It had not shown when the dress was worn; Frances McCalley, if the girl had been Frances McCalley, had never noticed it.

"Look," Pam said, pointing. "Can't we find out from that who she really is?"

"Listen, Mrs. North," Sergeant Mullins said. "It ain't that screwy. We know who she is—was. That we *do* know."

But he looked at the tag and, after a second, detached it. He leaned out of the door and called, and when a detective came, gave him the tag with instructions. Then he turned back.

"Just to make sure, Mrs. North," he said, "I'm having them check up. They'll tell us who cleaned it. But she was Frances McCalley, anyway." He looked firmly at all of them. "Anyway," he repeated. "People looked at her. Who knew her."

There was, he told them while they waited, nothing else in the small pile of the murdered girl's possessions which seemed to mean much. The envelope was addressed to Frances McCalley and Mullins pointed this out with modified triumph to Mrs. North. She had had two dollars and twelve cents in her purse when she was killed; she had bought the compact for a dollar at a glorified five-and-ten-cent store on Fifth Avenue. The purse had come from Fourteenth Street; her stockings had been rayon and so had her few underclothes. She had worn no girdle. She—

The detective came back and handed Mullins the cleaner's tag with a slip of paper clipped to it. "Clinton Cleaners," someone had written on the paper, and added a Madison Avenue address. Mullins looked pleased.

"Quick, those boys are," he said. "Put a description on the teletype and it comes right back at you." He nodded, approving the Police Department. "Laundry marks just the same," he said. He sat down at the desk and picked up a Manhattan telephone book. "Not that it's any use," he said. "It won't be open. Still—" He laid down the telephone book, asked for an outside line, and dialed a number. He waited and nothing happened. He was just about to hang up when someone answered.

The Clinton Cleaners was not, it appeared, closed, although it was closing and, evidently, glad of it. Mullins identified himself and read letters and numbers from the tag. He said, "Now, brother. When'd you think," and waited. He said, "Yeh," and wrote something on the pad in front of him. He said, "Thanks," and re-cradled the telephone. He sat for a moment looking at what he had written, a puzzled expression on his face.

"Seems to me I just—" he said, thoughtfully. Then he said, in a different tone, "Jeeze." He turned to the others, and surprise now was in control of his features.

"You know who they cleaned that dress for?" he demanded. The others looked at him. "Ann Lawrence, who lives on Gramercy Park. And she—"

He stopped because all three were nodding at him.

"Yes, Mullins," Jerry North said. "We know. She got killed tonight—too."

"Or," Pam said, "she got killed twice. Or—or this girl was a friend of hers and she gave her this dress, having it cleaned first. Or—"

She stopped and looked at them.

"They're tied up," she said. "It isn't two cases. It's only one case. We've got to go and tell Bill. Right away."

It was a jump, Jerry North thought. It was a frantic jump. Because it did not really follow, because Ann Lawrence had given a dress to Frances McCalley—if she had, which was unproved—that there was a connection between the deaths of the two girls. It meant, possibly, that they had known each other and—Then he had a new thought.

"Savings Shops!" he said. "Or something like that. Well-to-do women give their clothes to charities and charities run Savings Shops and girls like this buy expensive things there for very little and—"

Pam was agreeing.

"That was my other or," she said. "It's Thrift Shops, dear. And of course it could be. Only I don't believe it for a minute. I don't believe in things like that, because if I did there wouldn't be any sense to anything. And that would be too confusing." She paused and considered. "Things would be illogical," she said. "And what would we do then, except go round and round?"

There was obviously an answer to that one. Jerry North tried to think of it all the way to Gramercy Park, while Mullins pushed a police car, its red lights blinking in front, through the soft barrier of snow. They had pulled up among the other cars in front of Ann Lawrence's little house before Jerry realized that there wasn't any answer because, as it happened, Pam was perfectly right.

• 4 •

Tuesday, 8:50 p.m. to 9:45 p.m.

It meant hitting a policeman, preferably when the policeman wasn't looking. It also meant hitting him hard enough to be sure that, for as many minutes as could be managed, he was silent. John Elliot had taken that aspect of the situation into account. It also meant that, if they got hold of him afterward, as presumably they would, they'd have a small thing on him as well as the big thing. Whatever else they might or might not be able to prove in the end, they would unquestionably be able to prove he had hit a policeman. With a blunt instrument, by preference.

John Elliot thought of this and continued to sit easily in his chair, not seeming to look around. The policeman, who was fortunately only of medium size and seemed to have no club, stood in the middle of the room and part of the time he looked at John Elliot and part of the time he just looked around. Even when Elliot shifted in his chair the policeman looked at him only casually and then looked away again. To test it, Elliot shifted again. This time the policeman hardly looked at all. The policeman, Elliot thought, had merely decided that the suspect was getting restless. Which was true enough.

Elliot was long and thin and his blond hair made him look milder than he was. That was worth remembering, Elliot thought—blond hair

36

generally meant a mild person. If his hair had been black, now, the policeman might have been more diligent. That was worth remembering; some time he might use it. If he ever got another chance. He moved again and the policeman did not bother to look at all.

There was a table beside the chair in which Elliot sprawled—or now no longer quite sprawled. There were some objects on the table and, without making a point of it, Elliot looked at them. Most of them were obviously no good. Being struck with a vase of thin glass, for example, would only annoy a policeman and probably, in the end, get everybody cut and scratched. The bookend within reach was glass too, but glass of a different kind; it was a solid brick of glass. It was a polished example of the glass building brick. It would do very nicely. Idly, Elliot reached out his hand and let his fingers touch it. He still wasn't sure he'd try it.

The policeman really brought it on himself; he was a more alert policeman than Elliot had thought. This movement he did not ignore. He looked at Elliot and at his hand and then back into Elliot's face, and the policeman's eyes changed suddenly. He was no longer bland. He was suspicious and wary, and in a second he would move. It was finally by impulse that Elliot moved first; impulse was the end of his planning. He came out of the chair in a violent, almost explosive movement; he had reached the policeman before wariness had been quite replaced by certainty. The glass brick came with him and the policeman's hand was moving toward his side by the time Elliot was on his feet. But the policeman's uniform coat was over his holster and he was just pushing it aside when Elliot chucked the glass brick. He chucked it as if he were putting the shot. It was too heavy to throw easily and too awkward in the hand.

It cracked against the policeman's skull just above the ear with a soft, unpleasant sound. The policeman, with very surprised eyes, sagged and then fell. It was surprising how easy it was, but it would be a hell of a note if it had been too easy. If the policeman had a brittle skull, Elliot was in it deeper than ever—much deeper. There wouldn't be any argument about this.

The policeman had made no sound as he fell on the deep carpet and Elliot took a chance. He bent quickly and grabbed the policeman's wrist, feeling for a pulse. At first he could not find it, and he felt coldness coming over him in a wave. This had done it! Then his anxious fingers found a trembling and moved a little. There was a pulse, all right. Elliot sighed in relief. As far as he could tell, not knowing much about such things, the pulse seemed reasonably strong—slow, but strong. So probably the policeman was all right, or would be all right. Elliot looked at his victim an instant longer, and then the policeman's eyes began to open. He was going to be all right; he was going to be too damned all right. Elliot moved.

He had planned this, too. There was no use in trying to make it to the front, because the front door would be guarded. But there was a better way. In the wall under the curving stairs there was a door, and it opened on a flight of stairs leading down. Elliot went for it, moving fast and silently on the carpet. The door opened and Elliot went through it. He was pulling it behind him when he had another idea. The key—it was. His fingers groped on the wall beyond the door. The key ought to be—it was. Dutiful on its nail. It would be something if he needed it. Elliot took it along.

The stairs went down to a hall with doors opening off it. The one to the front was no good; it led to a storeroom and they would roust him out of that. The kitchen was the only way, and he hoped Mrs. Pennock would be somewhere else. He had no desire to meet Mrs. Pennock at any time and less now than at any other time. The kitchen was empty. He crossed it, moving still faster, and reached the door which opened on the paved court in the rear of the house. It was locked but the key was in it. Elliot went through, taking this key, also, with him. He closed the door and locked it from outside and started to throw the key away. Then he decided that it, too, might be useful. You couldn't plan far enough ahead to be sure.

Now it ought to be easy if they gave him a few minutes. The paved court was fenced, but a gate opened on a passageway between the house and the apartment building next door, which led to the street. It provided a service entrance which the house and the apartment building shared. But it meant coming out to the street beside the house, and in plain sight of the guard which would surely be on the sidewalk in front. That meant—Elliot looked around. You had to improvise.

There was an empty wooden box lying against the fence. It looked as if a delivery boy from a grocery had left it there after emptying it of bread and bottles and packages of food. You had to improvise. Elliot picked the box up and swung it on his shoulder. He went up the passageway and, when he neared the front of the house, began to whistle. He whistled "The Surrey with the Fringe on Top," not very well, but well enough. He stopped and tried to walk as he thought a delivery boy, perhaps done work for the day, would walk. He came out on the sidewalk whistling, saw a policeman standing in front of Ann's house as he had expected, and did not look at him. He turned and began to walk, not hurrying too much, toward Lexington Avenue. He crossed the street diagonally and began to walk along beside the park fence.

He was not very far along beside the fence when there were sounds behind him and the door of Ann's house was flung open and somebody yelled something angrily, presumably at the policeman on guard outside. Elliot did not hear clearly what was said, but he didn't need to. He hoped he was only a vague figure in the snow—a vague figure of a delivery boy with an empty box on his shoulder. But he was too close to run. There ought to be a gate along here somewhere.

He came to it almost as soon as he hoped. The key was going to be useful after all. But he couldn't carry the box in. Delivery boys didn't get into the only private park left in New York City; the only park owned by the property owners around it, kept sacred under lock to their moments of outdoor relaxation. Elliot put the box down and stood up straight and took his time unlocking the gate. But he took as little time as he could without hurrying. The gate was heavy and reluctant, but he pushed it open. He took the key out of the lock and closed the gate and locked it behind him. For a moment, anyway, they couldn't get to him.

But except for inadequate evergreens, the park was bare, offering little cover, leaving him visible from outside by anyone who wanted to look through the iron fence. And somebody would, probably, want to look through the iron fence. He moved unhurriedly along the path to the right and tried to look like a very respectable property owner taking a stroll in the open. But it was obviously an unlikely time to be taking a stroll.

He heard, then, the sounds of a heavy man running along the public walk outside the fence and he forced himself not to look around. He sauntered along, but the nerves crept at the back of his neck. Nobody was going to think he was merely walking in the snow for—then he thought of it. You could improvise, all right, when you had to.

An instant before the running feet outside were even with him, John Elliot stopped. He stopped near one of the evergreen bushes and held his right arm out toward it as if he were pointing. He held the right hand curved, as if it were lightly curved around something—a leash, perhaps. The feet stopped opposite him and Elliot turned to face the policeman, as a man in no fear of policemen might have done. The policeman stopped and looked in through the fence at John Elliot, staring through the curtain of falling snow.

"Hey, you!" the policeman said. Then he said, "Oh, sorry, mister."

"Yes, officer?" John Elliot said. "Did you want something?"

"Didja see a guy running up this way?" the policeman said. "A guy with a box, maybe?"

"No," said Elliot. "I didn't see anybody. Or hear anybody. Did somebody get away?"

"Well," the policeman said, "so you didn't see anybody, mister? Any guy running?"

"No," Elliot said. "I didn't see anybody. Maybe he ran the other way."

"Yeah," the policeman said. "Hell of a night, ain't it? But it don't mean nothing to them."

"Them?" Elliot repeated. Then he caught himself. "Oh," he said, and looked down in the direction of his pointing right hand. "Them. No, regardless of the weather, they—"

The policeman wasn't listening. He was turning away. He called back, "Thanks, mister," and went toward Ann's house through the snow. John Elliot figured it was all right, but he acted out the rest of it. He moved his right arm as if he were pulling something; he said, just audibly, "come on, you!" He walked away along the path, continuing to look as much as he could like a man walking a dog. He kept the hand which held the mythical leash a little out from his body, as if a dog were tugging at it.

He abandoned this when he was half around the park, and walked more briskly. He let himself out of the park opposite The Players and crossed the street diagonally, avoiding the club entrance and the entrance next to it. When he got to Irving Place he walked down it a block or two and waited for a bus. When the bus came he got on, shaking his overcoat and knocking snow off his hat and as he dropped his nickel in the coin box he told the driver it was a rotten night. The driver made an agreeing sound. Elliot took a seat on the left side of the bus, which went on around the park. As it went by Ann's house, Elliot stared out the window into the snow, although he wanted to see what was going on. As the bus turned north again he looked across it and out the windows on the right, and got a glimpse of the street in front of the house. A taxicab was stopping and a man was helping a woman out.

Elliot, feeling he had improvised to good purpose, stayed on the bus until it reached Grand Central. Then he got out and, after a little trouble, waved down a taxicab. He gave an address to the taxi-driver and got in. From now on, he would have to have some help.

Bill Weigand was not in a good humor. Once it was evident that Patrolman McKenna, who had stopped John Elliot's glass brick, was dented but basically sound, Bill Weigand gave Patrolman McKenna a description of himself. It was low-voiced, bitter and thorough; if Patrolman McKenna met himself soon, he would recognize himself with embarrassment. And then Weigand set things going. A description of John Elliot went out through the city, and through the adjacent states for good measure. Men of the precinct hurried through the neighborhood, looking unpleasantly at innocent men who happened to be, like Elliot, tall and thin. They found Elliot's box quite soon; the patrolman on guard outside remembered vaguely that somebody, carrying a box, had come out from between the house and the building next door. Weigand described the patrolman on outside guard more briefly, but with vigor. Then, sighing, Weigand telephoned Inspector O'Malley,

who when he answered had to leave the stud game with a king in the
hole and another showing, and a round—which long afterward O'Malley was still certain would have brought him another king, particularly
after he discovered that two pairs had taken the pot—coming up.

Inspector O'Malley listened and exploded into the telephone. Bill
Weigand listened to a description of himself which gave him several
new ideas. Bill hung up and sighed and turned impatiently to a patrolman who was beginning to make sounds at his elbow.

"Well?" Bill Weigand said. "Well?"

"Some people," the patrolman said. "Your wife and some people,
Lieutenant. A Mr. and Mrs.—"

"Yes," Weigand said. "I thought—" He broke off. "Ask my wife and
the Norths to come in here, Smith," he said. He waited in the living-
room, looking with continued disfavor at Patrolman McKenna, who
was lying on a couch and holding his head and now and then sighing
heavily. "Shut up," Weigand said. "Did baby bump its little head?"

"What?" said Pam North from the door. "What baby? Whose head?
And what's happened to you, Bill?"

Bill looked at the three and started to speak and gave it up.

"Nothing," he said. "Just that the boys let a murderer walk out on
them. Let him walk right through him. It seems to have annoyed the
inspector."

Pam said, "oh" and added that it was too bad. Dorian said, "Bill!
I'm sorry, dear."

Bill Weigand smiled at them, not broadly.

"Oh," he said, "we'll pick him up. In time. And I'll soothe the
inspector down. In time. Don't worry, children."

"Well, then," Pam said, "if it's really all right, we can tell you. She's
wearing her clothes."

Weigand looked at them.

"Please," Bill Weigand said. "Please, Pam."

"Frances," Pam said. "The girl in the cafeteria. *This* girl's clothes.
So it's really one case, after all."

Bill continued to look at them. He looked at them anxiously.

"That's right, Bill," Dorian said. "The girl who was killed in the restaurant. Frances somebody. She was wearing a dress which had been cleaned for the girl who was killed here. Ann something."

"McCalley," Jerry North said. "Lawrence."

"So," Pam said, "obviously one man killed them both. So it couldn't have been the girl's boy and we have to start all over. So it was right about the apple."

Weigand got it straightened out in a moment, and his interest rose as it straightened. But then he shook his head at Pam. He told her that she was jumping again. He said, as Jerry had, that the dress might have come from a thrift shop, and that it might be coincidence. Pam merely stared at him.

"All right," he said. "I don't like that either. Which doesn't prove it isn't true. Or the Martinelli boy may have killed them both, for some reason. Or the guy who got away from here may have killed them both. Or Martinelli may have killed the McCalley girl and Elliot may have killed Miss Lawrence. Or—"

"Or a couple of other fellows," Pam told him. "You don't believe any of it, Bill."

But Bill Weigand would not admit that. He shook his head. It might be anyway. A person they didn't know yet might have killed both girls; two people they didn't know yet might each have killed a girl.

Weigand looked beyond the Norths and Dorian, and Sergeant Mullins was standing in the doorway. He looked very unhappy. When he saw that Weigand was looking at him, Mullins shook his head dolefully and formed a word with his mouth. Mullins gave the whole affair a vote of no confidence.

"Yes, Mullins?" Bill Weigand said. "Oh, you came with the others? Right."

"Yeah," Mullins said. "So he got away, Loot? This guy who did it? Only now I guess he didn't."

"Why, Mullins?" Weigand wanted to know.

Mullins told him. It would be too simple. It would be like the way cases used to be.

"Before—" Mullins said, rather darkly, looking at Mr. and Mrs. North. "In the good old days, sort of."

Weigand told Mullins that the inspector didn't think it was too easy; that the inspector thought Elliot did it. The inspector had been touched and pleased when Elliot walked in.

"Walked in?" Pam North repeated.

Bill told her what Stein had told him, filling in details. Elliot had walked in after the body of Ann Lawrence had been found, and after police in the first radio patrol car had arrived. He had walked in, he said, to take Ann to a cocktail party, in accordance with an arrangement. He had been surprised and shocked. He had also been held.

"But doesn't that prove—?" Pam said. "No, of course it doesn't. Because if he was, he would have because it looked so innocent, wouldn't he?"

"Yes," Bill said. "That's why it didn't impress the inspector."

Then Bill Weigand was a little surprised at himself, because he had not been at all puzzled by what Pam North had said, and this was against nature. Evidently somebody's nature was changing. He let Pam's words echo faintly in his mind. It was his nature that was changing, all right. It was a little alarming to think that, because if it went on there might come a time when he could speak only to Pam North with any assurance of being understood. A closed corporation, like God and the Cabots. Or God and the Lowells? But Jerry North, whose nature had had a far longer time to adjust itself had ended in no such predicament. And he would always have Dorian—he hoped—as a counterbalance.

"But if he wasn't, he still would, assuming they did have," Dorian said.

Bill Weigand and Jerry North looked at each other.

"I don't know," Jerry said, gently and as if from far away. "I don't know, Bill. Is it something in all of them, do you suppose? Or just these?"

"Dorian!" Bill said firmly, chidingly. "Darling!"

"Well," Dorian said, "what's sauce for the goose is sauce for the goose. Or ought to be. What I meant, of course, was—"

"I know what you meant," Bill told her. "You meant that if they had had an engagement and if he was not the murderer, and didn't know of the murder, he would naturally come around at the time agreed upon to pick her up."

"Obviously," Dorian agreed. "Only people don't talk that way."

"Particularly here," Jerry said.

Pam said she thought they were all talking nonsense.

"Where did he go?" Pam said. "How did he do it?"

Bill Weigand knew by now, and told her what he knew. John Elliot had knocked out his guardian policeman, gone out the rear, carried a box past the policeman in front, entered Gramercy Park by using the key which belonged to the Lawrence house, and pretended to be walking a dog.

"Why," Pam said, "didn't the cop see the dog? The dog that wasn't there, I mean."

"Snow," Weigand told her. "And he thought it was behind a bush. If he thought."

Pam pointed out that Elliot wanted to get away very much, which was odd if he were innocent.

"Unless," she said, "he knew some way to prove he was innocent, but had to get away to do it. Which is possible."

"Listen," Mullins said. "I don't get this." He looked at all of them. "*Any* of it," he said, with finality.

Mullins brought Weigand back to immediate problems. One of them, which was to question Elliot, could not now be met. Another could. For that he could use helpers, and now he had them. He picked Dorian and Jerry and told them what to do; he took Pam with him to the third floor, where Mrs. Pennock dwelt alone, and to the bathroom from which she had heard the quarrel in Ann Lawrence's sitting-room. Pam sat down on the edge of the bed and Weigand closed the door and leaned against it. They listened to the ventilator. For a moment nothing came from it. Then Dorian's voice came, with remarkable clearness.

"Personally," she said, "I think it's a trick. To get up there alone. Don't you—*darling!*"

"Obviously," Jerry said, his voice also startlingly clear. "Our lawyers shall hear—Dorian!"

The last was in a voice which was filled with an emotion which for a moment struck Pam, who had never heard it, as one of anguish. Then she decided it was supposed to represent pleased surprise, colored with rapture. There was another sound through the ventilator and there was no doubt about it. Bill Weigand approached the ventilator in Mrs. Pennock's bathroom and spoke at it, firmly.

"Children," he said. "Children! No games."

"Do you suppose," Pam said, in a low voice, "that they really kissed? The way it sounded? I just wonder."

"Don't," Bill told her. "It will just encourage them." He spoke again to the ventilator. "Go away from there and do what I say," he told Dorian and Jerry. "Go out into the other room and do what I said."

There was a faint sound of movement from below, carried with reasonable clearness through the ventilator. Then there was a silence and then, much more distant, Dorian's voice.

"I've made up my mind too, Johnny. Unless you do—"

"It's a showdown, then," Jerry said. "You can't—"

"Was that what she heard?" Pam said. "The girl and this John Elliot? Saying that?"

"Or about that," Bill told her. "She could have, evidently. Now—"

New sounds came from the ventilator. Thudding sounds as of someone moving heavily on a carpeted floor; a louder sound, as if a chair had been knocked over.

"She heard that too," Bill Weigand told Pam. "Or says she did. Now listen."

There was a very faint sound, which they could hear only because they were listening closely, and which might have been the closing of the door between the sitting-room and the bath/dressing-room. Then, very far off, there was a continuing sound of voices. They seemed to be the voices of a man and a woman, but it would have been impossible to identify either speaker, or any of the words they used.

Weigand nodded. That fitted too; it seemed to work out as Mrs. Pennock said it worked out. So—He turned to open the door. But then Pam suddenly, quickly, shook her head and held up a warning hand and he stopped. Because there was another voice, neither Dorian's nor Jerry's, coming out of the ventilator, and the words could be distinguished.

"I hadn't," the voice said. It was unmodulated, decisive. "But I'd just as soon. They'd like to know. Why shouldn't I?"

There was a pause. Pam guessed at it first.

"Telephone," she said, very low. "Somebody talking on the telephone. Now the other person is talk—"

"That's right," the voice said. "Least said, soonest mended. For you, anyway."

There was another pause.

"What usually persuades people?" the voice said again. "You ought to know. In this case—plenty."

There was still another pause.

"All right," the voice said. "But it won't be cheap. I'll call you from outside in the morning. You'd better sleep on it. And visit your bank."

Weigand waited a moment, but there was no more.

"Who?" Pam said. "Do you know?"

"Pennock," Weigand said. "The housekeeper. Trying a shakedown on—on somebody. I'd better—"

But he broke off and looked through Pam for a moment, thinking. Then he shook his head.

"Not yet," he said. "As Mrs. Pennock would say, give enough rope."

"But—" Pam said. Then there was the sound of feet on the stairs, and a hammering on the bathroom door. Weigand opened it quickly and shook his head sharply at Jerry North. He motioned to Pam and she followed him out of the bathroom to the hall and he closed the door behind him.

"How long do you want us to go on?" Jerry demanded. "We're running out of remarks. As Ann and John Elliot, anyway. Do you want—"

Weigand said they had done plenty, and that it had been fine. He said it had been a very useful experiment.

"More than I expected," he said, and, leaving Pam to tell the rest, went downstairs. He went quickly to the living-room floor. Then he went to the door under the stairs and opened it with no effort at quiet and went down the stairs to the kitchen floor. Mrs. Pennock was in the kitchen. She was sitting in an easy chair, reading a copy of the *New York Post*. She looked up with moderate interest when Weigand appeared.

"Checking the way he went," Weigand told her. "Through here. Right?"

"He could have gone this way," Mrs. Pennock agreed. "I didn't see him." She smiled a little, with malice. "Seeing's believing," she reported. "The stout officer was right, I guess."

It looked that way, Weigand admitted, crossing the room. He opened the outer door. Flakes of snow swirled in. Weigand looked out into the snow, withdrew his head and closed the door. He crossed the kitchen again, taking it in with his eyes. There was a grill at one end which presumably connected with a ventilator. Under the grill, on a small wooden table, was a telephone.

Mrs. Pennock was worth keeping an eye on. Bill Weigand went upstairs to arrange for the eye. Mrs. Pennock was going to get herself into trouble, if she didn't watch out. Trouble of one kind or of another.

• 5 •

TUESDAY, 9:45 P.M. TO 11:25 P.M.

BILL WEIGAND stopped a moment to tell Detective Stein that an eye was to be kept on Mrs. Pennock and then went toward the sound of voices into the living-room. The Norths and Dorian, and Mullins too, were sitting in the living-room as if they lived in it. And Pam North was talking, with some intensity.

"Suppose he didn't," she said. "And he didn't because of the apple. Think how he feels—somebody killed the girl he was in love with and then the police grabbed him and tried to make him talk and wouldn't give him cigarettes or anything and then they just locked him up and didn't explain. Think how he feels. How would you feel?"

This evidently was to Mullins.

"Listen, Mrs. North," Mullins said. "We didn't hurt the kid. We just asked him questions, sort of. And maybe the apple is just an apple." Mullins paused. "That she ate," he said, earnestly.

Pam North shook her head.

"She got the apple after he went," she said. "She ate it and then somebody killed her. Because she couldn't get the apple the first time she tried and—"

"If he can prove that, the kid's all right," Bill said, from the doorway. He went on. "If she got the apple after he left, she was alive after

49

he left. And he didn't go back. There wasn't time between his leaving and his clocking in where he worked. But he can't prove she got the apple after he left."

"Well," Pam said, "I think she did. Because otherwise the apple doesn't mean anything. And it does, because it's an oddity and oddities always do." She paused, considering. "At least," she said, "they always have before."

"Which doesn't—" Jerry began.

"I know, Jerry," Pam said. "That's all very well to say. Like there being no proof that when you put a kettle of water on a stove the water will boil, because maybe it has always been an accident and maybe this time the accident won't happen. But that doesn't mean anything." Pam paused again. "That's *philosophy,*" she said, with a certain inflection. The inflection left philosophy with little to stand on.

"I wish, Pam," Bill said, "that you'd quit worrying about the apple so much. If you want to worry, help us worry about Elliot."

Pam said there was no use worrying about Elliot until they caught him. She said you couldn't worry about things you knew as little about as you did about John Elliot. At least, she couldn't. Whereas the apple—

"This girl who saw the boy leave," she said. "This—what was her name?"

"Harper," Mullins said. "Cleo." His face assumed an expression of doubt. "That's what she said," he insisted. "Cleo."

"Cleo Harper," Mrs. North said. "What did she have to eat?"

"My God, Pam," Bill said. "What do you think we are?"

He looked at Dorian, but instead of smiling, she was looking thoughtfully at nothing. Then she looked at him and shook her head.

"Suppose," she said, "she had a baked apple. Wouldn't that make a difference?"

Bill looked at her and then at Pam North. They had something there.

"Right," he said. "It would. Or it might. We'll go into it, eventually. But meanwhile, I've—"

He did not finish because Detective Stein came in, looking as if he were in a hurry. He spoke as if he were in a hurry.

"The commissioner!" he said. "On the telephone, Lieutenant. The commissioner *himself!*"

Weigand also moved quickly. He guessed that the telephone on a table near the door was an extension of the one Stein had answered. He lifted the telephone from its cradle and said, "Lieutenant Weigand, sir." The commissioner answered and, as he listened, Weigand motioned to Stein. He motioned toward the hall, where another telephone was and then pointed down toward the floor. Stein nodded, hung up the telephone in the hall, came back and opened the door which opened on stairs to the kitchen floor. He went down. He would stop Mrs. Pennock if she grew too curious.

"Yes, sir," Weigand said. "That is, we did have."

The police commissioner's voice was soft, almost tired.

"I don't get that, Lieutenant," he said. "You did have a man named John Elliot? And now you haven't?"

This wasn't good. But Weigand told him. "I was careless," Weigand told the police commissioner. That wasn't good either.

"Well," the commissioner said, "you'll have to get him back, Lieutenant. But probably you'll have to let him go again when you do. Dan Beck called up just now."

"Yes, sir?" Weigand said. "The commentator?"

The police commissioner said he was afraid Beck was more than that. His voice sounded very tired. He suggested that the lieutenant had better look Beck up, some time. However—

"Just now," the commissioner said, "you'd better go and talk to him, Lieutenant. He says Elliot couldn't have done it. He says he can alibi Elliot completely. He wants to talk to somebody." The commissioner sighed. "He wanted to talk to me," he said. "I suggested you."

"Yes, sir," Weigand said.

"He's important," the commissioner said. "I'm afraid he is quite important. So you'd better go up and listen to him. And then look him up."

"Yes, sir," Bill Weigand said.

"And," the commissioner said, "come in tomorrow and tell me about it, Lieutenant. He's quite an interesting man." The commissioner sighed again. "He's—" he said. "Good night, Lieutenant."

Bill Weigand replaced the telephone and stood staring at it. If he knew the commissioner, he was supposed to read more in that than the words told. He would have to count the sighs and the pauses. He would have to look Dan Beck up very thoroughly. He would have to know why Dan Beck made the commissioner, who was uncommonly alert and had been a policeman all his life, so very tired. He would have to decide for himself how softly he would tread. The commissioner liked detective lieutenants to be perceptive.

He was abstracted as he turned back to the others and when they waited expectantly he shook his head and his eyes warned Dorian.

"I've got to see a man," he said.

He let it lie there.

"Oh," Pam said. "Like that?"

"Just like that," Weigand told her. "So suppose all of you go home." He smiled. "Or calling," he added. This last was permissive. Since, he suspected, they would anyway. Or Pam would, and the others with her.

"Take Mullins if you go calling," he said.

The Hotel André rose high above Park Avenue and when you went as high as you could in the Hotel André you found Dan Beck. An elevator reserved for those fortunates who deserved suites in The Wing rose reverently with Bill Weigand, who was permitted to call on one of those so elected. The elevator left Weigand standing to his shoetops in carpet and descended with discretion. It was as if the elevator had backed out of the presence. A wide door faced the lieutenant; a single, perfect door. Weigand pressed a white button near it and chimes played within. He had an instant's feeling that they should play "Nearer, My God, to Thee."

But the woman in black who answered the door was motherly. Weigand did not know what he had expected, but it was not this. She was not tall and she was comfortably round; she had white hair which looked as if it deserved a bonnet. Her face was round and pink and a little wrinkled; she had blue eyes and was guileless. It was an odd place to find her; here and not comfortably rocking on a front porch, behind the green lawn and—yes, certainly—rambler roses. If Weigand, or another, came armed, he should be disarmed at this gently guarded threshold.

"Mr. Beck?" Bill said, and was surprised at the gentleness in his voice.

"Yes," she said. "Please. Is it Lieutenant Weigand?"

Bill admitted it was.

"Mr. Beck is expecting you," she said. "Please."

The "Please" meant to enter. Bill Weigand entered. The foyer was as large as a waiting-room. Apparently, as the woman—"the lady," Weigand corrected himself—murmurously brushed him toward a chair, it was a waiting-room.

"If you will wait a moment," she said, smiling at him. She did not smile anxiously. She smiled hopefully. It would, her attitude conveyed, be pleasant if Mr. Weigand, visiting simple people from a world of great affairs, would consent to feel momentarily at home. Bill Weigand smiled back at her and sat.

"I'll tell Mr. Beck that you are here, sir," she said.

The sir was anomalous. She should, Weigand thought, have called him "William." At the least. Or possibly "son."

She went through a door at the right. There was a pause. Then a man appeared through the door at the left. He was not Beck; he was evidently a butler.

He was about the age of the woman. He was taller. Very pink scalp showed through the very white, not very thick hair which marked the upper limit of a pink and comfortable face. His voice was respectful without unction. It said that if Lieutenant Weigand would come this way, Mr. Beck would see him. He trusted that Lieutenant Weigand had not been kept waiting unduly.

"I was attending Mr. Beck when you rang, sir," the butler said. "That was why Mary admitted you. Mary is the housekeeper, sir."

It was, apparently, merely friendly explanation. Or perhaps dignified apology at a tiny irregularity in procedure.

"My wife, sir," the butler presently added, "the housekeeper for Mr. Beck."

That, Bill decided, made it perfect. A charming and devoted couple, devotedly in attendance on the adored master. Weigand said, for no particular reason, "certainly," and got up. He followed the butler through the door on the left. It opened on a hall, wide and deeply carpeted. It ended in a wide room. Almost all the side of the room which you faced on entering was of windows and beyond the windows lay the city, misty in falling snow, dim in its shrouded lights. At the doorway the butler paused and made a small sound of being present—something which might have been a cough, if it had not been a murmur.

"Mr. Beck, sir," the butler said, with this preliminary accomplished. "Lieutenant Weigand to see you, sir."

The man standing in front of the windows, looking out, was short and square. He turned. He had a large, handsome face. He was short, Weigand noticed, in the noticing way of a man trained to remember, because his legs were short. His torso was substantial and imposing. Seated, as at a speaker's table, Mr. Dan Beck would loom as magnificently as any. Unseated he was, it was evident, a little at a disadvantage.

The voice of Mr. Beck betrayed no recognition of disadvantage. As he heard it, Bill realized that, in its presence, no disadvantage could exist. It was an amazing voice; it was a voice you could hardly believe in. It was, Bill Weigand knew, the most beautiful voice he had ever heard or was apt to hear. It was low without harshness; it left an odd vibration in the air. As soon as it was silenced you wanted it to begin again. There was a sensuous pleasure in hearing it. For the sake of hearing it, Weigand thought, you would be tempted to believe anything it said. It would be hard to believe that anything borne on so beautiful a voice could be anything but beautiful and true.

"Good evening, Lieutenant," Dan Beck said. "I am sorry to have had to bother you."

There was, of course, that—nothing anyone would commonly have to say would be worthy so majestic an utterance. It would risk sounding a nursery rhyme set to organ music.

"I am sorry to have had to bother you," Dan Beck repeated. "May I make amends by offering you a drink?"

Weigand expected to decline, which was normal procedure. He was surprised to hear himself assenting. His assent was a tribute to atmosphere. Of unlimited riches indicated by a smooth gesture of Beck's right hand, Weigand chose scotch. The butler bent over the table. He returned with scotch generously in a glass, with ice in a silver bucket, with soda in a small bottle. When Weigand nodded, he dropped ice on the scotch and poured soda bubbling over it.

"Thank you, William," Dan Beck said, almost tenderly. "And my milk, please."

He smiled after William as the butler turned away. It was a friendly smile. He transferred it to Bill Weigand.

"But," he said, "we mustn't keep you standing, Lieutenant. Unless you care to look at my view for a moment. It is—a very fine view."

His voice held deprecation of the inadequate adjective.

"It is," Weigand said. "Very fine."

He carried his glass across to the windows. Beck stood beside him and the two looked out for a moment without words.

"It is a beautiful city," Beck said. "In all weathers, in all lights. A miraculous city."

Weigand nodded. He found, oddly, that he did not relish the necessity of using his own voice. In the inevitable comparison to Beck's, it must inevitably be inappropriate. He took the low chair Beck indicated.

"Miraculous," Beck said, taking a last look. "But distracting. William, will you pull the curtains when you've brought my milk?"

William brought the milk. Dan Beck regarded it, in its slender goblet, while William drew heavy curtains across the windows. His pleasant nod dismissed William and William withdrew, with dignity.

"To this I am doomed, I'm afraid," Beck said, indicating the milk. He did not explain. He sipped milk and Weigand sipped scotch, waiting. It had now become time for explanation. Beck began it simply.

"I spoke to the commissioner," Dan Beck said. "A very able, intelligent man. Don't you think, Lieutenant."

"Very," Weigand agreed. He waited. Beck outwaited him. "You have something to tell us about a man named Elliot?" Weigand said. "Right?"

"John," Beck said. "John Elliot. I didn't want you to waste time on him, Lieutenant. He could not have killed Miss Lawrence."

"No?" Weigand said. "I thought he could. He ran away."

Beck said he knew about that. It was very foolish.

"He is excitable," Beck said, his voice hanging softly in the room. "He is a very young man, Lieutenant."

"Is he?" Weigand said.

"For his years," Dan Beck amplified. "For his years, Lieutenant. He is sensitive—perhaps immature, in a sense. And he was very disturbed, which was natural. You will admit that?"

"Right," Weigand said. "He was disturbed. He slugged a policeman and got away. He was evidently disturbed." Weigand found himself smiling slightly at Dan Beck as he spoke.

Beck made small, disapproving sounds. They deprecated John Elliot's youthful, but understandable, exuberance; his evident bad judgment in striking a policeman.

"Impulsive," Beck said. "Impulsive—and foolish. I don't defend him, Lieutenant. He should have been more trusting. He should have realized he was in no danger, so long as he was innocent. And he is innocent, Lieutenant. I assure you."

"I hope so," Weigand said. "Why is he innocent?"

"Because he wasn't there," Beck said. "Rather—because she was alive after he was there. There is no argument about that, Lieutenant."

"Isn't there?" Weigand said. "Why?"

"Because I talked to her after he had gone," Dan Beck said.

"You talked to her," Weigand repeated. "Right. And—?"

Beck told it. He told it quietly, as matter-of-factly as his voice permitted. To begin with, he also had been at Miss Lawrence's the evening before with other friends meeting at a convenient place for food and drink and conversation. He had left about 1 o'clock, most of the others remaining.

"I came here," Beck said. "I had some work to do. I work best at night, in a locked room, with no one else around. I do not even use a secretary."

"Right," Weigand said. "And—?"

At a quarter of three, Ann Lawrence had telephoned. Beck had answered impatiently; had grown more patient when he heard the girl's excited voice. She had wanted to know whether John Elliot had come to Beck's apartment. Beck had said, "No, why should he?"

"We had a dreadful quarrel," Ann had said, according to Beck. Beck remembered well, evidently. He could quote verbatim. "We had a dreadful quarrel and he rushed out. I want to talk to him. And he isn't at his apartment. I *have* to talk to him."

"She was very excited, Lieutenant," Beck said. "Very disturbed. She thought he might have come here. She was afraid that—well, that he might behave impulsively. It appeared that the quarrel was serious."

Beck had told her that Elliot had not come there, but had tried to reassure her. He promised that if Elliot did come, he would see that he telephoned her at once. But he was sure everything would be all right. He asked how long it had been since Elliot had left the house on Gramercy Park.

It had been about twenty minutes, she said, Beck told Weigand, who listened without comment. "I told her that that barely gave him time to get home. He lives over in the Sutton Place district. If he got a cab he might, with no traffic to speak of, just have done it. But cabs are hard to get now. I told her all that."

"By the way," Weigand said, "you're sure it was Miss Lawrence? You knew her voice?"

Dan Beck seemed surprised.

"Of course," he said. "There was no doubt in my mind—there isn't now. I knew her quite well." He paused. "A lovely girl," he said. There was a moment's pause. Bill Weigand sipped his drink.

"Right," Weigand said, then. "She said he had left, and she was still alive. But of course you see the hole in that, Mr. Beck."

"That he might have gone back," Beck said. "Of course, Lieutenant. But he didn't. I can testify that he didn't."

He did testify. Although he had tried to reassure Ann Lawrence that Elliot had come to no harm, Beck himself was worried. He was afraid that, if the quarrel with Ann had really been a serious one, John Elliot might do something—something—

"Rash?" Weigand said, supplying the inevitable.

"Rash," Dan Beck agreed.

So, after he had finished talking to Ann Lawrence and sat for a few minutes—not more than two or three—worrying, Dan Beck had telephoned Elliot at his apartment. And Elliot had answered.

"He had just come in," Beck explained. "He came in after Ann telephoned him, probably while she was talking to me."

Elliot was, Beck could tell from his voice, excited and unhappy and in no mood to remain alone. So Beck had urged the younger man to come to the André, and Elliot had agreed and come. He had, however, refused to telephone Ann and that Beck himself had done, a few minutes after three. He had told her that Elliot was all right, and would be more completely all right after he had slept on it. She had been relieved.

"And?" Weigand said.

And Elliot had stayed in Beck's apartment for a couple of hours, talking and having a few drinks. When he finally left he was much quieter and had agreed to call the girl and make things right the next day. He had been bitter when he came; he was not bitter when he left. He had left around five o'clock, planning to go home and to bed.

"So you see," Beck said, "he could not possibly have—harmed Ann. It was physically impossible, which is what you want to know. It was emotionally impossible, too. But that is not, I realize, a tangible point. The alibi is, isn't it?"

Weigand nodded. It was a very tangible point; it was tangible enough to clear John Elliot, if the Medical Examiner remained certain Ann Lawrence was dead at four that morning. This would annoy Deputy Chief Inspector Artemus O'Malley. If it held. With that testimony, from a man of Beck's standing, they would never convict Elliot.

He asked a few questions. Beck was certain he had really talked to Ann Lawrence; he was certain about the times. Weigand made notes and nodded.

"The second time you called her," he said. "The time you called to tell her Elliot was all right. Did she seem to be alone?"

"Alone?" Beck repeated, as if it were a new idea. "I didn't—wait, I see what you mean. Let me think." He thought. There was a slightly puzzled look on his face.

"I don't know," he said. "I hadn't thought. I heard no one else, certainly—no other sounds, as you do sometimes. But I'm not sure she *was* alone. Now it seems to me there was something in her voice—as if—as if—"

"As if there *were* someone else there?" Weigand suggested. "A—a conscious note? As if someone else were listening?"

Beck shook his head.

"Really," he said, "I'm not sure. It may be I am imagining it now, because you suggested it. But I'm not sure there wasn't something like that—a difference in her voice. But it is all very intangible."

Weigand stared at his glass. The case seemed to be made up of facts which were too abrupt and unrelated; of intangibles which were too elusive. Beck, he decided, was one of the abrupt and unrelated facts; the baked apple was at once a fact and an intangible. Weigand's mind felt cluttered. And if there had been someone, who was not John Elliot, with Ann when Beck called her back that made a small, annoying addition to the clutter. The beautiful voice of Dan Beck sounded again.

"I hope this isn't disconcerting, Lieutenant," Beck said. "I suppose, in a way, it must be. The boy's behavior—You must have felt that the case was cut and dried. But I knew you wouldn't want to make a mistake."

"No," Weigand agreed. "Of course not, Mr. Beck. We appreciate it, your help. Your promptness. People aren't always so helpful."

"I know," Dan Beck said, in his soft and beautiful voice. "I know. People—misunderstand. I have experienced that too, Lieutenant. We must—reason with them."

A half smile made the words only half serious, ringed them just perceptibly in marks of quotation. Bill Weigand found himself smiling in return, and in acquiescence. He finished his drink, glanced at the watch on his wrist, and stood up. Dan Beck looked up at him.

"I realize, of course, that you have much to do," Beck said. "But couldn't you have another drink, perhaps? Before you go?"

The voice was friendly, inviting. Weigand shook his head, with regret.

"Then," Beck said, standing up and holding out his hand, "it is pleasant to have met you, Lieutenant. I hope what I've told you hasn't really been—disconcerting."

"Murder is usually disconcerting, Mr. Beck," Bill Weigand said. "And full of complications. Probably you have merely removed a complication."

Bill took the offered hand. The grip was firm but not athletic. Behind Weigand at the door there was the small sound which meant the reappearance of William.

"Lieutenant Weigand is leaving, William," Dan Beck said, with polite regret.

"Yes sir," William said, also with the faintest hint of sorrow in his tone. "If you will come this way, sir."

Weigand, his hand shaken once more and released, went that way. It occurred to him that there must be a button in the arm of Beck's chair, convenient to summon William. Or William read minds—or listened at doors. The last seemed improbable, as below the dignity of the establishment.

Weigand followed William down the corridor and into the foyer. He went through the door William opened for him and found the elevator waiting. Apparently its operator, also, could read minds—or could be summoned by a signal operated from within the apartment. It would be comfortable to be of the elect, Weigand thought, entering the elevator. It started down as the door was still closing.

Weigand's face was level with the floor and the closing doors were still a crack. So his glimpse of the slightly opened door of the Beck apartment—the door William had closed behind him—was momentary and obstructed. Weigand had only time to glimpse a pink face surmounted by white hair; the face, from its height above the floor, of Mary, who was Mrs. William. For some reason she had decided to have a final look at him. Little old ladies could be curious, apparently. Weigand said, "hmm," under his breath.

The elevator carried Weigand to the lobby floor of the Hotel André.

Weigand's legs carried him to the hotel office and there he looked at telephone records. They were unsatisfactory. There was no record of incoming calls; there was no record of outgoing calls from the Beck apartment at the proper early morning times. But Weigand did not allow himself to be pleased, because he was afraid he knew the answer. He enquired, and got the answer. Beck had two telephones, one on a private line which did not pass through the switchboard. So he could call as he liked, and nobody the wiser.

Weigand tucked more facts into his mind and went out through revolving doors into a world where snow still fell placidly. He flicked the accumulation from his windshield with his gloves; he started the Buick's motor and let the wipers struggle with the snow that was left. After a little huffing and puffing, they managed it. Weigand drove east through quiet, slushy streets and came to a small, sedate apartment house in the Sutton Place district. He parked in front of it. He found the doorman inside, out of the snow and leaning confidingly against a boxed-in radiator.

Weigand did not expect to find much in John Elliot's apartment. He found more than he expected; to begin with, he found far more apartment. He would, he decided, looking at the apartment and the furniture in it, have to revise his tentative guess about Elliot's financial status. He was no indigent writer, scratching small checks out of the pulp paper on Grub Street. For a writer he was, evidently, doing fine.

The apartment had only a living-room, a small bedroom, a bath and something which was half a kitchen. But the living-room stretched for twenty feet or more along one side of the apartment building and was almost as wide as it was long. Its ceiling was high; heavy yellow curtains looped at each window from close to the ceiling to the floor and the floor was deep in carpet. The furniture, low and modern, had cost money. As a recent furnisher of an apartment, Weigand guessed that it cost a lot of money. Mr. Elliot had not stinted himself. Under book cases which ran along one wall there were cabinets and Weigand looked into them. Mr. Elliot had had a thirst, or expected one, and had not planned to stint himself.

Bill Weigand wondered why all this surprised him, since he had had no particular reason to think that Mr. Elliot was a poor man. Then he remembered. Mrs. Pennock had asserted that Elliot was after Ann

Lawrence's money. At the time he had had no reason not to accept this, but now he wondered. From the looks of things, Elliot had enough money of his own. Or—or perhaps, of course, he was already getting some of Ann Lawrence's money. Possibly he was a financed writer, on one basis or another. For his art? Or his arts? That would need finding out. But it was hard to believe that Ann Lawrence had needed to buy devotion. Her picture had not looked it; the descriptions of her had not sounded it. Another thing to check on. There were too many things to check on; too many facts with intangible meanings, too many intangibles without factual foundation. Weigand stood in the middle of the living-room and looked around it and sighed. Looking at the room, he tried to guess more about Elliot.

He was a man of taste, and money and leisure to gratify it. He probably dressed well. Bill went to the bedroom and opened the bedroom closet. He dressed well. He made himself comfortable as he worked. Bill went back to the living-room and crossed to a low desk and pulled at a handle. A typewriter came up out of the desk. Weigand looked at it, saw that the platen was unmarked by key impressions—why should it be? he wondered—and let it clunk back into the desk. Then the telephone on top of the desk rang and Bill, without hesitation, answered it.

"Finding anything?" a man's voice said, cheerfully.

Bill Weigand removed surprise from his voice before he answered.

"Who did you want?" he said.

The voice advised him to come off it.

"This is Elliot," he said. "John Elliot. You're in my apartment, whoever you are. Patrolman? Sergeant? Inspector, maybe?"

"Lieutenant," Weigand told him. "Why don't you come home, Mr. Elliot?"

The voice laughed.

"Wouldn't you like me to?" it enquired.

"It would save time," Weigand told him. "Just time, Mr. Elliot. If you are Mr. Elliot. You're being a damn fool, you know."

"How's the cop?" the voice enquired. "The one I had to slug?"

"Bad," Bill lied for him. "Very bad. You're in trouble there, too, Elliot."

"Hell," the voice said. "I don't believe you, Lieutenant. He was coming to when I left."

This was profitless, Bill Weigand thought. Elliot needed spanking, at the least.

"If you are Elliot," Bill said, "you'd better go to the nearest police station. Because we'll catch you. And we don't like guys who slug cops."

Weigand didn't, the voice told him, make it sound enticing. However, eventually, he might do just that. Go to a station house and give himself up.

"With my lawyer," he said. "Mouthpiece, you'd call it."

"You've been reading the wrong books," Bill told him. "I call it lawyer. You're still a damn fool, Elliot."

"Maybe," the man said. "But I've got things to do. I've got to see a person—about a murder. I've got to do that first."

His voice had changed, suddenly. He wasn't being amusing now. He sounded as if he meant to see a man about a murder.

"In a mirror?" Weigand asked. "Where are you?"

"Hell, no," the voice said. "I didn't kill anybody. Didn't his nibs tell you? And I'm near enough. And not too near."

He had to be, Weigand decided. Near enough to see who went into the apartment or—or to see a car with tell-tale red headlights. Probably that was it. And so he had gone somewhere near and telephoned. Why? Just to be cute?

"Listen," the voice said. "Are you still there?"

The man—call him Elliot—wasn't being playful now.

"I'll tell you," he said. "I know the person you want—maybe. I'm going to find out. If it works out the way I think it will, I can clean it up for you."

"If you know anything, spill it," Weigand said. "Don't mess around with it. You—"

But there was no use going on. A dead telephone wire would not be interested. Mr. Elliot, if it had been Mr. Elliot, had hung up and gone away. Cursing softly, Weigand dialed headquarters and said the right things to the right people. Elliot, if he had been in the neighborhood, had better move fast. But hell—he would move fast. You didn't catch men that way. Not in New York, anyway. Not with what the newspapers liked to call "cordons" "thrown" around areas. A cordon was merely a good many men, peering through a dimout made dimmer by falling snow. It wasn't a wire fence. The chances were prohibitive that Mr. Elliot would, for the time being, continue on whatever path he had laid out for himself.

There were too many people in this, Weigand decided; too many people behaving irrationally; too many who seemed determined to bang head-on into hostile stone walls. Mrs. Pennock, who was probably up to blackmail, which was dangerous. Mr. Elliot who, if he were not himself a murderer—and somehow Bill doubted at the moment that he was—was looking for trouble if he decided to turn detective. And Elliot wouldn't, Weigand thought, know what to do about trouble if he found it.

"I'd rather trust Pam," he thought, irrationally. She had a knack of getting out; a knack so far just equal to her knack for getting in.

Bill looked around the apartment again. He opened drawers and saw papers in them—papers that somebody would have to go over, as time went on. But not necessarily tonight. There was a part of a manuscript in one of the drawers and Weigand skimmed over a few pages. It appeared to be a novel. It gave Weigand an idea. He might as well use Elliot's telephone, and cost Elliot a call. He dialed the Norths' number and, after a moment, Jerry said "hello."

"Bill," Weigand said. "Do you know a writer named John Elliot? Did he ever send your firm a manuscript or anything?"

There was a brief pause.

"No," Jerry said. "It doesn't mean anything to me, offhand. Of course—"

"Of course," Weigand agreed. "The world's full of writers. You're only one publisher. But you never heard of him?"

"No," Jerry said. "I didn't. And listen—Pam's out somewhere. About that damned apple, I guess."

"And Dorian?" Weigand asked. His voice was quick.

"She's here," Jerry told him. "*She's* all right. But where's *my* wife?"

"Is Mullins with her?" Weigand asked. Jerry said he guessed so. That had been the plan, at any rate. He and Dorian had been told that four was a crowd and had gone to the Norths' to wait. They were still waiting. Jerry was acid.

"Damn your corpses," he said. "I am now going back and make another attack on Dorian's virtue."

He hung up. Bill hung up, grinning. He didn't think Pam North was in any danger. Yet, anyhow.

• 6 •

TUESDAY, 10:45 P.M. TO 11:30 P.M.

CLEO HARPER'S conversation was oddly eager; it was as if she had been hoarding words and had now, inexplicably, turned spendthrift. Pam North had been sorry for her from the moment she came down, her pale eyes reddened as if she had been crying, a moist handkerchief in her working fingers. She was too tall and too thin, her pale hair was too pale. She stood a little stooped because she was too tall and that embarrassed her. The room she came into was harsh and impersonal. It was a room in which nobody had ever lingered; Cleo Harper was a girl with whom nobody had ever lingered. They belonged together, Pam thought—a girl who was going nowhere and a room to which nobody ever willingly went; a room in which, probably, young men had waited uneasily for girls to come down to them from the upstairs rooms of Breckley House, and from which young men and their girls had fled a little anxiously, as from something inimical.

For the first time, Pam thought, watching Cleo Harper sitting uncomfortably on an uncomfortable chair, worrying a damp handkerchief—for the first time I understand what places like this are for; sterilized places like this, in which girls voluntarily live in dormitories, hygienically. They are for girls like Cleo Harper, with whom nobody will ever really want to live. They are for tall girls with flat chests and inevitably damp handkerchiefs, and always with slight colds in the head.

Cleo Harper had a slight cold in the head and as she talked she sniffled. It was also evident after a moment that she had been crying and was ready to cry again. She cried again, unbecomingly, when Mullins identified himself, and introduced Mrs. North without identification, and said that he wanted to go over again the circumstances of her meeting Frank Martinelli that afternoon. The tall, pale girl bent her head and gulped. You could, Pam found, be very sorry for her, without liking her.

"Oh," Cleo Harper said, "it was dreadful—dreadful. To do a thing like that—to Fran. To Fran of all people. To dear Fran."

Her words are inadequate, too, Pam North thought. She means more than that.

"She was my best friend," Cleo said and dabbed at her nose. "Ever since I went to the company she was my best friend. She understood."

Cleo Harper did not say what Frances McCalley had understood—what there had been to understand. It was as if she had merely used the word which lay nearest.

"And she's dead," Cleo said. "I just can't believe it. I just can't. What a horrible thing to do."

"It was horrible," Pam North said. "I know how you must feel."

But I don't, Pam thought. I can never know how she feels. It's as if she were feeling in a different language.

"About this boy," Mullins said. "This Martinelli."

But it was not easy to guide Cleo Harper. She was insistent that they know about Frances McCalley, who had been her dearest friend, with whom she had "always been," with whom she had gone to movies and walked home from work, with whom once she had gone to a camp on summer vacation, with whom—in summer—she had ridden back and forth on the Staten Island ferry. You could see the two of them, as she talked; perhaps, Pam thought, you could see more than she meant them to see, or more than she knew.

Because there was nothing to indicate that Frances McCalley had been a girl whom Cleo Harper would have contented. You could only guess at Frances now, and guess with little knowledge. But Martinelli, murderer or not, was a dark, angry youth and, murderer or not, he appeared to have had a dark, angry attachment to Frances McCalley. And a girl who was, contentedly, Cleo Harper's best friend would hardly, you could suspect, engender such an attachment. People who are killed violently, unless they are killed by accident, usually have in some fashion been violently alive. Or so Pam North, listening to words which got them nowhere, thought as she listened. No one would, for example, kill Cleo Harper.

"Unless," Pam said to herself, "they were married to her. But nobody ever would be."

Pam heard herself think this and was suddenly shocked. I'm cruel, she thought; I'm contemptuous because she isn't attractive, I'm cruel because Jerry loves me and nobody will ever love her—no man and, not really, any woman. She's just trying to make herself believe that Fran was her dearest friend; that she was dear to Fran. She is making it up for herself so that she can have it as a memory and—

"Until she met that horrible boy," Cleo said. "That horrible, black, dirty boy. She must have been crazy—it wasn't like her. She was never that way."

There was an odd emphasis on the word "that." Cleo Harper spoke as if there were a kind of unspeakable loathesomeness about being "that way." But as far as appeared, she meant merely that Frances had been normally responsive—had been at any rate interested—in a young man.

"He did something to her," Cleo said. And now there was a new note in her thin voice. Before she had been sorry for herself, and writing ineffectual drama about her own not quite believable bereavement. But there was a new note now, not immediately decipherable. If Cleo had seemed strong enough to hate, you might have thought it hate. It caught Pam North's attention.

"It ought to be him," the girl said. "Him lying there, all cut and with blood all over him. Somebody ought to have killed him and then none of it would have happened."

Cleo Harper gulped and dabbed at her eyes. Then she looked up and it occurred to Pam that perhaps she was not altogether ineffectual. There was something odd about her eyes.

"The dirty little beast," the girl said. "The dirty—*thing!*"

There was no doubt about the note in her voice now. It was venom. There was room in the thin body and the thin mind of Cleo Harper for one large emotion—hatred. It was surprising.

"Now, miss," Mullins said. "Now, miss. You don't want to work yourself up. O.K.?"

"You ought to kill him for it," Cleo Harper said. "You ought— you've got a right. He killed her—he changed her and then he killed her. Somebody ought to kill him. He oughtn't to be alive."

It was abashing. That was the only word for it. It was so naked; it was so much more than people said to other people. It spread emotions out too openly, let you see too deep. I don't want to know that much about her, Pam thought. It is more than anybody ought to know about anybody else. It's—ugly.

And it lay in the tone, in the inflection.

"Now, miss," Mullins said. "You oughtn't to talk that way. It ain't—"

He broke off, looking puzzled. Pam had a disturbing notion that Mullins had been about to say it wasn't ladylike. Or perhaps he had really seen, and almost said, that it was not human.

Mullins looked at Mrs. North, with a kind of anxiety. It was, his look told her, getting beyond him.

It was beyond Pam too, she thought. Or she hoped it was—or she hoped she was wrong. She hoped that Cleo Harper hated Frank Martinelli because she believed he had killed her friend; that she felt a hatred which, although extreme, would still be comprehensible. Pam hoped that all this venom, which was not like anything she had seen before or wanted to see, was directed against a murderer, and not merely against a man—because he was a man and so had "changed" the feelings of a girl.

I don't care what people do, Pam thought. It isn't that. Or how they feel, because any way of feeling can be natural and all right. Or I suppose it can—for some. But this would be ugly.

Pam North groped for a word more accurate. When she found it she hesitated to use it even in her own mind because it was too big a word for people. For ordinary people, anyway. But the word was "evil."

Looking at Cleo Harper, hearing her bitter words continue, Pam thought that there was something evil, and unexpected, in the room. Or that there might be. It was not clear. Possibly, Pam thought, she was now herself a writer of melodrama, inventing motives, imagining mysteries in simple things. Probably Cleo Harper was merely an overwrought, not very effectual, person who had lost a friend and lacked self-control.

It was easier to think that. More comfortable. Thinking that made the world more comprehensible and, in a way, more tolerable. That, Pam decided, was why people had quit believing in evil. It was too uncomfortable a belief. It was too unseemly. Even now, with something enormous that was surely evil loose in the world, and not yet bound, it was hard to believe in evil on a smaller, more human scale. It was easier and less alarming to think that you were merely making things up.

People did not believe in big emotions, except, of course, their own emotions, which they always considered big. They—

"Philosophy," Pam said to herself, alarmed, deciding to stop it at once.

"Huh?" Mullins said. Cleo Harper merely stopped talking for a moment and looked at Pam through reddened eyes. Pam realized she had done it again.

"I'm sorry," she said. "I must have been thinking out loud. I do, you know. Even when I think I'm not. Like now."

"Why philosophy?" Mullins said. "I don't get it."

"Neither do I, Mr. Mullins," Cleo Harper said. "I'm trying to tell you—and she—"

"I'm really sorry," Pam said. "It was just a thought. I was really listening. You were going to tell us about seeing the Martinelli boy at the cafeteria."

Cleo Harper hadn't been, precisely. She had been telling them what ought to be done with Franklin Martinelli. But she was oddly obedient. She took up a new line of thought without protest and now Pam did listen.

"He was running," she said. "His face was all twisted up. And—I just remembered. He had one hand in his pocket, like he was holding something. The knife!"

Mullins shook his head, chiefly in answer to the question in Mrs. North's eyes. It couldn't have been the knife, he said. They had found the knife, on the floor where it had been dropped, apparently, as soon as its work was done. It was a clasp knife with one long blade and a rough handle which was smeared, but not usefully imprinted, by the hand which grasped it.

"A sticker," Mullins said. "Sort of a Boy Scout knife. Like a kid might have had."

"His hand was in his pocket, anyway," the tall, thin girl insisted. "I thought it was a knife—afterward. He was almost running because he had just killed her and—"

It was difficult to keep her even remotely objective. Martinelli had, it appeared, gone very rapidly through a revolving door, setting it swirling. Cleo had been indignant and turned to say something to him and recognized him.

"He looked terrible," she said. "Like he was crazy. So I didn't say anything. He turned and ran up the street."

"Ran?" Pam repeated.

"It was almost running," the girl said. "Because he was afraid—because of what he'd done. And the knife in his pocket, all bloody."

"Listen," Mullins said. "He didn't have the knife. Whoever did it left the knife."

"I don't believe it," the girl said. "You're trying to pretend he didn't do it. You're crooked and he's paid you something or—"

"Jeeze," Mullins said. "Jeeze, miss." He looked at her as if he were measuring her for something. "You've got some mighty funny ideas, miss," he said, with unexpected mildness.

"You oughtn't to say things like that, Miss Harper," Pam North told her. "They're confusing. You don't understand about things like that. People don't pay for murders." She paused to consider. "Not that way, anyhow," she said. "Like buying a license. Not from Sergeant Mullins."

"You don't know," the girl said, looking at Pam. "How *could* you know?"

This, Pam thought, is one of the strangest conversations. One of the very strangest.

"Listen," she said. "Can't you just pretend you *don't* know the boy killed her? And just tell us what happened?"

"He ran," the girl said. "With his face all twisted and with the knife in his pocket."

Of course, Pam thought, she could be just a little queer, perhaps only because of strain. Or she could be—what was the word?—psychotic. Or, of course, she could be, for some purpose which was not clear, pretending to be these things. She was difficult.

"And to think," Pam said to herself, "that I thought she was just a flat-chested girl, who didn't mean anything! Just something facts would come out of if you pressed a button."

Then Pam looked a little alarmed at the others, thinking that again she might have thought out loud. But apparently this time she hadn't.

"Suppose," Mullins said, "I just ask some questions. And you just answer them. O.K.?"

"What do you want to know?" the girl said. "I told you about seeing him."

What he wanted to know Mullins got slowly. She had stared after Franklin Martinelli for a moment while he ran—or perhaps merely walked rapidly—up the street. Then she had gone on into the restaurant. She had gone up to the counter. She had got her lunch.

"What?" Pam said.

"I got my lunch," the girl said.

Pam was impatient.

"I know," she said. "What for lunch?"

"Oh," the girl said. "Stew. Irish stew."

It was incongruous. Pam had expected—

"Oh," she said. "Not just a sandwich? Cream cheese and jelly or something?"

"Stew," the girl said. "I was hungry. I didn't know then that—"

"Of course not," Pam said. "I didn't mean that. And then what?"

"Then I ate it," the girl said.

Pam shook her head.

"For dessert," she said. "What did you have for dessert?" She paused. "A baked apple?" she said. She said it casually.

"No," the girl said. "Why? What made you think a baked apple?"

"I didn't," Pam said. "I was just—suggesting. As if I'd been in and you came in from outside and I said 'is it clearing up?' or something like that. Meaning, what is it doing?"

"Oh," the girl said. "I had a fruit salad. I looked at the baked apples, but I don't really—"

"What!" Pam said. She said it very suddenly.

"—like baked apples particularly," Cleo Harper said. "There are always those little hard slivers around the core."

"There shouldn't be," Pam told her. "That's just careless preparation. You ought to—"

She broke off. It was hard enough to keep Cleo Harper on the subject, without helping her this way.

"Listen," Pam said. "Forget about that. You saw the baked apples?"

The girl nodded.

"The man just put them down," she said. "A tray full of them. That's why I looked. Usually I don't even look at them, but these just came in."

"A full tray?" Pam insisted. "I mean—a completely full tray? Not even one gone?"

"Listen," the girl said. "I think you're nuts, whoever you are. What difference does it make?"

"Well," Pam said. "It makes all—"

Again she broke off, because Mullins suddenly shook his head at her.

"It doesn't make any," she said. "I don't know why I asked. It doesn't mean anything."

Cleo Harper looked at Pam North with great and evident doubt. Then she shook her head.

"So I looked at the apples," she said. "And I got a fruit salad and I went over and sat with a girl I knew and ate lunch. And then—when I was leaving—somebody screamed and—and—"

"You went over?" Pam asked. Her voice was gentle. Whatever the girl was, you had to be gentle.

Cleo Harper nodded without speaking. She drew in her breath in a quick, shivering gasp.

"Don't remember it," Pam said. "It doesn't do any good."

It was good advice, and obviously futile.

Mullins waited a moment and then he took over. He got a guess that Cleo Harper had taken about twenty minutes to eat her lunch, talking with the other girl as she ate. So it was perhaps twenty-five minutes after she had come in, and seen the Martinelli boy going out, that the scream had come. Pamela North broke in, her question to Mullins.

"Couldn't you have told?" she asked. "From the outside booth, I mean. Somebody looking in? Doesn't the mere fact that it was almost half an hour mean that the boy couldn't have done it because somebody would have found her in that time?"

Mullins shook his head. It was not light in the booth—not glaringly light. The Greystone Coffee Shop went in for subdued lighting. It had not been unduly crowded; a person sitting alone in a booth had a reasonable chance of remaining alone. A person passing and looking in casually, and not actually sitting down opposite, might have assumed that she was merely sitting there. The woman who discovered her had done so because, with the restaurant filling up, she *had* started to sit down opposite the huddled girl. Then she had screamed.

"But," Mullins said, looking at Mrs. North questioningly, "that doesn't matter now because—don't you get it, Mrs. North?"

"Of course," Mrs. North said. "Who thought of it? Who brought it out, Sergeant? I just wondered whether we needed it."

The girl looked at Mullins and then at Mrs. North.

"You talk and talk," she said. "It doesn't make sense. The Martinelli boy killed her and you just sit here and talk and talk. And don't make sense."

"You're sure the tray was *full* of apples?" Pam insisted. "You have to remember."

"But I do remember," the girl said. "They just brought it in—a man just brought it in. Why shouldn't it be full?"

"Because if it was," Pam said, "the Martinelli boy couldn't have. Because—"

Mullins stood up.

"I wouldn't say any more, Mrs. North," he said. "We won't bother Miss Harper with all that. O.K.?"

"I don't—" Pam began. But Mullins shook his head at her. She still didn't see why not, and thought of saying so, but decided it wasn't important. Then she went out with Mullins, leaving the thin girl with a damp handkerchief clutched in one hand in the room. Cleo Harper looked after them, apparently not understanding.

Outside, Mullins indicated, with a kind of bumbling tact, that Mrs. North sometimes talked too much.

"She'd deny it in a minute to get at the kid," he said. "If she knew what to deny—and maybe, from what you said, she does now. But there's no reason giving her a blueprint, Mrs. North."

"All right," Mrs. North said. "But it is a blueprint, isn't it? As plain as, or plainer. Plainer, I should think. In black and white, not blue."

"I—" Mullins began. He paused.

"You know," he said, in quiet wonderment, "sometimes I understand you, Mrs. North." Mullins considered himself with a kind of awe. "Honest to God," he said. "Sometimes it ain't screwy at all, really."

They were, Mrs. North told him, almost sternly, talking about blueprints. Not about her.

"And baked apples," she said. "And an alibi." She paused. "And you know," she said, "it really *is* an alibi. Not something people just *call* an alibi. He really was somewhere else when it happened. He must have been—punching the time clock, maybe. Where he worked. Or perhaps actually working."

Mullins was not really happy about it. But he said "yeah" and added that he guessed it was.

"Since it must have been *after* the Harper girl came in," Pam pointed out. "Because there weren't any apples earlier, and a full tray came in when Cleo did and Frances *had* eaten one. The poor kid!" Pam thought a moment. "It's kind of sadder that way," she said. "Nothing but a baked apple at the last, with all the other things—all the good things—in the world. Things with fine, sharp tastes and good smells and all the strange things she's never—And in the end just a baked apple."

She was not in the least facetious. Mullins didn't think she was. He thought it over and said, "yeah," again.

"Only," he said, "maybe she liked them better than anything else."

Pam shook her head.

"That wouldn't be possible," she said. "Baked apples aren't like that, even if you like them. They're just—all right. At best that's all they are. Not like olives or—or—something with a new sauce. Or beefsteak outdoors over charcoal. Or—"

"Or cornbeef," Mullins said, suddenly. "The kind that crumbles, sort of. I guess you're right, Mrs. North."

They looked at each other, a little hungrily. Sergeant Mullins was the first to break it.

"Of course," he said, but without conviction, "there could have been *another* tray of apples. Making three in all. And she could have had one from that. While Martinelli was still there."

"I don't believe it," Pam said. "Neither do you, Sergeant. Not really. That would be too many baked apples. Altogether."

There was, Mullins told her, a way to check up on that. They were walking through the snow, away from the safe, uninteresting neighborhood picked by the founders of Breckley House as appropriate to safe and uninteresting lives. They were looking, without optimism, for a taxicab.

"Remember how many there used to be?" Pam said, waving at one which went on disdainfully, with successful passengers gloating behind windows. Mullins agreed without emphasis, giving matter-of-fact acknowledgment to departed luxuries. He was looking for something else; he found it in the lights of a cigar store, doubly dimmed out by the falling snow. He led Mrs. North to it. It had a soda fountain, too, and Mrs. North sat promptly.

"Oh yes," she said, "and really good vichyssoise. But meanwhile, I'm going to have coffee. Aren't you, Mr. Mullins?"

Mullins said he was, in a minute. He pulled out a notebook and went through its pages, said, "yeah," abstractedly and found a telephone booth. He was gone a good while, and Mrs. North drank coffee. Then he came back and sat beside her.

"Two was all," he said. "I got the manager and he got somebody else—the baked apple department, I guess. There was only two trays of apples, so I guess you're right."

Pam nodded and said she thought so. Because otherwise, what was the sense of it?

"And sometimes I don't," Mullins said. "There's sometimes, Mrs. North, that you stop me." He paused. "Cold," he said. "How's about some coffee, bud?"

Bud produced coffee. Mullins drank. Mrs. North seemed impatient.

"Well," she said. "We'll have to go tell him. The poor kid."

"In the morning," Mullins said. "After we see the Loot."

"Now," Mrs. North insisted. "We don't have to get him out, or anything. But we have to talk to him right away, now that we know he didn't do it."

"Why?" said Mullins, gulping.

"Because," Pam said, "he knew the girl. So maybe he knows why somebody would want to kill her." She paused.

"And if he does," she added, simply, "I think we ought to ask him. Don't you?"

Sergeant Mullins looked at her, started to say something, withdrew it and shook his head.

"Sometimes—" he said, indefinitely. He abandoned it. "O.K., Mrs. North," he said. "He's in the precinct. We'll talk to him like you say."

· 7 ·

TUESDAY, 11:31 P.M. TO WEDNESDAY, 1:15 A.M.

JERRY NORTH said, in the tone of one whose worst expectations are more than fulfilled, "What? What, Pam?"

"The police station," Pam told him, patiently. "Only not to stay."

"Well," Jerry said, "that's good. That's fine. Why, Pam?"

"Because it was just as we thought," Pam told him, using a generous plural to mollify. "He couldn't have done it on account of the apple. Only it's too complicated to go into on the telephone, Jerry. And now we're going over to tell him he didn't do it."

"Doesn't he know?" Jerry said. "I mean—do you have to tell him?" He paused, apparently listening to himself. "Anybody knows if he *didn't* commit a murder," Jerry went on, clarifying. "It isn't as if everything had gone black, Pam."

"Gone black?" Pam said, interested. "What's gone black?" She paused momentarily in turn. "Jerry!" she said. "Did you eat something?"

"Eat something?" Jerry said. "What do you mean, did I eat something?"

"Ptomaine," Pam said. "That's what it sounds like. All right, in just a minute."

"Pamela!" Jerry said, with severity. "What's happened to you, for God's sake?"

"Mullins," Pam said. "Knocking on the door. Of the booth. He seems to think we ought to go to jail."

"Maybe—" Jerry said, and broke off. "I think you'd better come home, Pam. After all, Dorian's here."

"Good," Pam said. "Put him on, won't you, dear?"

"Not Bill," Jerry explained. "Just Dorian. Waiting. Also, I'm waiting. Pretty soon Bill will be here."

"Tell him to wait," Pam said. "I'll have Mullins bring the Martinelli boy, too. Because even if he didn't himself, maybe he knows. I mean, if anybody murdered you, for example, dear, I'd know right away. Because I know so much about you."

"Well," Jerry said, a little helplessly. "It seems—I mean. . . ."

"Or," Pam said, "if somebody murdered *me,* then you'd know. Sauce for the goose, you know."

"No," Jerry said, firmly. "I don't know. It's much more difficult over the telephone, somehow. I think you'd better come home."

"Of course," Pam said. "Right away, dear. That's what I called up about. As soon as we've been to jail. All right, I'm just hanging up. I was explaining to Jerry about the apple."

"What?" Jerry said.

"Mullins," Pam told him. "Impatient. I was just telling him I was just hanging up. Goodbye, Jerry. Tell Bill to wait and that we're bringing the Martinelli boy. And you can play three-handed bridge, or something."

"I hate—" Jerry said, just as she was hanging up. She quickly took the receiver off the hook and said, "What, dear?" But this time, apparently, Jerry had hung up.

"Three-handed bridge," Pam said to herself as she emerged from the booth. "He says he'd rather match quarters."

"Sure," Mullins said. "Who wouldn't? Or gin. Three-handed bridge is a low sort of game."

"All right," Pam said. "Why don't we go? We're going to get the boy and take him over to our place and Bill is going to wait and help us talk to him."

Mullins looked doubtful, but was carried along. They scuffed through snow for a block, waving fruitlessly at taxicabs. Then they got one. Mullins gave the address of the precinct and they skidded through slush. The lights of the precinct house were dim in the snow fog. It was a red brick building, tall and too thin for its height—like Cleo Harper, Pam thought—and it was a little drawn away from other buildings, as if other buildings shunned it as a symbol of misfortune. They went through slush across the sidewalk and through double doors and across a worn wooden floor to a desk with a uniformed policeman behind it. Pam waited while Mullins talked to the policeman; she followed Mullins through a doorway into a small, grimy room with plastered walls painted an unhappy green and with one window which had bars across it. After a few minutes they brought Franklin Martinelli into the room.

He was a little under middle height and his shoulders were broad under a blue shirt open at the neck. He had a dark, square face and damp black hair and he looked at them with defiance and hatred—and bitterness. He stood with his feet a little apart and fixed black eyes on Mullins and said nothing.

"Sit down, kid," Mullins said.

The boy's gaze did not waver. He did not sit down. It was as if Mullins had not spoken. Mullins waited. After a moment he spoke again.

"I don't care, kid," he said. "Sit down. *Or* stand up. It ain't my feet."

Mullins sat down. The boy—Pam thought he could not be over eighteen and that he was too angry for eighteen—stood without saying anything.

"This lady," Sergeant Mullins said, with a half gesture toward Pam. "This lady—Mrs. North—thinks you didn't kill the girl. Maybe she's got something."

"What the hell," the boy said, without inflection. "What the hell, copper."

"She was alive when you left," Pam said. "The sergeant knows that too, Mr. Martinelli."

The boy's black eyes fixed on her, unwinking.

"Yeah?" He said. "Yeah?"

But the voice was not quite the same.

"Because she ate—something," Pam said. "And it had to be after you left. So there was somebody else with her. Somebody else killed her."

"She was smiling," the boy said. His voice still had little inflection. "Like I said, she was smiling. She—"

Suddenly he turned his back to them and walked over to the wall near the window and put one arm against the wall and rested his head on it. With the other hand he made a fist and then he began, softly, as if he were counting, to pound the wall with the fist. He said nothing more, but hid his face from them and pounded the wall softly, as if he were counting with the beats. Pam watched him a moment and half stood and then sat down again. She and Mullins sat and looked at the boy and he went on softly pounding against the wall. And then he ended it, with his fist against the wall, and let the fist slide slowly down as if he were very tired. And then, finally, he turned to them again. He had been crying, but he made no sound.

For a moment nobody said anything and now the boy looked at the floor. Then Pam spoke.

"We want to find out who did it," she said. "Who did—that—to Frances. We want you to help us."

"I wanted us to get married," the boy said. "Before I go in the army. She—she was thinking about it. I tried to make her hurry up and she wouldn't have it and I got mad, maybe. But just because I wanted us to get married. Like you do at people you like. At a girl you like."

"Yes," Pam said. "I know what you mean."

"To hell with it," the boy said. "What good does that do, lady?"

Sergeant Mullins started to say something but Pamela North stopped him with a gesture.

"None," she said. "It doesn't do any good, Franklin. Except I *do* know what you mean."

"Thanks," the boy said. He said it with irony. "Thanks, lady. So you know what I mean."

"And," Pam said, patiently, "that you didn't do it. I know that, too."

"O.K.," the boy said. "So I'm not in jail, huh?"

The boy's young, heavy irony curled the words. Pam North seemed not to hear it.

"No," she said. "We're going to take you out."

"Yeah," the boy said. "To where?"

"To my apartment, first," Pam said. "Sergeant Mullins and I. So Lieutenant Weigand can talk to you. Then, I think, wherever you want to go. Isn't that right, Sergeant?"

It was, Mullins qualified, up to the Loot. But his tone did not discourage the idea. The boy looked at him hard and then looked a little puzzled.

"Is this a new one?" he said. "A new racket the cops have got? With the lady in it?"

Pam said, still patiently, that it wasn't a racket. The boy still looked at Mullins. He looked at Mullins as if he did not like what he saw and Mullins looked at him as if he were part of the wall. When Mullins spoke, his voice, too, was without expression.

"You're a very smart kid," he said. "A very smart kid. You know all the answers. Come on."

The boy looked at Mullins, decided Mullins meant it, and came on. They got his jacket and a thin overcoat and stood by him as he put them on; they got a little pile of things from the property clerk—an envelope with a letter in it, some change, a flat billfold, a single key. Pam looked at the key and thought it was odd, and pathetic, for a boy to have only one key—only one thing of his own, or a little room of his own, to be locked and unlocked. Pam had keys, even in the little leather case in her purse, to say nothing of desk drawers at home, whose keyholes were ancient, never to be solved mysteries.

As they went across town through the snow in a borrowed precinct car she thought about keys, and how some people have a great many so that they can lock up a great many things—sometimes including things they no longer owned, like early cars which had departed and left stray keys behind as mementos—and some people had only one key. Some people, probably, had no keys at all, which was a kind of dispossession. Or a symbol of dispossession.

The precinct car drew up in front of the brick walkup downtown where the Norths lived. Pam, fumbling in her purse, discovered that she had apparently lost the little leather case which held all her keys.

"There is a symbolism here, if I can only work it out," she thought, and rang the bell so that Jerry would click them in. Jerry clicked them in. His clicking, Pam thought, sounded relieved and impatient. She smiled secretly to herself, pleased, and tucked the key symbolism away to think of later.

Nobody looked approvingly at Mrs. North or Franklin Martinelli and Bill Weigand looked with marked disapproval at Sergeant Mullins. Bill Weigand's voice was cold.

"Well, Sergeant?" he said. "Well?"

Mrs. North answered quickly for Mullins, who looked at her hopefully.

"I made him, Bill," she said. "Because we found out it couldn't have been Franklin and of course, if he isn't a murderer he's a witness. Because he knew the girl better than anybody. And—"

Mullins looked at Lieutenant Weigand with some anxiety.

"It ain't regular, Loot," he said, breaking in. "I don't argue it's regular." He looked at Mrs. North and then back at the lieutenant. "Mostly things aren't regular any more," he said, and now he was clearly wistful. "Not like they used to be." He looked through the lieutenant, remembering. "Back before we knew the Norths," he said. "When we were just cops, sort of. And—"

"And you could round up a couple of guys and give them a going over," Pam finished for him. "We know about the good old days, Sergeant. And we're sorry. Aren't we, Jerry."

"Yes," Jerry said, without equivocation in word or tone.

"Well," Pam said. "A little sorry. But it seems to me we all meet very interesting people nowadays."

"Yeah," Mullins said. "Only most of them are dead."

Franklin Martinelli looked from one speaker to another and his eyes stopped on Bill Weigand.

"Look," he said. "What the hell goes on, Lieutenant?"

Weigand told him, crisply, that he could drop that tone. Plenty went on; Martinelli was not yet out of what went on.

"But he is," Pam said, and told why. She told of Cleo Harper and what Cleo had said, and explained how that made it impossible that Franklin Martinelli could have killed Frances. "Because she thought—thinks—he *did* do it," Pam North pointed out. "So she must have been telling the truth because what motive would she have had?"

Bill Weigand listened and when Mrs. North finished he was nodding slowly. He looked at Martinelli, still dark and angry; expressing anger even while he stood and said nothing. Bill said the story helped Martinelli.

"Yeah," Martinelli said. "Maybe you'll lay off me."

"Maybe," Weigand said. "Who would have wanted to kill Frances?"

"Harper," Martinelli said, without kindness. "That Harper—"

"O.K.," Mullins said. "Can it, kid."

"Was she?" Pam said, finishing the thought the boy had not finished.

"She's nuts," Franklin Martinelli said, still surly. "I don't get dames like that. What did she want? Always trying to break things up."

"Between you and Frances?" Weigand asked.

The boy nodded.

"Like Franny belonged to her," he said. "Like I was something—I don't know. Like I was a disease or something. I didn't get it. Like she wasn't a girl—the Harper. What's the matter with her?"

Weigand said he didn't know. He looked at Pam North, who looked at Jerry. Jerry raised his eyebrows.

"What's the matter with her, Pam?" Jerry said.

Pam North's slender shoulders moved slightly.

"It seems to me," Dorian Weigand said, from deep in a chair, "that we're all being very innocent. And that it doesn't become us."

"No," Pam said. "It isn't that clear. I mean the way you mean—it isn't as clear as that. It's a lot of things all mixed together."

Martinelli grew red and angrier. He said, suddenly, that they made him sick.

"She wasn't like that," he said. "Franny wasn't like that."

Nobody, Pam told him, had said she was—had suggested she was. Like anything. But Frances McCalley's being one way did not prevent Cleo Harper's being another. In theory, at any rate. But Pam didn't, she said—she repeated—think it was a simple thing at all, even from the point of view of Cleo Harper. Particularly from the point of view of Cleo Harper.

Sergeant Mullins followed the conversation from speaker to speaker. He followed it anxiously, as if it were an elusive ball.

"Listen," he said, as if it were an entirely new point. "Dames like that kill other dames. Queer dames."

"Yes, Sergeant," Weigand said. "That could be on the cards. And the killing of the other girl a coincidence." He was talking more to himself than to anyone. Dorian, who was more himself than anyone, answered.

"And the dress, Bill?" she said. "Two girls who were linked somehow, killed the same day, or almost the same day? A few blocks apart? Two girls who were connected, somehow? All coincidence."

Bill Weigand looked at her, thoughtfully. He said it wasn't a big coincidence. Ann Lawrence had given Frances McCalley a dress and Frances had been killed in it, ten hours or so after Ann Lawrence had been killed. If she had given her the dress.

"You mean," Martinelli broke in, "somebody killed the Lawrence girl? Miss God Almighty?"

They all looked at him.

"What do you know about Miss Lawrence?" Bill Weigand asked him.

Franklin Martinelli glowered at them. He said he knew plenty.

"She was another one," he said. "Trying to tell Franny what to do. Trying to break it up between us."

"Why?" Weigand asked.

"I wasn't good enough," Martinelli said. His voice was bitter. "I was just a wop laborer. I wasn't good enough for any of those dames— except Franny. And they wouldn't leave us alone. See?"

"No," Pam said. "Not entirely. What did she do? Miss Lawrence, I mean?"

It was difficult to get it out of him, because the thought of Ann Lawrence made him angrier than even the thought of Cleo Harper. He was angry at the world, young Franklin Martinelli. Even after they got him to sit down he sat on the edge of a chair, with his elbows on his knees and his chin in his cupped hands, his black hair falling over his forehead, his words spilling with fury, and then freezing up with fury. And it was not, in any case, tangible.

Ann Lawrence had not done anything that even the boy could put his hard fist on. And his words were not built for nuances. She had influenced Frances McCalley, and influenced her against the boy. She had upset Frances, as Cleo Harper had never done.

"She would talk like Lawrence sometimes," Martinelli said. He reserved prefixes and first names for one girl, and her dead. "Sometimes you'd think it was Lawrence talking."

You could build something on that, if you thought about it. An alien attitude showing through familiar words; new standards, to the boy inimical standards, appearing and disappearing among accustomed things.

"That one I *could* have killed," he said. "She was spoiling things. And for nothing. She didn't give a damn, really."

You could visualize one girl, educated and serene and without the world's ordinary worries, noticing another girl and—what would be the phrase?—"taking a fancy" to her. No more than that, nothing deeper. And trying to "improve" her; to bring her "up." Pam could visualize something like that—some light-hearted meddling, with the fingertips, in another life. And with the best of motives; with only casual kindness meant. The results would remain, probably, intangible and impermanent. But to other people—to Franklin Martinelli, who was likely to be insufficient by Ann Lawrence's standards—inimical.

It would be a gradual thing, the estrangement which might result from that; gradual and subtle. It would be hard for a very young, very violent, boy to understand; difficult for such a boy to combat. Except—

"That one I *could* have killed," Pam heard the boy saying, as if in an echo. "*That* one I *could* have killed."

That would be irony, certainly. If half-meant kindness, utterly casual

interference—and interference hardly realized by the one who inter-
fered—if that could lead to the violence of a poker's point in the brain—
that would be a strange thing. But no stranger than other things. All over
the world it had come to that; extermination had been the answer to the
subtlety of the mind, to intricate thought and motive, formed in the web
of the brain. Brain tissue had spilled out of skulls for that; out of skulls
as young as Ann Lawrence's. Pam had stopped listening to what the boy
was saying, and thought of all the horrible things in the world at war;
things so much more horrible than this one small horror of a girl killed
with a poker and another girl with a knife. The quietest second in the
world brought death more horrible than either.

"Pam!" Jerry said. His voice was uneasy and he was beside her.
"What is it, dear? Your eyes—what are you thinking about, Pam?"

At first his voice was a long way off. Then it was nearer; then it was
Jerry's voice, quite close to her.

"Oh," she said. "About—about everything, Jerry."

He looked at her and nodded.

"Yes," he said. "About that. Yes. Only—"

Pam said she knew. And that she was all right, now.

"Only," she said, "it's an ugly world, Jerry. Except a little of it;
except the little parts of it."

They were all, she found, looking at her. Dorian Weigand spoke
again, from deep in the chair.

"So," she said, "the little parts can't be broken. Not without protest.
Not without some sort of action. You have to keep the little things. And
so—and so you can't have murder. Even in a world of murder. Isn't that
it, Bill?"

Bill Weigand nodded. He said that that was part of it, at any rate.
And also that it was simpler—you had to have law, even in a lawless
world. A little law, somewhere; a little order. Among other things, murder was a violation of order—of society's order, most simply. And of
the order of ideas.

Franklin Martinelli was staring at the floor, in a world of his own.
As soon as they had stopped listening to him, his mind had gone away.

"All right," Pam said, "I'm sorry. I'm all right, now. Where were we?"

They were, Bill Weigand said, at an odd place. Martinelli had just indicated that Ann Lawrence was somebody he could have killed; someone for whose murder he felt he had a motive.

"Perhaps he did kill her," he added, as if Martinelli were not there, his hard chin propped in his hard hands, glaring at them. Martinelli glared, then, particularly at Weigand and spoke rapidly and with venom in Italian.

"No," Weigand said, "I'm not. And talk English."

Martinelli said it again in English. Mullins got up and started for him, not angry, not excited, extremely formidable. Bill Weigand told him to sit down.

"Where were you this morning, Martinelli?" Weigand asked, as if Martinelli had said nothing.

There was a definite wait before Martinelli answered.

"In my room," he said. "Asleep. Where the hell did you think?"

Weigand said he hadn't thought. He had asked. He kept on asking. Martinelli had been alone in a room he rented in a tenement in Carmine Street. He had gone to his room about eleven o'clock the night before, after going to a movie with Frances McCalley; he had gone home early because they both were tired.

"Because we'd been working all day," he said. "Ever hear of people who work all day?"

Nobody rose to that, although the boy gave them a chance. He seemed a little surprised. Weigand kept at it. He had gone to bed almost at once and slept until around seven. He always woke up around seven. He had dressed, got coffee and doughnuts at a lunch-room and gone to work. He had got to work in time to ring in at 8:30. And he could prove none of this. Weigand let him see that he could prove none of it. He let it sink in. He sat across from the boy and looked at him and waited, letting it sink in.

The boy wilted under it; the toughness softened and collapsed. He looked at Bill Weigand out of dark eyes which held fear.

"I didn't go near there," he said. "Where she was killed."

"Where was she killed, Martinelli?" Weigand said. "Just where was she killed?"

"Why—" the boy said. "In her house." He looked at all of them, then, and looked wildly. "You said in her house!"

Weigand shook his head. Nobody, he told the boy, had said she was killed in her house. Nobody had said anything about where she was killed, or how. Weigand said that and waited again.

"I guessed it," the boy said. "I just guessed it. Like anybody would."

"Maybe," Weigand admitted, in a tone which admitted nothing. "Maybe you were there. Maybe you did kill her—because she was turning your girl away from you. Maybe you got mad and killed her."

The boy shook his head, with violence.

"I didn't kill anybody," he said. "What are you trying to do to me?"

He stuck to that; stuck to it endlessly. And Weigand had, and knew he had, too little to go on. He let up after a time and asked other questions—about Frances, about the people she knew. She knew only the people you might expect, except for Ann Lawrence; nobody hated her; nobody except the boy seemed to have had strong feelings about her.

"How," Bill Weigand said, "did she come to know Miss Lawrence?"

"A guy named Elliot," Martinelli said, with the innocence of one who does not know his answer is loaded. "Franny was a sort of relative of a guy named Elliot. A cousin, maybe—some kind of a cousin. And he was a friend of the Lawrence dame and I guess he asked her to do something for Franny. That was way back—two years ago anyhow."

Weigand wanted to know why Frances McCalley had needed something done for her. The boy was vague as to details; it happened before he knew Frances McCalley. But there was something about Frances's having been sick and Elliot's having heard of it, and thinking she needed help. And Ann Lawrence had helped.

"Like Franny was a stray cat, I guess," the boy said, bitter again.

So then they had a link, for what good it might do them. It was a link to test but, looking at his watch, Weigand decided it was a link to test tomorrow. Weigand used the telephone in Mr. North's study and, ten minutes or so later, told Franklin Martinelli he could go—and to stay in town, and home at nights, so they could get him if they wanted him.

Mrs. North was surprised at that and, when the boy had left, said so.

"On a string," Mullins told her. "Didn't you see the Loot telephone? He's on a string; we can pull him in if we want to."

"Oh," Pam said, and thought. "Was he there?" she said. "How did he know where she was killed?"

He might have guessed, Weigand told her. Or he might have been there, inside or outside; he might have seen something; he might merely have seen her and, knowing she had been home—rather late, perhaps— had assumed she was still at home when she was killed. He might have gone to see her in a rage, or not in a rage—or not at all. He might have blamed her for the other girl's hesitancy about marrying him; there might have been more wrong between him and Frances McCalley than he now admitted, and he might have blamed it on Ann Lawrence.

"Might," Pam said. "Might. Might."

Bill Weigand nodded and smiled faintly and gathered up his wife. They stood in the doorway and Bill Weigand pointed out that tomorrow was another day. And a busy one.

"As far as might goes," Pam said, "Franklin Martinelli, who isn't as nice a boy as I thought, might have killed Ann Lawrence. And John Elliot might have killed Frances McCalley. Except that it would be upside down. But it would balance."

"A perfect balance is a worthy thing," Bill told her, pushing Dorian ahead of him gently. "Good night."

The Norths stood side by side and watched their guests go down the stairs. Jerry North yawned widely. He said that murder certainly kept people up late.

• 8 •

WEDNESDAY, 9:15 A.M. TO 9:35 A.M.

BILL WEIGAND sat at his desk, looked at the papers on it, and tapped its surface gently with his fingers. There were too many papers, representing too many things. There was too little that was tangible, too much that almost certainly meant nothing. And there was more to be got; men were getting it. They were getting it, with care and patience, knowing that almost surely their work was time and effort wasted. But they would get it and put it on Weigand's desk and he would, in effect, pat them and they would go away. And he would try to make sense out of it.

Mullins came in and he had some of it. It was about a man named Wilkins—a man named Herbert Wilkins. Thirty-seven years old Wilkins was, and 4F because of something which did not, evidently, impede him greatly in civilian life. In civilian life he did publicity for a department store. He was five feet eight inches, about, and rather heavy and had receding blond hair and he was the subject assigned to one Detective McKenney, who had gone to work on him only about half an hour before. He had gone to work on Wilkins half an hour after Detective Stein had got from Mrs. Florence Pennock, who regarded with outspoken contempt this indication that the police were not fully content with John Elliot as murderer, a list of the men and women who had been at Ann Lawrence's party the night before.

He was one of those who had dropped in after dinner. He had dropped in, had a drink or two, met some old friends and been introduced to some people he didn't know, and dropped out again. He had then gone home to his apartment in the east Fifties and gone to bed and to sleep. He had known Ann Lawrence for a couple of years, casually; he had wished her well and was sorry she was dead. He had no idea who killed her and he had, when interviewed, had some dictation to get out.

Weigand read the report through and put it down and sighed. Eight at dinner, he remembered. Four or five after it. People who had known Ann Lawrence, well and not so well. People of whom, but for the chance that they were free on the night of the eighth of March and had gone to see Ann Lawrence in her home, he would never have heard. People from whom, almost certainly, he would derive no profit now that he had heard of them. Because there was no reason to believe, particularly, that Ann had been killed by someone who had been at her smallish, gay and casual party. If someone had poisoned her food at dinner; if someone had stabbed her with a fruit knife and one was missing after the meal; if—but there was no sense in the ifs. She had died of a broken skull, crushed by a poker in someone's hand. And her dinner guests were no more suspect than—well, than anyone.

It didn't, Weigand thought as he tossed all that he knew about a man named Wilkins into a wire basket, boil down to anything. He drew a sheet of paper toward him and drew a picture of a house on it, for no reason. It was a child's picture of a house. Carefully, Bill Weigand put a child's picture of a tree in front of the house. Then he drew a path from the front door of the house down to the edge of the paper. The path widened as it approached the edge of the paper, presenting a child's version of perspective. Bill Weigand drew a curl of smoke from the chimney of the house and looked at the result carefully, with apparent interest. Then he folded the paper methodically, again and again, until it was a packet a couple of inches square. Then he dropped it into the wastepaper basket. He was not really conscious of doing any of this.

Two young women murdered; their names and stories in the morning newspapers. But grouped only by newspaper makeup, as representing similar tragedies, and not written together as facets of a single crime. And not played prominently, because of the war. And with the account of Frances McCalley's murder much shorter than the account of Ann Lawrence's, and run under it like an afterthought. For reasons which would surprise no newspaper reader and displease no amateur of murder. The newspapers did not, as yet, suspect any link but coincidence.

There were two possibilities, as to that. The newspapers might be right, in spite of the facts nobody had told them. The facts were insufficient proof of anything; two girls might know each other and be killed the same day and their deaths be unconnected. It was not, of necessity, an orderly world. That much Weigand was prepared to admit, as theory. But he was not prepared to act upon it, because he believed the newspapers were not right. He believed the two had died within a single pattern of crime.

"Sit down, Mullins," he said. He pushed cigarettes toward the sergeant, who sat at the end of the desk. Mullins said, "O.K., Loot," and took a cigarette. He took a lighter out of his pocket, opened it and twirled steel against flint. Fire appeared.

"Mrs. North," Mullins said, taking a long drag.

"What?" Weigand said.

Mullins waved the lighter.

"Gave it to me," he said. "This. For my birthday."

Weigand said he didn't know Mullins had had a birthday.

"Yeah," Mullins said. "I had a birthday. Mrs. North gave me this. I don't know where she got it, nowadays."

"I do," Weigand said. "Don't use it when Jerry's around, Sergeant. He gave it to her. She could never remember to fill it."

"Oh," Mullins said.

Conversation languished momentarily.

"Listen, Loot," Mullins said after a time, "who—?"

"I don't know," Bill Weigand said.

Mullins looked disappointed. He looked more disappointed when

Weigand said that eight men and women who had dined at Ann
Lawrence's and the four or five who had dropped in later would be
assigned to the Mullins province. Mullins was delegated to think about
them. Mullins said, "O.K.," without enthusiasm.

"Routine," Weigand said.

"Ain't it?" Mullins agreed.

So far, Weigand said, it all was. He talked for Mullins to listen and
advise, getting facts straight in his own mind. He drew another sheet of
paper to him and wrote names on it.

He wrote the name "Lawrence"—he printed it clearly as a headline.
He wrote "1–3:30," which indicated the time limits between which, on
medical evidence obtained during the night, she had probably been
killed. He wrote "skull," to fill out the record.

That was what they knew. He wrote down "John Elliot."

Elliot, he told Mullins, who nodded, was still the most likely, if for
the moment you arbitrarily rubbed out his alibi. Mrs. Pennock would
swear he had quarreled with the girl; she would swear there had been a
scuffle. Elliot had come around the next day to keep an appointment
with the dead girl, but that would be an obvious step for an intelligent
man to take. Elliot had hit a policeman and escaped, which was the
obvious thing for a guilty man to do. But it was not—and here was an
evident flaw in logic—the obvious thing for an intelligent man to do.

"Hell," Mullins said. "Sometimes guys is bright and the next minute
they ain't. You know that, Loot."

"Right," Weigand said. As Mullins indicated, it was an abstract
point which faded as you examined it. But the alibi did not fade. On
evidence they couldn't, at the moment, go behind, Ann was alive after
Elliot had left her. She died while Elliot was sitting in Dan Beck's
comfortable apartment, talking comfortably with Dan Beck.

"Unless this Beck guy is lying," Mullins pointed out.

"Why?" Weigand asked.

Mullins shook his head. Then he brightened.

"Why not?" he said.

Weigand shook his head this time. He didn't know; he didn't know
either way. He tapped his desk softly.

"All right," he said. "I'll take Beck off your list. That leaves only eleven or twelve. Take Beck off, unless something comes up. That leaves ten or eleven. I'm making things easy for you."

"Yeah," Mullins said, without conviction. "O.K., Loot." He ruminated. "You know, Loot," he said, "it ud better be Elliot. On account of if it isn't, who have we got?"

Weigand shrugged. Mullins had put a finger on it. Or call it a thumb. They suffered from a paucity of everything except the obvious. And Dan Beck's alibi stood in the way of the obvious.

"Somehow," Mullins went on, pressing his point, "this guy Elliot got around Beck. Maybe it was a phonograph."

Weigand looked at Mullins, as sometimes he looked at Mrs. North.

"Maybe what was a phonograph, for God's sake?" he said.

"The voice," Mullins said. "That Beck heard on the telephone. Maybe it was a transcription, sort of. Of the Lawrence girl's voice."

It was, Weigand pointed out, quite a transcription. It had carried on a conversation with Beck. It was not a transcription; it was a mechanical miracle.

"Yeah," Mullins said. "You got something there, Loot." He paused for a word. "A flaw," he said, finding it. "But maybe he did it some other way. Maybe—maybe he fooled with a clock somehow."

Weigand looked at Mullins with growing suspicion. He accused Mullins of having been reading books. Mullins, indignant, shook his head. He said, "What I read is newspapers, Loot. And reports on guys who had dinner with the Lawrence girl before she was cooled."

"Right," Weigand said, dismissing it. "Sorry, Sergeant. So we have Elliot, if we can break his alibi. Opportunity; motive. We have Mrs. Pennock. Opportunity. No motive we know of. We have Franklin Martinelli. Motive, possibly. Opportunity—possibly. And there's this to be said for Martinelli—he's violent. If he killed it would be—convulsively."

Mullins considered the word and nodded.

"Now," Weigand went on, after a moment, "for the other murder. We have Martinelli to begin with. Motive—yes, if he is lying about a reconciliation between him and the girl, and if he killed her he would be. Opportunity—not if his alibi is good. And his alibi is pretty good and it doesn't depend on somebody's telling the truth, unless—" He broke off, contemplating.

"Unless, of course," he said, "the Harper girl is lying. Come to think of it, his alibi does depend on the truth of what somebody says. It's good—if he *was* coming out of the restaurant when the Harper girl went in. But—"

Mullins was looking negative. He shook his head heavily.

"She wants him to fry," he said. "She wouldn't help him out of anything. If she saw him frying she'd think it was funny as hell."

"Or," Weigand pointed out, "she wants you to believe that. But suppose she's just acting you a little play, with Martinelli helping her. Suppose they worked it out between them, he to kill Frances and she to give him an alibi. Not an obvious alibi—one that would look accidental and unwilling. What do you think of that, Mullins?"

"Lousy," Mullins said, with emphasis. "Why?"

"Because they both wanted to get rid of Frances," Weigand said. "Because they wanted to get together and she was in their way. Maybe she was going to have a baby. Maybe she and Martinelli were really married."

"Hell," Mullins said. "It's you who's been reading books, Loot."

Weigand paid no attention to him, but tapped on the desk.

"Or," he said, "she might have killed Frances herself and alibied the boy without knowing it. Because Frances was leaving her for the boy, before you come in with your 'why?' How do you like that one, Mullins?"

Mullins was not so quick, this time. Finally he nodded slowly and said he liked it better.

"But still not very good," he said. "Who else?"

Weigand lifted his shoulders and let them fall again. Almost anybody in New York, he admitted. He pushed the papers back on his desk and looked at them. He crumpled the one on which he had started to write and dropped the ball he made into the wastebasket.

"The fact is," he said, "we haven't begun. And we'd better."

"Yeah," Mullins agreed. He stood up. "Maybe," he said suddenly, "Elliot killed both of them. Maybe they had something on him we don't know about so he killed them both. Because, Loot, when you come to think about it—*he was the only one we've come across who knew them both.* Martinelli just knew *about* the Lawrence girl, the way I see it." He stopped and stared down at the lieutenant. "What was the matter with the McCalley girl when she was sick that time?" he demanded. "Did you think about that, Loot?"

Weigand looked at Sergeant Mullins for a moment without answering. His eyes closed a little, reflectively. He was frank, and said he hadn't.

"But," he said, "I think we'd better find out, Sergeant. I think it might be interesting to know."

The telephone rang, and Weigand scooped it up.

· 9 ·

WEDNESDAY, 9:40 A.M. TO 10:55 A.M.

ROUGHY put her forepaws on the edge of the bathtub and stared in at Pamela North with round, interested and unblinking eyes. Roughy spoke at length. Pamela North, comfortably stretched at full length under steamy water, regarded Roughy.

"Why?" Pam said. "Why, Roughy?"

Roughy always answered when spoken to. She answered now and Pam North listened with every evidence of close attention.

"You had breakfast," Pam told Roughy. "Hours ago. Don't you remember?"

Roughy spoke at greater length. Her voice, which was attractive without being melodious—peculiarly without being melodious—was beyond question the voice of a Siamese cat. But Roughy was as unquestionably a small gray-and-white cat with nothing in appearance to suggest that she was a product of miscegenation. Roughy talked at length and, it seemed to Pam, with growing alarm.

"It's all right, Roughy," Pam assured her. "I won't drown. I can get out at any time. See?"

To prove it, Pam lifted one leg out of water and waved it slightly. Roughy followed the movement of the leg with her round eyes. Pam let it subside into the water. Roughy watched it disappear, looked into Pam's face, and wept.

"Of course," Pam admitted, "I have been in here a long time. But I really can get out, Roughy."

Roughy seemed to doubt it. The whole business puzzled Roughy. She looked with what Pam thought must be anxiety at the water. Then she reached down and touched the water gently with a white paw. She made a surprised and incredulous sound, withdrew the paw, looked at it, shook it and began to lick it hurriedly.

"I'm thinking, Roughy," Pam told her. "That's why I stay so long. Really." The last was said with rather forced conviction. "I'm trying to think who killed the girls. Who do you think, Roughy?"

Roughy looked at her mistress and made a small, purely formal sound of acknowledgment. She lifted her paws from the edge of the tub and lowered them to the floor. She looked around the bathroom as if she had never seen it before, turned slightly and floated to the top of the clothes hamper.

"You're the best jumper we've ever had," Pam told her. "By far."

Roughy looked down at Pam from this new vantage point with fixed interest. It was so fixed as to be slightly discomforting. Pam looked away and tried to forget the small, disapproving cat. It was, Pam thought, really time she got out of the tub. It had been an hour, anyway, since Jerry had gone, and she had really done nothing in all that hour but take a bath. Probably, she thought, it constituted a record. Probably if she stayed under much longer she would dissolve. On the other hand—

Pam could, she found, reach the hot water faucet with the toes of her right foot and, with a little effort, turn it. She turned it, letting more hot water flow into the tub. The new hot water lapped her toes and advanced. By the time the line of demarcation reached her ankles, her toes were too hot. She turned the hot water off with the toes of her left foot, relaxed a moment and suddenly sat up. She hesitated a moment indecisively, decided that the time had really come and got out of the tub. She flicked water from her wet fingers at Roughy, who made a small, startled sound, bounced from the clothes hamper and made a soft thud on the tiles. Pam opened the door and Roughy rubbed against it purring, looking up at her mistress with deep emotion. She rubbed against the edge of the door and did not go out but only curved indecisively. Pam pushed her with the toes of one foot and Roughy collapsed suddenly, lying luxuriously on her back. Pam rubbed her abstractedly with a foot and Roughy expressed ecstasy. Pam stopped, and Roughy protested at length. The foot did not return and, after a moment, Roughy rolled effortlessly onto her feet, listened with apparently shocked intensity to some inaudible sound and dashed headlong out of the bathroom. Pam closed the door behind her and toweled herself, wondering about cats. Anybody who could fully understand cats, Pam thought, ought to have no trouble at all with murders, which were, after all, customarily done by humans. And no human, certainly, was half so intricate as a cat.

The trouble was, of course, that nobody understood cats, probably including other cats. So it got you nowhere.

She turned her mind with resolution to the problem of murder. It worried her to discover that she had no theories, except theories about people who had not killed Ann Lawrence and Frances McCalley. She did not think that Franklin Martinelli had killed them, or that John Elliot had—not really, although there was something funny there—or that Mrs. Florence Pennock, the housekeeper, had. (Although there was something funny there, too.) She thought that there was also something funny about Cleo Harper, but she did not really think that Cleo had murdered the two girls. It was all very negative.

"Too damned negative," Pam told herself, aloud, and opened the door of the wall cabinet abstractedly. Several things fell out with the celerity of things which have been waiting for a long time to fall out. Pam caught a container of tooth powder but a small bottle of iodine fell into the bathroom glass and an old toothbrush—kept long past its days of usefulness for reasons which, if they had ever existed, could no longer be remembered—fell to the floor and bounced disconsolately. It occurred to Pam that she might forget the murders for a time and devote herself to reorganizing the bathroom cabinet, which clearly needed it. Pam dismissed this thought as dull and, in a sense, escapist. She found the bottle she was looking for, sat down on the edge of the tub, and painted on stockings. She stood in front of the long mirror in the door and regarded herself and thought she looked very odd with painted stockings and nothing else and turned sideways and regarded herself from that angle. Possibly, she thought, I ought to give up potatoes for a few days. But it was a moot question. She considered herself further in reflection, thought of Jerry, blushed slightly and inexplicably and returned her mind to harsher things. She left the bathroom and for a moment the air in the hall and the bedroom seemed cold, but after a moment it was no longer cold. She was very careful not to rub her legs against anything and sat on the edge of the bed, holding them well out, and waved them up and down. But whatever she did, they would certainly rub off on whatever she wore.

Cleo Harper, she decided, was really the oddest of all of them. The others were strange and seemed to be doing strange things. Elliot was hiding himself, for example, and Martinelli was hiding something else. Where he had been when Ann was killed, probably. And if he had more than the most casual, oblique relationship with Ann he was hiding that, too. But Cleo Harper was, as the others were not, contradictory. The others might be, and that included even Mrs. Pennock, quite usual people in an unusual situation. Cleo would be odd even in the most usual situation.

And even as she formed it, Pam realized that that conviction was based on a feeling rather than on anything tangible. Being in the same room with Cleo Harper, you felt her as odd and contradictory; you felt that you knew, really, nothing about her. You did not approve or disapprove; you were merely perplexed and made uneasy. And you suspected that, if you were more alert, you would find out something which it was important to know.

So, Pam thought, I had better try to find out more about Cleo Harper. Pam waved her legs and touched one of them doubtfully. It did not come off and she touched the other. It did not come off either. So probably they were dry, or as dry as they were going to get. And how could you find out more about Cleo Harper? The answer to that seemed to be—see her and find out more. But you ought, in human decency—as a tribute to human circumlocution—to have an excuse. You could not merely go to Cleo Harper and say: "Listen, I want to find out more about you."

That would be too simple and direct, and too sensible. And probably it would be unproductive. It would surprise Cleo and surprise would make her sullen and secretive and uneasy. There had to be some excuse. Pam pondered an excuse. She might, she supposed, merely call Cleo up and suggest they have lunch somewhere and a good talk, and plead a sudden fondness for Cleo to justify the obviously rather inexplicable advance. This would not, Pam realized, seem convincing to anyone; her own attitude, which was one of moderate distaste for Cleo, would inevitably show through. The excuse would have to be something specific.

Pam continued to contemplate as she continued to dress. Dressing was very simple; it consisted primarily of a girdle—which looked oddly disconsolate with no stockings to tie to—and a grayish brown dress of light-weight wool. Her shoes were brown (and felt strange on merely painted feet) and the brown hat matched. Pam regarded the final product without disapproval and looked up the number of Breckley House in the telephone book.

Cleo Harper was not at Breckley House, an impersonal voice told her. Miss Harper was at her office. There was an implication in the voice that that was too obvious to need reporting; there was a further implication that, by this time, all the world should be at its office. It was not customary, the voice said, to give office addresses of residents of Breckley House to unidentified voices on the telephone.

"Why?" said Pam, with sincere interest.

"It is not at all customary," the voice said, even more impersonally. "Not at all."

"But I'm a very old friend," Pam said, urgently. "And I'm only in town for a few hours and I simply must see Cleo. *Dear* Cleo," she added, to clinch it.

"Well—" the voice said. "It is really not at all customary. However—in the event of a special case. I'll see if we have it."

There was a pause and the small, elusive sounds which come

through a telephone laid on a desk. There were tappings and distant voices and, dimly, someone saying, "Well, she'll have to, that's all." Then feet tapped on the floor and there was the sound of the telephone being lifted and that curious moment when the other end of the telephone line became sentient. The voice at the other end of the line drew in a preparatory breath and said that this wasn't in the least customary.

"However," the voice said. "Under the circumstances. Her card says Estates Incorporated." The voice hesitated. Then, with the final barrier overcome by new resolution, it gave an address on Madison Avenue. Near the beginning of Madison Avenue. Pamela North thanked the voice and hung up.

One thing, Pam thought, was a little interesting about all of this. All of it centered within a relatively few blocks of which Madison Square was roughly the center. Ann had lived a little south and east; Cleo had worked and Frances had worked a little north; Frances had died only a few doors from where she worked and Cleo lived only four or five blocks north and west, between Madison and Fifth.

This was convenient but not, so far as Pam could see, illuminating. She put on a fur coat over the grayish brown—or brownish gray, as Jerry insisted?—dress and went out. It wasn't snowing today, but there was melting snow in Washington Square. The rest of the snow had almost vanished. Pamela got a cab with surprisingly little difficulty.

Estates Incorporated was evidently a large affair. When you stepped from the elevator, you stepped at once into it, facing a bare desk behind which was a crisp young woman who was anything but bare. She was expertly furbished. She looked at Mrs. North with polite inquiry. Mrs. North advanced to the desk and the young woman stood.

"I want to see Miss Cleo Harper," Mrs. North said. The young woman sat down again. Her action was comment, and adverse. She said, "Oh," making the comment more explicit.

"Have you a Miss Harper?" Pam said, when the conversation seemed to lag.

"Harper?" the young woman said. "Harper? Oh, *Harper.*" Her tone implied that Mrs. North was guilty of deliberate and confusing mispronunciation. "You mean Cleo Harper?"

Mrs. North was patient. She said she did.

"I believe there *is* a Miss *Cleo* Harper," the young woman said, indicating at once disapproval of Miss Harper's name and annoyance that Mrs. North had begun by asking for—say—a Miss *Jane* Harper. "I believe she files, however."

"However what?" Mrs. North said. "Why however?"

"What?" the young woman said, looking at Mrs. North without fondness.

"What I mean is," Mrs. North said. "Why do you say 'however'? She files, however. Do you mean that because she files I can't see her? Or what? And what is Estates Incorporated, anyway?"

Mrs. North added this because it had been bothering her and she wanted to know. The other looked at her and there was worry in the clear, businesslike eyes.

"What do you mean what is Estates Incorporated?" the young woman said. Her voice was uneasy. "It's the company."

"Of course," Mrs. North said. "I know that. What is it?"

"Listen," the girl at the desk said, leaning forward and putting her elbows on the desk. "What the hell do you want, Miss?"

"Cleo Harper," Mrs. North said. "Unless she's filed. Permanently, I mean. And to know what Estates Incorporated is, since you brought it up."

"*I* brought it up?" the other said. "*I* brought it up?"

"Look," Mrs. North said. "I came in here just like anybody else to see somebody. Cleo Harper who files, however. Is there any reason why I can't see Miss Harper?"

"What do you want, anyway," the other said. "What are you trying to pull, Miss?"

"I wish," Mrs. North said, "you wouldn't call me miss. Or get so excited. I just came to see somebody who works here. Like you do. Is that so very—so very uncustomary?"

"She's just a file clerk," the girl said. "Why don't you see her at home if you want to see her?"

"Because," Mrs. North said, "she isn't at home. She's here."

"Oh God," the young woman said. "Oh God!"

She was no longer bright and impersonal. Her accent was no longer bright and impersonal. It puzzled Pamela North somewhat, but she waited.

"It manages estates," the young woman said. "It just manages estates. For people who have estates."

Pam North looked at her a moment.

"Did it manage Ann Lawrence's estate?" she said suddenly.

"Yes," the receptionist said. "I mean, I don't know. You'll have to see Mr. Pierson."

"Why?" Mrs. North said. "Why instead of Miss Harper?"

"If you want to talk about estates you'll have to see Mr. Pierson," the receptionist said. She said it as if it were a final truth to cling to. "Everybody does."

"All right," Pam said, quite unexpectedly to herself. "Let me see Mr. Pierson."

It was as if she had touched a button. It was a button which made everything regular again. She could see the young woman become, instantly, competent and alert and assured. Things were regularized; somebody was asked for who might, within the rules laid down, suitably be asked for.

"I am afraid Mr. Pierson is engaged," the receptionist said, and now even her accent was assured and untroubled. "Whom shall I say is calling?"

It ought, Mrs. North thought, to be "who." But she wasn't quite sure and she decided to ignore it.

"Mrs. Gerald North," she said. "Although I don't suppose the name will mean anything to him."

"Mrs. Gerald North," the receptionist repeated, writing it down on a pad, in a space set apart for names so submitted. Now everything was beautifully regular.

"In regard to—?" the receptionist said, and paused.

"In regard to seeing Miss Cleo Harper," Mrs. North said.

The poised pencil trembled slightly.

"Please," the receptionist said. "Please, Mrs. North."

It was entreaty.

"All right," Mrs. North said. "In regard to whether you handle—handled—Miss Ann Lawrence's estate."

The pencil started to write. Then it paused. The eyes—they were blue eyes—above the pencil looked at Mrs. North.

"She was killed," the receptionist said. "Is it something about that? Because there's a man with Mr. Pierson now about that. A—a Mr. Mullins. A sergeant, but he isn't dressed like a sergeant. Not like the sergeants I know."

"He's a detective sergeant," Mrs. North explained. "He's just dressed like anybody." She paused, visualizing Sergeant Mullins. "Or almost," she added, in the interest of strict accuracy. "Look. I'd like to see Mr. Mullins, as long as he's here. Will you tell him, please?"

The receptionist looked at Mrs. North sadly.

"First," she said, "you wanted to see Miss Harper. Then you wanted to see Mr. Pierson. Now you want to see this Mr.—this Sergeant Mullins. Whom do you want to see?"

"Any of them," Pam said. "All of them. Let's start with Mr. Mullins."

The girl looked at Mrs. North again and shook her head. But she picked up a telephone and pressed a button and then she said, softly, "A Mrs. North would like to speak to Mr. Mullins." She waited. "No," she said, "she's right here." She looked up at Mrs. North. "Right here," she repeated, with rather odd emphasis. She waited and said "thank you" and then, to Mrs. North, she said: "They say to come in, Mrs. North."

She pointed the way and, after Mrs. North had started down a corridor, she looked after Mrs. North with a strange, awed expression. Then she sat and stared at the elevator door, but she stared at it with eyes which held foreboding.

Alfred Pierson had been the third name on Sergeant Mullins' list of those who had been at Ann Lawrence's house the evening before she was killed. But the first name was that of a man who had left on an overnight sleeper for Washington and the second that of a woman who had left, at a remarkably early hour that morning, for a shopping tour which, Mullins gathered from her maid, promised to be extensive. So Mullins had come to Estates Incorporated and Mr. Pierson at a few minutes before ten o'clock.

Mullins had been obscurely surprised to see Mr. Pierson, because he had visualized him as quite different from what he was. Mullins, for no good reason, unless names have a character of their own, which is doubtful, had anticipated meeting a grayish man in middle life. He met a blackish man in, evidently, his early thirties.

Alfred Pierson had black hair with a wave in it, and black eyes; he was slender and graceful; his dark suit managed not to look like a dark suit a man would wear to an office and his face, lightly tanned, looked as if a barber had only just finished with it. He looked very well taken care of and, Mullins admitted a shade reluctantly, as if he could very well take care of things. Particularly, Mullins added to himself, of women.

He was quick when he met Mullins, but he was at the same time unhurried. He offered cigarettes quickly, with a deft movement; he waited quietly while Mullins lighted the cigarette and until Mullins spoke. He nodded when Mullins spoke and there was a suitable expression of gravity on his face, and nothing more.

"Yes," he said. "I read about it this morning. In the *Times*. A horrible thing—almost unbelievable. Was it a case of someone—breaking in? One of those—one of *those* murders?"

His emphasis clarified his words.

"No," Mullins said. "Not so far as we know. If you mean was she raped, no. She was just killed."

"Tragic," Alfred Pierson said. "Utterly tragic. She was a lovely person. It is hard to believe."

Nevertheless, Mullins indicated, it had to be believed. It had also to be investigated. Which brought him—

"Of course," Mr. Pierson said. "I was there a few hours before it happened. If, as the *Times* said, it happened some time very early yesterday morning. I and a number of others. You want to know if I saw anything—well, anything that would help. Anything suspicious."

It simplified matters for people to question themselves. Mullins merely nodded.

"Let me think," the black-eyed Mr. Pierson said. "There was nothing at the time, of course. It was all very pleasant and gay and—unexciting. You want to know whether, looking back, I remember anything strange in view of what happened. The answer is, I don't."

He paused.

"Nothing," he said, with finality. "A few people who knew one another in the home of a girl we all knew and liked. Or, in some instances, more than liked." He broke off. "In several cases, more than liked," he added, thoughtfully.

"Who?" Mullins wanted to know. He explained. "We've gotta find out everything we can about her, you know," he said. "We always do. Most of it don't help, but we always do."

"Who more than liked her?" Pierson repeated. "Elliot—a chap named John Elliot. For one."

"Yes," Mullins said, appearing to make a note of it. "John Elliot. We've heard of him. Who else?"

Pierson shrugged. No one else, in quite the same sense. Elliot made no bones about it. His attitude toward Ann Lawrence, and hers toward him, were accepted things. They were acknowledged.

"But most men who knew her had—well, had notions," he said. He smiled slightly, rather sadly. "I did—once. For a little while. I suppose I was thinking of that as much as anything. I don't really know how other men felt."

"No," Mullins agreed. "A guy can't always tell. But who would you think?"

"Does it make any difference, now?" Pierson wanted to know. "Any real difference?"

"We don't know," Mullins said. "It could. We don't know why she was killed. Maybe it was somebody who hated her. Maybe she was in somebody's way. Maybe it was somebody who was crazy about her. All kind of things happen."

Pierson nodded.

"And all men—" he said, and let it drop. Mullins nodded. That was one allusion he knew.

"Yeah," he said. "It happens."

"Probably," Pierson said, "I ought to tell you, under the circumstances, that I wasn't—well, violently in love with Ann. I just thought about it sometimes, the way a man does. You know?"

"Sure," Mullins said. "Who don't? She must of been quite a girl."

"Well," Pierson said, "she made you—think about it. I don't suppose she intended to, or not more than most. You know what I mean? It seems the hell of a way to talk about her, now."

"Yeah," Mullins said. "I know how you feel. And that was all there was to it?"

"Yes," Pierson said. "There was Elliot, anyway, if I had other ideas. And there were other people. I was merely trying to give you an idea the way other men might have felt. I don't know what anybody else felt, of course."

"O.K.," Mullins said. "But who else might have felt the way you did? Or more so?"

Pierson looked at nothing, obviously remembering.

"A guy named Beck, maybe," he said. "I don't know. The guy on the radio. A funny little guy with a hell of a voice."

"Beck," Mullins repeated.

"He made it look fatherly, if anything," Pierson said. "And even that wasn't obvious. Probably there wasn't anything else. I tell you I don't know."

"I know," Mullins said. "I'm not holding you to anything, Mr. Pierson. We're just—fishing around. Trying to find out something about her. What kind of a girl she was; that sort of thing."

"She was a swell girl," Pierson said. "Don't get any ideas. She didn't—how do you want me to say it?"

"Play around?" Mullins suggested. "We know that, Mr. Pierson. She hadn't played around, that way. What else about her?"

"Oh," Pierson said, "I don't know. What do you want to know? She had a lot of money from her parents, who were dead. She had an aunt somewhere—upstate, I think. She went to a good school and awhile to college—Bryn Mawr, I think. She was engaged to some guy once and didn't marry him and she knew a lot of people and she did some kind of war work—driving a car, I think. And she didn't wear a uniform, if she had a uniform, except when she was driving the car. And it was her own car—and she could drive it. She was just a nice girl with plenty of money, but not worrying about it, and plenty of people who liked her. She went a lot of places around town, the way people do, and she had a house up in Connecticut somewhere and people used to go up there weekends and play tennis and things. In the summer."

Mullins said it sounded like a pretty good way to live.

"Yes," Pierson said, "it's an all right way to live. Or was, until recently. I suppose she was a little—unsatisfied—lately. Like everybody. And not just because it was hard to get gas, and food for weekends and that sort of thing. I mean she was—well, keyed up—like almost everybody."

"Sure," Mullins said. "I know what you mean."

"You got it too, Sergeant?" Pierson asked, looking at Mullins with a new expression.

"Sure," Mullins said. "I was in the last one, but sure. What the hell'd you think?"

"Look," Pierson said, "they say I've got a bad heart. And my own doctor says they're crazy. What do you do about that, Sergeant. Do you know any way?"

"No," Mullins said. "I don't know any way, Mr. Pierson. I heard about another guy like that. There didn't seem to be any way."

"Of course," Pierson said. "That was for a commission. Maybe the draft board will feel different."

There was a pause while they regarded this possibility. It was now a comfortable, friendly conversation and Mullins, during the pause, awoke to the fact that it was no longer leading anywhere. There had been a few points, but they seemed to have passed. He sighed slightly and became again a policeman.

"So," he said, "I gather nothing out of the ordinary happened at the dinner or afterward. Nothing we ought to know about."

Pierson, coming back, said there wasn't. If anything occurred to him, he'd let Sergeant Mullins know. But he didn't suppose anything would.

Mullins had already stood up to leave when Pamela North was

announced by the receptionist. Mullins was surprised, but not greatly. When Pierson raised eyebrows, Mullins said only that Mrs. North was a friend of the lieutenant's. Mrs. North could speak for herself.

Mrs. North, looking very trim and very interested, came through the door. Her eyes flickered over Mr. Pierson politely and came to rest on Sergeant Mullins. Mrs. North spoke for herself.

"Mr. Mullins," she said. "I might have known you'd be here first. Isn't it a coincidence that Cleo Harper works here?"

"What?" Mullins said. Then he remembered a note on Cleo Harper which he had forgotten; a note which explained why, as he came to its offices, the name Estates Incorporated had seemed familiar. But he still didn't quite see why it was a coincidence.

"Why?" Mullins said.

"Why because it handles her estate, of course," Mrs. North said. "Ann's estate. This—this company does. Doesn't it, Mr. Pierson?"

Now she looked at Mr. Pierson with interest. He looked back at her, and Mullins, intercepting the look, decided that it was at least with interest. Possibly, Mullins thought suddenly, there was even more than interest in the look with which Mr. Pierson greeted Mrs. North's announcement.

But all he said was, "Why yes, as a matter of fact, I believe it does."

Mullins looked at Mr. Pierson for almost a minute with considerable intentness. But when he spoke, his voice was mild. Mr. Pierson hadn't, Mullins pointed out, got around to mentioning that point.

"And don't," Mullins added, "tell me I didn't ask."

But precisely, Pierson explained, that was what he would have to tell Mullins. Mullins hadn't asked. It did not occur to him to volunteer the information any more than it would have occurred to him to volunteer the information that Miss Lawrence had had a checking account in the Corn Exchange Bank Trust Company or—or that she owned a Cadillac. That Estates Incorporated managed her estate was, to his mind, extraneous. He still thought it was extraneous.

"Were you in charge of her estate yourself, Mr. Pierson?" Pam North asked in the light tone of one who merely wanted to know. Pierson examined the idea and examined Pam North. He said that the handling of an estate by the company was never, in any real sense, a one-man job.

"Well," Pam said. "Not in a real sense. In a—in a titular sense?"

Mr. Pierson was in no hurry to answer. He thought it over, giving a great impression of a man thinking over an abstruse—and academic—point. But finally he nodded.

"In a sense," he said. "Only in a sense. I advised her. When she came to ask questions or sign papers, I saw her. No doubt the impression was given that I was her adviser. But it was a corporation responsibility. I was merely—well, a contact man."

It sounded all right, Pam thought. It sounded fine. But—

"Was that how you met her?" Mullins asked. "Did you get to be friends, or whatever it was, because you advised her about her estate? Or did you know her before?"

Pierson didn't see what that had to do with it. Mullins remained bland. No doubt it had nothing to do with it.

"The lieutenant will want to know," Mullins said. "I've got to anticipate what the lieutenant will want to know. I don't know what he'll do with it, myself."

Pam looked at Mullins quickly and looked away. Mullins was being very innocent. You'd think he didn't have an idea of his own. But Pam thought he must have several ideas of his own.

"As a matter of fact," Pierson said, "I did know her before. My father and her father were friends; the families used to get together now and then. I knew her when she was a little girl. And later."

"Before you joined this company?" Mullins asked.

"Oh yes," Pierson said. "Naturally. I was in college when she was a little girl. I knew her then—before then. But we weren't childhood sweethearts or anything, if that's what you mean."

"I don't mean anything," Mullins said. "I just want to get the picture. For the lieutenant."

"Well," Pierson said. "Don't get the wrong picture. She was just a little girl in a family my family knew. I only really began to know her a few years ago."

"Sure," Mullins said. "I'll explain to the lieutenant."

Mullins stood up and his eyes signaled Mrs. North.

"Well," he said, "I guess that's all the lieutenant would want to know. Don't you think so, Mrs. North?"

"Oh yes," Mrs. North said. "I'd think so. Wouldn't you, Mr. Pierson?"

Mr. Pierson looked at her a little darkly, but perhaps only because he was a dark man. And handsome, if you liked dark men—very dark men—Mrs. North decided.

"I'd think a great deal more than the lieutenant would find interesting," he said. "But I don't know the lieutenant."

"Weigand," Pam explained, wide-eyed. "William Weigand. He's very nice. But curious, sort of."

Pierson stood up.

"For example," Mrs. North went on. "I just thought. He'd wonder, I expect, if you advised Miss Lawrence about her investments and things—whatever you *did* advise her about, you know—before you became whatever you are here. A partner or something. He'd wonder whether—well, whether you sort of brought her business in when you came, you know. He's *very* curious, Bill is."

Pierson looked at her and she thought his eyes were guarded.

"He must be," Pierson said, dryly. "Perhaps if he wants to know so much he'd better come around and ask himself."

Pam North smiled pleasantly.

"Oh," she said. "I expect he will. He's very curious about things like that. He thinks so much murder comes from money. And vice versa, of course."

Mullins and Mrs. North used that as a curtain line, leaving Mr. Pierson looking after them—darkly, but no doubt only because he was such a dark man. When they got out on the street, Mullins said, still blandly, that he was afraid Mrs. North had irritated Mr. Pierson there toward the end. Mullins made a deprecatory sound with his tongue and teeth about that and Mrs. North said she was sorry.

"But I do think the lieutenant will be interested," she said. "Because I do think that he got his job because he had control of Ann Lawrence's money and—sort of brought it with him. And that makes you wonder if he's still got it, doesn't it?"

"It could," Mullins said. "It could make you wonder that. I guess the Loot will want to have auditors find out, probably."

Pam nodded.

"And," she said, "you said something that made me wonder whether there was something between Mr. Pierson and Ann. Something emotional, I mean."

"Yeah," Mullins said. "I guess there was something. But he says it wasn't anything much." Mullins pondered it. "Of course," he said, still carrying out the game, "the lieutenant might think he was holding back something. The lieutenant's apt to be suspicious, sometimes."

Pam agreed that he was. Particularly, she pointed out, when there was a good deal of money around. Say, she added, that somebody was handling a girl's estate and some of the estate got lost and that he tried to marry her to make it all right—because he could cover up that way—and she wouldn't marry him because she was in love with somebody else. And then suppose she found out that some of the estate had got lost and threatened to do something about it and—

"Yeah," Mullins said. "Suppose all that. Where does the other girl fit in?"

That, Pam told him, was simple. The other girl had worked there—at Estates Incorporated. Working there, she might have found out something. She might have found it out and told Ann. She might have known enough to send Mr. Pierson to jail. Or, maybe, to the electric chair.

"Because," Pam amplified, waving at a taxicab which continued indifferently on its way, "Frances might have known that he had a motive for killing Ann. Because of the money he stole and the fact that she wouldn't marry him."

"Listen, Mrs. North," Mullins said, waving at a taxicab, which stopped. "We don't even know he stole any money."

"Oh," Pam said, "I think he must have, really. He looks like it. And he didn't like me at all, and why wouldn't he if he hadn't?"

• 10 •

WEDNESDAY, 11:10 A.M. TO 11:45 A.M.

BILL WEIGAND contemplated in retrospect the conversation he had just had with the commissioner and tried to fit it in. Deputy Chief Inspector Artemus O'Malley had been present, but more or less formally. Inspector O'Malley had, he made it clear to Weigand and to the commissioner, turned the case over, so far as detail went, to Lieutenant Weigand. O'Malley was still in there thinking, but the lieutenant was doing the spade work. The commissioner, who was wiry and deceptively soft-voiced and had been a policeman all his life, accepted this gravely and directed most of his remarks to Lieutenant Weigand.

The commissioner did not, he said, want to interfere or to suggest a line of inquiry. That was up to Weigand. But he did want to hear what Weigand thought of Dan Beck—since Dan Beck had somehow come into it. The commissioner assumed that Weigand had followed his suggestion and looked Beck up.

Fortunately, Weigand had, on his way from his own office to Head-quarters, after receiving the commissioner's telephoned summons. Weigand had done it by the simple method of stopping by a newspaper office and having a look at the morgue, this being usually the easiest way of finding out a little about anything. Among the clips Weigand skimmed had been one rather long one, reviewing Beck's career in connection with a book which Beck had recently written—the kind of book which is reported in the news columns as well as in the book reviews. (Mr. Beck's book had further been a stick to beat the New Deal with, which had helped.)

Since Beck was, if not fully on the right side—he advocated change, after all—still against the wrong side, the report on his career had been reasonably favorable. He had been, which was in his favor, a businessman of sorts and no professor. He was the originator of the Beck System of Industrial Management, which had had, a few years earlier, almost the popularity of the Culbertson System of Contract Bridge. Industry had used it widely, workmen had struck almost as widely because of it, it had been tried out in Germany. It measured the output of each worker in a unit rather intricately compounded of time spent, product achieved, price of product to consumer and supply of labor available for the fabrication of the product, together with the amount of capital involved in the making of each item in the total product and a further component which, to Bill Weigand a little mystically, involved the commodity index averaged over a preceding six-month period.

Mr. Beck, or people representing him, had stirred all these elements together in the case of an individual industry which desired to install the Beck System of Industrial Management and given figures applicable, together with a survey showing how the plant could be more efficiently run. The management then paid a fee and happily installed the System. Then, commonly, the workers in the plant walked out growling and modifications set in. The modifications, Weigand gathered, never reached as far as the fee paid to Dan Beck, who was also Dan Beck Systems, Inc., in the United States, Beck, Ltd., in England and Der Beckische Fabrikwerkengesellschaften-system in Germany before Hitler took it over and interned the executives, en masse, as representatives of international Jewish plutocratic bolshevism.

That period in Mr. Beck's career had reached its height almost ten years before. It had been preceded by a period during which Mr. Beck was by turns an auditor, a stock salesman and, briefly, publisher of something called the Volume of Wisdom which had had a fairly wide sale before it, and Mr. Beck, became mysteriously involved in litigation which appeared to have a charge of plagiarism somewhere at bottom— the newspaper account was politely vague at this point. The litigation had faded out, as had the Volume of Wisdom and, for a year or more, Mr. Beck himself. Then the Beck System had begun in a small way and burgeoned and it had continued to burgeon, in a modified way, even after 1929. But after the spring of 1933, industry, involved in new complexities, apparently had had less time for the complexities of the Beck System, even when lucidly explained by the Beck Representatives, and Mr. Beck himself appeared to have spent several years on the Riviera, during which he entertained several very distinguished personages, one of whom had, while visiting Mr. Beck, undergone a very distinguished theft of jewels. (The jewels had later been recovered in a lock box in the Grand Central Terminal under circumstances rather more mysterious than those surrounding their original theft, which had been accomplished by the use of a ladder leading to a second-story bedroom. Weigand remembered the case, now he had run into it, and was less perplexed than the newspaper was, or chose to be, about the recovery of the jewels. A good many things like that had happened about then, prior to the sudden death of an almost mythological private detective.)

Mr. Beck had returned to the United States unassumingly a few months before the start of the war and it was six months later that he emerged gently from obscurity. He emerged, a little to the surprise of everyone, as a radio commentator, speaking fluently—and very mellifluously—as an expert on Europe, and displaying a command of oratory of which no one had previously suspected him. Miracles of inflation were occurring in those days, and almost before anybody knew it, Mr. Beck had expanded from a single small station to a chain and from a man who could talk entertainingly, and with considerable eloquence, about the European scene into a man who had definite and, from the start, persuasive theories on the redrawing of the American one. Mr. Beck was now on the largest, most national hookup of them all, speaking Tuesdays, Wednesdays and Thursdays just as people were getting up from dinner and weakened by the early labors of digestion. It had proved easier for hundreds of thousands to listen to Mr. Beck than to walk to the radio and turn him off, and by then remote control devices were quietly breaking down throughout the country and were, in face of a new haughtiness on the part of radio technicians, remaining unrepaired. So Mr. Beck thrived.

"There's more to it than that," the commissioner had pointed out when Weigand, in rather different words, had reviewed Mr. Beck's career to this point. "The man's infernally dangerous. He ought—something ought to be done."

"He ought to be thrown off the air," Inspector O'Malley said, flatly.

The commissioner shook his head. Nobody ought to be thrown off the air for saying what he thought, and there was no way of proving that Beck wasn't saying what he thought. No way, indeed, of bringing up that academic point.

"It is hard to put your finger on," the commissioner said. "There's no way we can put a finger on it. It's hard even to say what's wrong with it, except that the whole picture he paints is false and emotionally—attractive. It's like the universal old-age pension schemes, although less definite; it's like Father Coughlin—it's an invitation to an emotional debauch in the economic field. It's—well, it could be a leader coming up again, using American terms, promising things we all dimly remember as good things. It—"

"What it amounts to," Weigand said, when the commissioner paused and did not continue. "What it amounts to is that you think Beck is organizing a mob. A mob he could lead—almost anywhere. To the destruction of almost anything. An American leader."

The commissioner nodded slowly and said that probably that was what he did mean. Even now, the commissioner said, he had—well, influence. Enough so that he could call up the commissioner and reach him on the telephone and ask that the man handling the Lawrence case come around, and be justified in confidence—well, say in certainty—that the officer in charge of the Lawrence case would be told to come.

"That's for this room," the commissioner said. "I'm not saying it would work—yet—in anything big. It wouldn't as long as I'm here. But the things in which it will work are getting—well, they're getting bigger." He broke off and looked at Weigand. "You saw him last night?" he said, knowing Weigand had.

Weigand nodded.

"He was very agreeable," Weigand said. "Very polite—very—folksy. We were just pals together. He alibied Elliot." Weigand looked at Inspector O'Malley. "I'm sorry, Inspector," he said. "It's a pretty good alibi."

"There's a hole in it," the inspector said. "There's got to be."

Weigand was polite, as becomes a lieutenant in contradicting an inspector, but he didn't think so. At least, he saw none.

"You've read my report, sir," he said to the commissioner. "Do you see any?"

"No," the commissioner said. "I don't see any. But that's up to you. I wouldn't be too easy on it."

Naturally, Bill Weigand indicated, he was not going to be easy on it.

"Of course," the commissioner said, "it alibies Beck too, doesn't it? Now if—"

He let that hang and Weigand was a little surprised. It continued to hang, needing some response.

"There's nothing to tie Beck in that I can see," he told the commissioner. "Except that he knew Elliot and Miss Lawrence. There's no motive. And he alibied Elliot, which he wouldn't have done, so far as I can see, if he'd been involved himself. At least, I never heard of a murderer alibiing another possible suspect."

"And himself," the commissioner reiterated. "It works both ways."

Tactfully, Weigand corrected that. It was an alibi for Elliot, in the sense that it was independent evidence that he was not at the scene, at the time. In the case of Beck, since Elliot had not substantiated the story, it was merely an unsupported denial. Only if Elliot said the same thing would Beck be alibied, in any real sense of a misused term.

"And Elliot ain't around," Inspector O'Malley pointed out. "Elliot's hiding out. How do you figure that, Weigand?"

Weigand admitted he didn't figure it. Not yet. The commissioner was having his own thoughts. When he spoke it was without inflection.

"Of course," he said, "there oughtn't to be any finageling with the law. No subterfuge. Capone should have gone up for murder, not for beating the income tax. But—it would be convenient to find that Mr. Beck had stepped out of line somewhere, in addition to being out of line everywhere. It would be—convenient."

Weigand contemplated this and he was a little surprised. The commissioner must regard Mr. Beck as a very considerable menace, indeed, if he was willing to suggest, even without inflection, what he seemed to be suggesting.

"A murder rap," Weigand said, "is a good way out of line, commissioner. It's a hell of a long way out of line. For convenience."

The commissioner smiled faintly and advised Bill Weigand not to be too literal.

"I never framed anybody for murder," he said, still without inflection. "Or had it done—for murder. Or—allowed it to be done, since I've been in a position to allow anything. It would be convenient if Mr. Beck were even suspected of murder—publicly. If there are grounds for suspecting him. I don't say there are."

Weigand was stubborn and felt himself being stubborn.

"I don't see any, commissioner," he said. "Perhaps—perhaps the inspector has somebody available with—better eyes."

The commissioner looked at Weigand with something like amusement and advised him to be his age. He said that Weigand's eyes were all right and always had been.

"They're good enough for the Army, probably," Weigand said, forcing it. "My kind of the army."

"Forget it, Lieutenant," the commissioner said. "They're good enough where they are—and useful enough. You young cops."

Weigand thought he was not so young as all that; not by a good bit. He also felt, obscurely, as if he were lacking in tact. The commissioner seemed amused.

"Forget Mr. Beck, Lieutenant," he said. "No doubt you're right. It would be—too convenient. Probably the inspector here's right—probably it is young Mr. Elliot. It usually is."

The commissioner did not mean, as he seemed to mean, that it was usually young Mr. Elliot. He meant it was usually the man who ran away. The most obvious man. He meant that the inspector, as a man a long time a cop, would usually be right about the man they were looking for.

And probably, Weigand thought, sitting at his desk and making small, meaningless marks on paper, and drumming his fingers on the desk and waiting for the boys to bring in the dope—probably Inspector O'Malley is right this time. Probably it is John Elliot. Because nine times out of ten, ninety-nine out of a hundred, it is the most obvious man or the most obvious woman. Usually it is so obvious that it hits you between the eyes; usually it is as obvious from the start as it was that Ruth Snyder was lying when she told her pathetic story of being bound by a grotesque intruder who had then killed her husband with a sash-weight. Usually it leaps at you from between the lines of newsprint. Usually, for all their pathetic efforts, murderers are as obvious as their crimes.

So still Elliot was the man to start with—his was the name to write at the top of the list. Elliot, Martinelli—thereafter your list began to run out. Add Cleo Harper, in consideration of oddities noted by Mrs. North, who had an eye—as well as a tongue—for oddities. By the same frail token, add Mrs. Florence Pennock, who was also odd. Add Dan Beck, because it would be convenient—and because he had put in an appearance, even if the nature of the appearance seemed to vouch for its innocence. Put Beck in, in other words, because the commissioner evidently liked the idea, hoping against hope; because the commissioner was a policeman and hated, almost by instinct, mobs and the leaders of mobs—hated and feared them.

It wasn't, Weigand thought, much of a list. He crumpled it into the waste-basket, which seemed, this time, to be getting more than its share of useless notation.

Weigand looked at what else the boys had brought in. They had brought in two women and a man who had been at Ann Lawrence's house before she was killed and none of their names meant anything and none of their stories meant anything. They had, in two cases, eaten dinner at Ann's and stayed the evening; the man had come later and stayed the evening. They had been friends of Ann and were shocked at her death; they had noticed nothing unusual during the evening. They were supernumeraries—or quicker-witted than the detectives who had questioned them.

Weigand leaned back in his chair and thought of Ann Lawrence's last party. He thought of the small house on the park, and of the kind of easy elegance which its size and the money spent on it had given it. He thought of cars stopping in front of it and people getting out—young people, for the most part. Probably attractive people. He thought of the door opening and light coming out through it and people moving into the light from the dimmed-out street. He thought of Ann Lawrence, who was young and attractive and had everything before her and friends with her and a dress she liked and a feeling of being rested and a little excited. He thought of her waiting that final fifteen minutes between the time she was ready for the first of her guests and the time the doorbell first rang and perhaps using it to straighten a flower or to move some small object on a table. (Dorian did that, and even when it was not a special party she was a little happy and excited, and she would go out into the kitchen to see if the canapés were attractive and attractively arranged.)

Bill Weigand thought of Ann's waiting for the party to begin, and of what the party must have been like in the living room which occupied so much of the ground floor of the little house, and was so comfortable and quietly bright. He thought of Mrs. Pennock—or, more probably— a maid brought in for the occasion, passing canapés and cocktails, and of people in little groups of twos and threes, talking about other people with no more than a reasonable amount of malice, and Ann talking with them and moving from one small group to another. He thought of this, and of the rest of it—of the dinner and the further drinks after din- ner, and of the party breaking up with Elliot remaining later than the others, and he could not see that the party would be likely to have had anything to do with the murder. He wished he knew what did.

And then Pam North and Mullins came in, and Pam was full of something she believed did have to do with it. Bill listened to her account of Pierson, and to Mullins's steadying contributions, and it was interesting. It was a new name for the list—perhaps it was a name to top the list. Weigand got another sheet of paper and wrote it there—

Alfred Pierson.

It looked fine and tangible and maybe, Weigand thought, this was it. When he had all the story he lifted the telephone and called the district attorney's office. The district attorney's office saw it the way he did and within an hour, and with the permission—the ostensibly cordial permission—of the executive secretary of Estates Incorporated, auditors were adding and subtracting and checking the accuracy of the figures which represented, as a result of one of society's more convenient conventions, a largely mythical substance which had enabled Miss Ann Lawrence to live in very tangible comfort in her little house. It became almost immediately apparent that Miss Lawrence's substance was uncommonly mythical even for a convenient social myth. If Miss Lawrence had not been killed, she would very shortly have had to make a living.

• 11 •

WEDNESDAY, 2:33 P.M. TO 10:40 P.M.

DETECTIVE HANSON, sitting on a bench just inside Gramercy Park, and commanding an excellent view of the little house of Ann Lawrence, deceased, and at the same time looking merely like a somewhat eccentric man of leisure who chose to sit in a park on a chilly March day, saw movement and looked at his watch. His watch said 2:29, from which Detective Hanson knew it was 2:33. The movement, in the areaway beside the Lawrence house, established itself as Mrs. Florence Pennock, outward bound.

Detective Hanson, who had been feeling the chill, was pleased. At least he would get to walk a bit. He sauntered to the gate, keeping an artfully casual eye on Mrs. Pennock, and emerged on the sidewalk. He looked up and down it, like a man undecided as to his future course, and turned after Mrs. Pennock, who was going east. He stayed on the Park side of the street, since she was on the other side. At the intersection, she turned north and Hanson quickened his pace. He crossed diagonally and came in behind her—about half a block behind. At the next intersection, she turned east again.

It was not, as Hanson had felt from the first, much of an assignment. Presumably, if "they"—"they" being the Homicide people, to whom Hanson was on loan from the precinct—wanted to know where Mrs.

Pennock went and what she did, somebody had to follow her around. What Hanson did not see was why he should be the one. Hanson had a theory of his own about the whole business, and Mrs. Pennock was not involved in it. Hanson thought Miss Lawrence had been murdered by a bloke who was after her jewels. He was pretty sure she would have had jewels, because people who lived by themselves in complete—even if tiny—houses always had jewels. So far as Hanson's experience went, this was a minor law of nature.

All right then, Hanson thought, crossing the street after Mrs. Pennock, some guy had got in and tried to get the jewels. He had come in during the party, when it was always easy to get into a house. Probably he had gone around to the back and got in through the kitchen, waiting outside until Mrs. Pennock and whoever was helping her was upstairs serving. Then this guy, after the jewels, had gone on upstairs at a convenient opportunity—Hanson was not quite sure how the convenient opportunity had been managed, since the stairs from the kitchen ended in the living-room, in which everyone still was—but he figured there must have been some way—and started looking in the upstairs sitting-room. And Miss Lawrence had surprised him there and started to scream and the guy had hit her, probably just to shut her up. When he saw how much more he had done than merely shut her up, he had run like hell.

That, Hanson decided, watching Mrs. Pennock cross the street diagonally, was almost certainly what had happened. The Homicide boys liked to make them fancy and kept digging around for motives and things. But so far as Hanson could see, jewels were plenty of motive and all you had to do was to figure it out from that. He'd be willing to bet, he told himself, that the boys from Homicide had never thought of anything so simple. Probably they hadn't even bothered to find out if the Lawrence babe had had jewels, or if they were still in the house.

Mrs. Pennock turned another corner and in due course, Hanson turned it after her. He was just in time to see her go into a drug store halfway up the block. Hanson followed her in without hesitation, confident that she had never seen him before. Without seeming to look around the store, he moved to the soda fountain and ordered a coke.

Then, holding it, he half-turned from the counter and looked around the store, abstractedly. It was a busy store and people kept coming in and going out and it was hard to locate one person. But unless it had another exit, which Hanson thought it hadn't, Mrs. Pennock was still in it. It merely required system.

Hanson looked down one side of the busy store and up the other, checking off the people who were not Mrs. Pennock. The rather short man buying aspirin was not Mrs. Pennock, nor was the rather dark man waiting for—apparently—a tube of shaving cream. The tall, thin girl who was evidently with the much broader, much shorter girl, and seemed to be helping her decide on a shade of face powder was not Mrs. Pennock, nor was the swarthy young man who was looking at a tray of fountain pens, although he was not, at a casual glance, the sort of young man who would have much use for a fountain pen. There was a gentle old couple sitting together at the end of the soda fountain, finishing coffee, and neither of them was Mrs. Pennock, although the woman was about the right age. They left the counter as Hanson looked past them and went toward the rear of the store, toward the section which said "Prescriptions."

Following them with his eyes, and looking beyond them, Hanson saw Mrs. Pennock. She had joined a little group waiting outside a short line of telephone booths. Hanson finished off his coke and sauntered down. There was quite a little crowd around the telephone booths, and through the glass he could see the fortunate ones who had worked their way into them. All the people in the booths—three women and a man—were relaxed and unhurried. Two of the women were talking vivaciously into the transmitters; the other woman was dialing slowly from a number written down on a slip of paper—and apparently making a mistake and hanging up and starting over—and the man was leaning back against the wall of the booth with the receiver in his hand and listening with no apparent interest to someone else who was doing all the talking. Now and then the man would nod, apparently without saying anything, which struck Hanson as an odd gesture under the circumstances.

Detective Hanson joined the outer fringes of the little group and

looked like a man mildly interested in calling somebody on the telephone if the occasion offered. Watching him—as more than one person
was—you would have thought that his interest in telephoning was very
mild indeed, since he managed to keep consistently on the fringes of
the group as new people joined it; as the vivacious women finished
talking and were replaced by, respectively, a very businesslike man and
an elderly woman in black, who, on entering, put down an enormous
handbag on a very small ledge, held it there precariously by pushing
against it, and began an anxious, but still unhurried, search through it.
After a nickel, apparently. Hanson kept an eye on Mrs. Pennock, who
was now second in line from one of the booths, and pursued his
thoughts.

He could argue later—and did argue later—that he had not been
careless in his observation, although clearly he had missed something
which was worth observing. He could, and did, give reasonably complete descriptions of several of the people who had, at one time and
another, been waiting to get into the telephones while he and Mrs. Pennock also were waiting, and after she had got in. But he could not, he
had to admit, tell with any assurance which of them were there early,
and had left before Mrs. Pennock went into the booth, and which had
been around the booth while she was inside it and who had come after
when people were waiting, with growing impatience, for Mrs. Pennock
to finish a rather protracted conversation.

He knew that there had been several men and women in the group—
rather more, he thought—than at any other time, when Mrs. Pennock's
turn came and she went into the booth, neatly filling it. He had watched
her idly as she dialed and he had, properly, moved closer to the booth on
the chance she might leave the door partly open and so be subject to
eavesdropping. He had had little confidence in this maneuver, and little
confidence had been justified. She had closed the door firmly. He had
thought of getting near enough to the booth to press his ear against it,
and had concluded—rightly, it was admitted even by those who, by that
time, were not at all pleased with him—that clamping his ear against the
wall of a telephone booth would make him rather more conspicuous
than a good detective ought to be. And he had not, in any case, assumed

that what Mrs. Pennock would be saying would have anything to do with the case, because he did not figure *she* had anything to do with the case. Detective Hanson thought it was a matter of jewels.

(Even much later, walking his beat in deepest Staten Island, former Detective, then Patrolman, Hanson was convinced that he had been constructively right. It hadn't been jewels, unless the Homicide boys were wrong about the whole thing—as they still might be, when you thought about it. But it might just as well have been jewels; the theory that it was jewels was still the theory at which any sensible cop would have arrived at the time. Given the whole thing to do over again, Patrolman Hanson decided, he would still have thought it was jewels. Hanson's conscience was clear. If you had to be in deepest Staten Island, it was some consolation to have a clear conscience. Not much, maybe, but some.)

Hanson was not, admittedly, able to reconstruct the situation afterward from what he had seen at the time. It was easy enough to reconstruct it from what happened; there was only one way it could have happened. But Hanson did not see it happen; he did not know any of the people involved and so could not say whether any of them was in the group around the booth. He had merely stood by, making sure that he knew where Mrs. Pennock was, and hardly bothering to think that she was taking a good while. He knew that during almost all the time she was in the booth there had been a little group in front of it, pressing closer to let somebody by who wanted to go to a further booth—she was in the second of the five—and billowing out again when the person had passed. He could not, certainly, say who was in the group and when they showed him pictures of people who might have been, he identified several of them as possibilities, but no more than that. The only thing Detective Hanson was really sure about was what happened at the end.

At the end, Max Silverstone, who had a deal to close and wanted to close it, noticed that Mrs. Pennock didn't seem to be talking any more, but was merely standing in the booth abstractedly and had put the receiver down on the little ledge. She was, in short, occupying a telephone booth and not using the telephone, and Mr. Silverstone had a deal to close—right then. Right then if ever. He waited for a minute or so even after he had noticed this, being a gentleman, and when he decided nobody could be expected to wait longer he had, at first, merely rapped on the glass with a coin—with a nickel, to be exact. She had paid no attention.

Then, thoroughly exasperated, Mr. Silverstone had pushed in on the door. It pressed against Mrs. Pennock, who did not move for a moment and then gave suddenly. Then Mrs. Pennock fell out of the booth onto Mr. Silverstone. She covered Mr. Silverstone's good-looking gray suit with blood. She had been standing in blood on the floor of the booth and when the door was open it ran out, smearing Mr. Silverstone's brown shoes. And more blood ran out of Mrs. Pennock.

Mr. Silverstone let out a strangled sort of sound and tried to push Mrs. Pennock back into the booth, but she wouldn't go. Mr. Silverstone held Mrs. Pennock away with one hand and brushed at the blood on his suit with the other and then, just as Detective Hanson caught Mrs. Pennock's body, Mr. Silverstone fainted. He fell in the blood which had flowed out onto the floor.

The ambulance surgeon, when he arrived, examined Mr. Silverstone, who was by then sitting in a chair with sweat standing out on his white forehead, and said he would be all right. Mr. Silverstone had looked down at the blood on his gray suit and shuddered, and kept on shuddering.

The ambulance surgeon had said, in effect, that Mrs. Pennock was all right where she was, which was on the floor just outside the booth. Hanson had lowered her there after Mr. Silverstone had been removed. Mrs. Pennock was as all right on the floor as she would be anywhere, until the Medical Examiner sent somebody. She had been dead, when the ambulance surgeon looked at her, for about half an hour. She had been stabbed through the left side of the back, and through the heart; she had lost consciousness instantly and the time she had lived after that was a matter of purely medical interest. For all other purposes she had been dead when the knife was pulled out and the blood followed it.

The knife was on the floor of the booth. It was long and slim and sharp and apparently had been much used. It was the sort of knife, ground down by repeated sharpenings, that expert carvers use in carv-

ing meat; the kind that professional carvers use in view of passers-by
as they work on thick slabs of meat, reducing them to thin sandwiches.

Pure reflex, they supposed, had led to its being drawn out and not
left in the ugly wound it had made. Thought had followed reflex and
the knife had been dropped. It had caught momentarily in Mrs. Pennock's clothing, apparently, and so had not made much sound when it
struck the floor. And by that time the door of the booth had obviously
been closed again.

Because, Bill Weigand told Sergeant Mullins, who agreed, there
was only one way it could have been done. It was hard to think of its
being done that way, but it was impossible to think of its being done
any other way. Somebody in the group around the booth, hiding the
knife with his body, had opened the folding door with his left hand
and, concealing the knife now by holding it along his arm—it had to
have been that way, Bill thought—appeared to tap Mrs. Pennock on the
shoulder. As if he were a friend, and wanted to remind her of something, probably. And when he appeared to tap her on the shoulder, he
had actually driven the very sharp knife into her back.

"He" could have been of either sex. The blow took little pressure,
unless the knife met a bone, and it had not. Actually, it was, if anything, easier to think of the murderer as a woman, who could have concealed the knife in her handbag, or by holding it against her handbag,
and who might more naturally have reached in to call the attention of
another woman to something by touching her on the shoulder. Unless
somebody was watching carefully, and if the murderer were assured
and confident and did not attract attention by hesitancy, it might have
been done that way.

"Hell," Mullins said. "It was done that way, wasn't it? Sure, it could
have been."

Mullins repeated this remark late in the afternoon, at the bar in
Charles', and both the Norths and Dorian Weigand agreed that there
could be no quarrel with his logic. Bill Weigand, although his face was
set—Deputy Chief Inspector Artemeus O'Malley had not been cordial
when he heard the news—smiled faintly. He admitted that Mullins had
something.

But the smile faded faintly. He drank his martini.

"Of course," he said, "I shouldn't have used Hanson. The man must be half-witted. But I had to use somebody and—well, I didn't actually figure anything would happen to Mrs. Pennock. Even now, I can't see why anything should have. Which is about what Hanson says, incidentally. He keeps talking about her not having the jewels."

"You couldn't know," Dorian said. "How could you know, Bill? And you have to turn some of it over to other men. You can't be everywhere."

The trouble seemed to be, Bill said with some bitterness, that apparently he couldn't be anywhere. Not anywhere that did any good.

"To be perfectly honest," he said, "I haven't the damnedest idea what's going on. That's what's the matter, really. I'm just groping around in a fog. And somebody's going around in the fog, seeing everything he wants to see, and killing people. And that's what I'm supposed to stop."

He paused and looked at them.

"Good God," he said. "That's my only excuse. If I can't stop this sort of thing, I haven't any excuse at all."

"Bill, dear," Dorian said. "You'll stop it. Of course you will."

Bill Weigand smiled, but his smile was unhappy.

"Sure," he said. "I'll stop it, eventually. Or it will just stop—when this guy in the fog gets through. When he has everything all tidied up. Eventually everybody'll be dead but him, and then I can arrest him. Which is a hell of a way to be a policeman."

"Jerry had another examination," Pam said, after a moment during which nobody answered. "He still can't see anything. Not anything they want him to see. You'd think for what he can do it wouldn't matter, wouldn't you?"

"How many is that, Jerry?" Dorian said.

Jerry North grinned, putting a face on it.

"Four," he said. "I came up a point with the right one, this time. Only I went back a point with the left. Even squinting."

"You and me," Bill said, not to be diverted. "We can't see a thing. You haven't got any eyes; me, I haven't got any mind. Between us, we ought to fall flat on our faces."

"Quit feeling sorry for yourself, Bill," Pam told him. "Quit being so sunk. Why did they?"

"Because she knew something, obviously," Bill said. "Which doesn't fit. That's why, I guess, I didn't—"

"Why doesn't it fit?" Pam North insisted.

There were, Bill Weigand told her,—and now, she and Dorian noted, he was leaving himself out of it—several reasons why it didn't fit. Primarily, because she had seemed so certain, and so anxious to make them certain, that John Elliot had killed Ann. And in trying to make them certain she had told everything, apparently, that she knew against Elliot. Anyway, she had told enough. So—Elliot, who was the only one she appeared to suspect, the only one she had tried to involve, would have no reason to kill her.

"Because she had already done him all the damage she could," Pam North agreed, voicing it for the rest of them. Bill nodded.

"I wondered about that when she seemed to be trying to shake somebody down on the telephone," he said. "It didn't fit, if she really believed Elliot had killed the girl. That's why I decided to keep an eye on her. Half an eye, as it turned out—Hanson. But I didn't take it very seriously. She was such—such a character. I suppose I didn't ever take her seriously."

"Well," Jerry said, "somebody did."

He considered and shook his head. He said he didn't get it, completely.

"Apparently," he said, "we have to assume that the whole story she told about Elliot was a fake, set up to distract us from the man she really suspected until she had a chance to shake this other man—or woman—down. She was just giving us a false scent, so she could be free to follow the true one, and so we—you, Bill, I mean—wouldn't catch the right person until she had had a chance to make something out of it."

"Well," Weigand said, "it doesn't have to be all a fake—her story about Elliot, I mean. Maybe that was true—maybe something like that happened. But maybe she knew something else about somebody else, and thought this other person would pay not to have what she knew told. I mean—she might really have thought that Elliot killed the girl, but knew enough to involve this other person if he didn't come through. Perhaps she actually thought there were merely appearances against this other person, and that she might pick up a little something if she didn't let the appearances come out. But perhaps she was wrong about that—perhaps what she had on the other person wasn't merely an appearance, as she thought, but the real thing. Perhaps—perhaps she went hunting for a rabbit and caught a bear."

"Like the parson, one lovely Sunday morning, although it was powerfully against his religion," Pam North said. Everybody looked at her. "The jingle," she said. "And on his way returning, a great big grizzly bear. Although the parson caught the bear, not the other way around."

"Oh," Jerry said. "But there's nothing in it about rabbits, Pam."

"And one dum dumply hare," Pam said. "A rabbit's a hare, isn't it?"

"Sort of," Jerry agreed. "He was really hunting quail, I always thought."

"You two," Dorian said. "What else, Bill?"

"So," Bill said, "she went out to telephone this other person, on whom she had so much more than she thought. She went to a public telephone because she thought we might have had the one at the house tapped."

"Did you?" Pam wanted to know.

Bill merely smiled at her.

"So—" Bill started again, and then he stopped and a line came between his eyes.

"It doesn't fit, does it?" Pam said.

Bill Weigand shook his head.

"Not if she was talking," he said. "And Hanson had sense enough to notice that she was. It was his high point of the day."

"Why—" Jerry began. Then he said, "oh, of course!"

"It would be pretty hard to be stabbed by somebody you were talking to on the telephone," he said. "Particularly in the back."

Everybody looked at him.

"*I* see what you mean, dear," Pam said. "It's perfectly logical, really. Until you think about it, of course."

"All right," Jerry said, amused. "This one's on me, people. But the fact remains—"

They agreed that the fact remained. If Mrs. Pennock had gone several blocks to a public telephone to blackmail a suspected murderer, and had got him on the telephone, it was hard to see how that same person could be waiting outside the telephone booth to stab her in the back. So, presumably, she was not talking to the person she was blackmailing. This last from Dorian.

"Or," Jerry said, "she was talking to a servant of the person she was blackmailing and learning he was not at home. And he wasn't at home because he was right outside the booth with a knife. How did he know she would be there, incidentally?"

"Followed her," Bill said. "Unless she had made an appointment to meet him—or her—in the drug store and filled in time waiting for him by telephoning. That's possible. Except that the amazing Mr. Hanson seems to think she went right to the telephone booths without looking around for anyone, or waiting at all, which isn't natural. She went there as if she had gone to telephone, not to meet somebody."

Pam said it was very confused. She studied it.

"Of course," she said, "she may have been wrong again. Perhaps there was another murderer. Making three, in all."

They looked at her, anxiously, for enlightenment.

"You'd have to use letters, or something," she said. "Suppose Mr. Elliot is Mr. A."

She paused and looked around for acceptance of this.

"All right, dear," Jerry said. "Anything you say. Mr. Elliot is Mr. A."

"Then," Pam said. "This other person is Mr. B.—this first other person. The one Mrs. Pennock thought had really done the murder—or had a lot to explain about it. The one she was using Mr. Elliot as a red herring for."

"Listen," Jerry said, "Mr. Elliot was Mr. A. just a minute ago. Now he's Mr. Elliot again."

"A. for Elliot," Pam said. "I don't care, really, I was just trying to make it clear."

"All right," Jerry said. "Maybe it is, Pam. So—?"

"So," Pam said, "she went out to telephone Mr. B. to try to—to shake him down. But all the time there was a Mr. C. The real murderer. Because she was wrong about Mr. A. *and* Mr. B. And Mr. C. killed her while she was talking to Mr. B. and trying to make him give her some money."

"Yes, but—" Bill and Dorian and Jerry said that almost together. Mullins said, "But listen, Mrs. North."

"I know," Mrs. North said. "Why should Mr. C.? Because she thought it was Mr. B., if she didn't think it was Mr. A. Well because—because she *should* have realized it was Mr. C. and Mr. C. thought she *did*. Maybe he thought she had seen him killing Ann, when really she hadn't. But maybe she had said something which made him think she had. So he was just playing safe. Maybe he thought she was thinking about the whole thing too much, and would eventually think the right thing."

They thought that over.

"Then," Bill said, "she was really killed by mistake, Pam? It could be, of course."

"Or, anyway, too soon," Pam said. "Before she got around to being right."

They thought of that one.

"Of course," Dorian said, "maybe whoever it was—Mr. B.—just hired somebody. Maybe he has a faithful old retainer who stabs people out of devotion."

Bill looked at his wife with interest.

"Beck has a faithful old retainer," he said. "Two of them, by count."

"Would they stab somebody?" Dorian asked with interest. "Either—or both."

Bill said he should think so. Pam shook her head.

"I don't believe in faithful old retainers," she said. "Not the stabbing kind, for love of the mahster. Or even the massa."

"If you come to that," Jerry said, "you don't really believe in murder. You don't think anybody would. But they do. So do retainers, for all we know." He paused. "Not that I think Martha would, for us," he said.

They tried to think of fat Martha murdering for the Norths, and were unsuccessful.

"Maybe," Pam said, then, "she was blackmailing *both* Mr. B. and Mr. C. at the same time, because both of them were there, or something, or had threatened Ann or something. And while she was blackmailing Mr. B. or Mr. C., the other one—the one she wasn't actually blackmailing at the time—followed her to the store and killed her."

They were thinking of that, and that they had now about all the reasonable combinations, when Hugo came and stood behind Weigand. Bill looked around.

"Telephone, Captain Weigand," Hugo said, adhering to his custom of promoting all good customers by at least one grade.

Bill followed Hugo to the telephone booth wedged into a corner of the small, secure cocktail lounge. Hugo waved the detective on and Bill, not quite hesitating as he entered the booth—but not avoiding a thought of the final condition of the booth in which Mrs. Pennock had done her telephoning—went in and closed the door behind him. He said, "Hello."

"Hello," John Elliot said. "I see he got another one."

The voice was familiar to Bill Weigand; much too familiar. It was infuriating.

"You mean *you* got another one," Bill said. "And you seem to think it's part of a game. We'll teach you about that, Elliot."

"When you catch me," Elliot commented, with truth. But his voice was not flippant; it was merely reporting the obvious. "But I'm still not the one you want to catch. I haven't killed anybody. And I think you know it, Weigand."

"I don't know it," Weigand said. "You're a killer, Elliot, or the damnedest fool I ever met. You're acting like—like a perverted schoolboy."

"I know," Elliot said. "It must seem that way. But I'm not a killer. *Or* a fool. I know something you don't know and I've got to work on it."

"If you didn't kill Ann Lawrence and the McCalley girl you're a damned fool to hide out," Weigand told him. "Because we'll catch you anyway."

"You haven't so far," Elliot reminded him. "And why don't you include Mrs. Pennock?"

Weigand was triumphant.

"Because I wanted you to mention her," he said. "Because you couldn't have known about her unless—"

Elliot broke in.

"Unless I listened to the radio," he said. "I did listen to the radio. It's part—"

He stopped there for a moment. Then he went on.

"It was on the radio half an hour ago," he told Weigand. "Didn't you know that, Lieutenant?"

Weigand hadn't. He would know why it was on the radio and somebody would wish it hadn't been. But meanwhile, he was inclined to believe Elliot, because a lie would be too easy to check.

"All right," Weigand said. "You heard it on the radio. And you called me up to tell me how smart you are. Is that it?"

Elliot said it wasn't.

"And incidentally," he said, "I'm not anywhere around now, so that roundup of the neighborhood won't work. I just took a chance you'd be at Charles'. Knowing your methods, Sherlock."

"One trouble with you, Elliot," Weigand said, "is that you haven't grown up. One trouble."

"And one trouble with you, Weigand, is that you can't see your nose on your face. Or your hand in front of your eyes, or whatever it is. Or a murderer who's sticking out a mile."

"I can talk to him," Weigand said. "On the telephone. And get him, eventually."

Elliot said they weren't getting anywhere.

"All right," Weigand said. "Where do you want to get?"

"Damn it all, man," Elliot said. "I'm trying to help. I wasn't sure before; now I'm sure. It's one of two. In about an hour I'm going to ask a couple of questions. Then I'll know—then I'll hand it to you."

His voice was serious. It would be easy to believe him.

"Elliot," Weigand said, "you're still being a fool. Maybe you're telling the truth. If you are you don't know what you're getting into.

Just on the chance you're telling the truth—for God's sake show some sense. Don't go around asking questions of murderers. Don't—"

"I can take care of myself, Lieutenant," Elliot said. "Thanks all the same."

"Mrs. Pennock thought she could take care of herself," Weigand said, and his voice was harsh. "She's in a bin at the morgue, Elliot."

There was a slight pause.

"She didn't know what she was up against," Elliot said, but his voice momentarily sounded less sure. "I know what I'm up against."

Weigand said nothing. He listened to Elliot breathing on the other end of the phone. But before Elliot spoke again, Weigand knew he had lost the round.

"And," Elliot said, now with no hesitancy, "she wasn't even right. She thought she knew something she didn't know. This time it's different."

With him it was different, he meant. He believed it again. There was nothing to say to convince him. Weigand's voice was weary when he answered.

"Right," he said. "With you it's different, Rover boy. You'll catch a murderer for the dumb cops. Or he'll catch you, and then we'll have to catch him for that, too. What do you want from me—a testimonial?"

"No," Elliot said. He paused, apparently searching for words. He spoke more slowly.

"Listen," he said. "I'm not a fool, whatever you think. I know it's—risky. If I could prove anything—but I can't. Not now. I could just give you a theory. You'd think it was a crazy theory. It wouldn't make sense. But I can—trick him. I think I can."

"I think you're a fool," Weigand said, driving it in.

"You don't know how it is," Elliot said. "I know what I can do. In this case. With this—this guy. Something nobody else could do. Because of—well, say special circumstances. And there's no use trying to talk me out of it."

"Right," Weigand said. "It's your neck. If you're telling the truth. And I'll say this—I don't get the game if you're not."

He had not meant to say that much. There was something in the earnestness of the other's voice which had brought it out.

"It's my neck," Elliot said. "And I'll take care of it. And—I'll be seeing you. Tomorrow, maybe."

"Any time," Weigand said, with marked politeness. "Any time at all, Mr. Elliot. Just drop in. And bring your murderer."

"Maybe I will, Lieutenant," Elliot said. "Maybe I'll do just that. Or maybe I'll just let you hear about it, as I did about Mrs. Pennock. On the radio."

Suddenly, it seemed to Weigand, there was a jeer in the end of it. It was as if Elliot were laughing at him about something; had been laughing at him all the time. And Weigand started talking with contained violence before he realized that part of the cause of his fury was that Elliot had, at the end of that sentence, hung up the receiver.

Weigand went back to the others and he was both exasperated and uneasy. He was being played for something—and he didn't know just what. There was a game going on, under his nose, and he didn't know the rules. And there seemed to be nothing he could do about it, except to catch Elliot and shake it out of him. And so far, he hadn't caught Elliot. He felt as if he were "it" in a game of blind-man's bluff. Over another round of drinks, he told the others of Elliot's call, and of his own confusion. His confusion did not lighten; it remained after they had left the bar for a table. It persisted through dinner.

They had finished and were no longer talking much when Detective Stein appeared, excited interest in his quick, mobile face. Stein did not wait to be spoken to.

"I think we've got him, Lieutenant," he said. "The auditors found it; a baby could have found it."

"What?" Weigand said, not bothering to sit down. It didn't sound as if it would be worth while sitting down.

Stein told him, quickly and precisely. Alfred Pierson, who had brought Ann Lawrence's account into Estates Incorporated, and continued to handle it, had milked it almost dry. By substituting securities at first; finally merely by hypothecating securities. He had, in short, brought it down from a great deal to almost nothing, and he had done it with amazing rapidity. Ann's pleasantly adequate fortune had, within four years, turned liquid and flowed into Pierson's pockets. What remained were real estate holdings of no liquidity whatever; what remained was a series of tax liabilities.

They looked at one another as Stein finished. So there it was—there was motive, all wool and a yard wide. At least a yard wide.

"It's uncanny," Pam North said, in a bemused way. "It's just as I suspected. And he was in love with her, too."

"Or," Weigand pointed out, "he wanted to marry her to keep the truth in the family. And—where is he now, Stein?"

He was around, Stein said. He had gone out to lunch about one and come back a little after three. By that time it had begun to become clear, but they said nothing to him. He had gone out again a little before five, but this time he had not gone alone. A small, almost invisible, man had gone with him.

"I took a chance on that," Stein said. "I couldn't reach you. You'd just left the precinct after the checkup on the Pennock kill. So I took a chance. O.K.?"

"Right," Weigand said. "Who's on him?"

"Krenke," Stein said.

Weigand was relieved and said, "Right," again. Krenke was no Hanson; Krenke would be right along with Mr. Pierson, wherever Mr. Pierson went. And Krenke would be keeping in touch.

Weigand decided he was right not to have sat down. It was a time to stand up and get going. The fog, he decided, was lifting. Or a corner of it was lifting. He and Stein and Mullins left the Norths and Dorian sitting over coffee and went away from there. Weigand's Buick snarled at intersections between Charles' and the headquarters of the Homicide Squad.

Krenke had kept in touch. It had not been difficult. The reports he had managed to telephone in between a little before five o'clock and ten minutes ago told the story of an easy chase. Pierson had stopped for a cocktail, alone. He had gone home—home being an apartment in the Murray Hill district—and had stayed until about seven-thirty. Then he had gone to a Longchamps and had a couple more cocktails and dinner.

Then he had gone home again. He was home now; Krenke was in the lobby of Mr. Pierson's home.

They got going again. They went fast until, off Madison, they turned east toward the street number Krenke had given them. Then, so unexpectedly that the others started forward in their seats, Weigand slowed the car. He slowed it until it crept. He pointed.

Walking ahead of them on the sidewalk at their right, and only a door or so away from the apartment house, they saw a short, broad-shouldered youth, poorly dressed but moving with a kind of angry swagger. They crept behind him for a moment, watching. He turned into the entrance of the apartment house.

Weigand looked back quickly. A heavy man, well dressed and at peace with the world, was sauntering after the youth with the air of one before whom time stretches comfortably. But when the youth turned into the entrance, the heavy man quickened his pace, as if time had suddenly shrunk. Weigand touched Mullins beside him and indicated with a movement of his head. Mullins extended his right hand from the window and made a downward gesture. The heavy man, who had been going wherever Franklin Martinelli went, slowed down. He sauntered again and crossed the street diagonally. On the other side he began to look at street numbers.

Weigand edged the car up to the curb and switched off the ignition.

"What the hell?" Mullins inquired, with interest.

"I wouldn't know, Sergeant," Weigand told him. "I really wouldn't know. But we might find out. Right?"

"Yeah," Mullins said. "I'd sorta like to know, sorta."

They left the car and Detective Stein in it. Stein whistled lightly as they walked toward the apartment-house entrance and the heavy man, who was still looking at addresses on the other side of the street, started and turned. He beamed a surprised beam and crossed to the car. Stein held the door open for him and he got in, still surprised and beaming at meeting a friend in so unexpected a fashion.

One of the elevator indicators showed its car stopped at the eighth floor. The other car waited. As they moved toward it, the indicator of the first car moved to the left as the car descended. Weigand and Mullins got into the waiting elevator.

"Mr. Pierson," Weigand said. "Alfred Pierson. Eight, isn't it?"

"Yes, sir," the boy in the elevator said. "Is Mr. Pierson expecting you?"

"Oh, yes," Weigand said. "I'm sure Mr. Pierson is expecting us."

"Eight-C," the boy said. "To your left."

Weigand rang the bell. The door opened instantly, as if somebody had been standing just inside it. The somebody was Alfred Pierson, who said, "Yes?" with a rising inflection. Then he saw Sergeant Mullins. He said, "Yes," again, without the rising inflection. He stepped aside.

"This is the lieutenant," Mullins said, with a kind of pride.

"Yes," Mr. Pierson said, without inflection. "I supposed it was. You wanted to see me?"

"Oh yes," Weigand said. He went in the obvious direction across the foyer to the living room beyond. Franklin Martinelli was standing in the center of the living room, with his hat on.

"And Mr. Martinelli," Weigand said, with a tone of pleased surprise. "*And* Mr. Martinelli."

"Hello, copper," Franklin said, with a minimum of animosity. "So you finally got wise."

Weigand had not even looked around to see whether Pierson and Mullins were following. He knew Mullins would attend to that.

"Oh yes, son," he said. "We got wise. Finally, as you say. And just what are you doing here, son?"

"Hell," Martinelli said. "I give a guy a chance. Maybe he had some reason."

"Some reason for what?" Weigand asked. He made his voice sound as if the question were purely casual, the answer already evident.

"For being at the Lawrence dame's," Martinelli said. "That night. I was just going to ask him."

"Were you?" Weigand said. But he heard Mullins, behind him, draw in a quick breath. Weigand turned suddenly.

"And what were you going to answer, Pierson?" he asked, his voice quick and hard.

"I don't know what he's talking about," Pierson said, with belligerence. "Who the hell is he?"

"Don't you know?" Weigand asked. "You let him in. Didn't you ask him?"

"He said he was a friend of Miss McCalley," Pierson said. "A—a girl who used to work at the office."

"Until she got killed," Martinelli said. "Until some so-and-so stuck a knife in her."

"Until she got killed," Pierson agreed. "But I don't know what he means, I was at Ann's that night. Except at the dinner, of course."

Martinelli laughed, artificially and boisterously. They looked at him.

"At *dinner,*" he mimicked. "At dinner, he says. And I suppose you didn't come back afterward, Mr. Pierson."

"No," Pierson said. "I don't know what you mean."

But there was no conviction in his voice.

"Sure you know what I mean," Martinelli said. "Sure you know what I mean. You went away when the others did, maybe—I don't know about that. I wasn't there—*then*. All I know is you come back about one, maybe—one-thirty?"

"Oh," Pierson said. "That!" He said it as if he had just remembered. "I—I had forgotten something. A—cigarette case."

"Oh, for God's sake, Mr. Pierson," Weigand said. "Oh, for God's sake."

"You were inside half an hour, maybe," Martinelli said. "Maybe forty-five minutes. I saw you."

Weigand turned suddenly on Martinelli.

"And how did you see him?" Weigand wanted to know. "You were at home. In bed. Don't you remember?"

"Hell," the boy said. "What did you expect me to say? What did you expect, copper?"

"About what I got," Weigand said. "Lies—all around. What were you doing there?"

Martinelli looked sullen. He shook his head.

"Then," Weigand said, "you're lying now, Martinelli. Lying to involve Mr. Pierson. You weren't there."

Young Martinelli hesitated, uncertain. He looked at Weigand and then at Pierson.

"All right," he said. "I was there. Outside—in that little alley thing beside the house. Waiting for the kid."

"What kid?" Weigand said. "Frances?"

The boy nodded, reluctantly.

"All right," he said. "She was going away. Miss Lawrence was taking her somewhere on a trip. Anyway, she said it was a trip. I couldn't talk her out of it."

"And—?" Weigand prompted.

"All right," the boy said, angrily. "I was going to—catch her as she went in. I wasn't going to let that Lawrence babe get her hands on her. The Lawrence talked too damn much—she kept telling Frances I wasn't any good."

Weigand's questions came rapidly. Frances had not appeared; it developed that Martinelli had only deduced she was going to Ann's that evening, to stay overnight in preparation for leaving early the next day. It was, Weigand gathered, to have been a kind of treat for Frances—the gift of a holiday. Presumably she would have gone more or less as a companion.

Frances had not appeared, but Alfred Pierson had. Martinelli knew him; Frances had pointed him out one time, as her employer—as one of the bosses of the firm. He had gone up to the door and opened it and walked in. "Like he lived there." Martinelli's identification was certain. He had seen Pierson's face as he passed a street light. He had stayed inside half an hour, maybe forty-five minutes. Then he had come out again. He had probably come out not later than two o'clock. Shortly after he left, Martinelli had decided Frances was not coming and had gone home. He had come around that evening to give Pierson a chance to explain.

"Hell," he said, "I wouldn't turn a guy over to the cops until he had a chance. Not to the cops."

It seemed to Weigand, watching him, that Pierson did not take this as hard as he might have. He did not interrupt and did not deny again. But when Martinelli finished he laughed shortly.

"Now I'll tell one," he said. "I—"

But Weigand stopped him.

"Not yet," he said. "I'm going to arrest you first, Pierson."

Pierson was startled and outraged. Then he was suddenly shrewd and his eyes narrowed.

"I suppose you've got a warrant," he said. He said it in a tone which made clear that he supposed Weigand didn't have. Weigand shook his head, blandly.

"A warrant?" he said. "I don't need a warrant. This is on suspicion of homicide, Pierson. What did you think?"

Pierson looked at him, steadily.

"When you came here," he said, "you didn't know about this—kid's story. Why did you come?"

"Oh," Weigand said, "you're worrying about that. Yes, we'd need a warrant for that—for grand larceny. Are you in an awful hurry about it, Pierson?"

Pierson said that Weigand couldn't prove a damn thing. He said it with a violence which sounded hollow.

"I had her order for everything I did," he said.

"Well," Weigand said. "That will be just fine. That will give us something else to talk about, as the night goes on, Mr. Pierson."

Mullins asked about Martinelli as they were leaving. Weigand said they might as well take him along—too.

"As a material witness," he said. "Don't you think, Mullins?"

"O.K., Loot," Mullins said.

Pam and Jerry and Dorian listened to the radio when they went back to the Norths' apartment after dinner. They listened because Pamela wanted to hear the news. There was fifteen minutes of news, ten of it about the war and almost three of it about the Lawrence-McCalley murders, with emphasis on the killing of Mrs. Pennock, Ann Lawrence's faithful servant.

The commentator had a good deal to say about that, and almost as much to say about a mysterious young man—not named in that connection, but named a few seconds later so that only the law, in the remote contingency of a suit if things did not work out properly, would fail to note the implication—who had been missing since almost the beginning and continued to outwit the police. The commentator, who clearly fancied himself as a man of logic, summarized the whole case, with times, and seemed to have a very clear theory which he chose only to hint at.

The Norths and Dorian listened very carefully, and Pamela, a little to the surprise of the others, made several notes. Then the news period ended and, before they got around to turning off the radio, Dan Beck began. Jerry moved over quickly to stop him, but Pam shook her head and said they might as well listen. They heard Mr. Beck through.

Jerry turned the radio off then and they sat for a time digesting the news, and, of course, Mr. Beck. And then Pamela North spoke.

"You know," she said, "there's something funny about it. The more I think about it, the funnier it seems."

The others, of course, wanted to know what was funny, but Pam North shook her head. It was just a notion, she said, and she would have to think about it before she said anything. Probably it was crazy—completely crazy. But all the same it was funny. Even after Dorian got a telephone call from Bill, telling of Pierson's arrest and saying that he would be up the rest of the night with it, and went home. Pam would not tell Jerry what was so funny about "it." She would not even say what "it" was, except of course that it had to do with the murders.

• 12 •

Thursday, 6:40 A.M. to 9:50 A.M.

It was no satisfaction to Bill Weigand to know that he had been right; that he had seen danger and warned of it. He stood with his back to the slanting rain, the collar of his raincoat turned up and his hat pulled low, and looked at what the pointing lights showed him. A semicircle of men, most of them in uniform, looked where Weigand was looking, impersonally and without emotion. One man crouched and his hands moved and then he stood up and rubbed his hands as if he were dusting something off them. He looked at his hands and thrust them in the side pockets of his raincoat.

"Twelve hours," he said. "More or less. At a guess."

Weigand's voice was dull.

"Right," he said. "O.K., Doc."

There was nothing more to do there and Weigand turned away. Mullins walked after him and neither of them said anything. They got into the car and Mullins got behind the wheel and still neither said anything. Finally Mullins spoke.

"You told him, Loot," he said. "The fool kid."

"Sure," Weigand said, bitterly. "I told him. That was damned bright of me, Sergeant. I told him to be careful and not get in any trouble and went back and finished dinner. I was very bright."

147

"Well," Mullins said, reasonably, "what could you do, Loot?" He left a moment for an answer and none came. "Anybody can hide out for a day or so," he said. "Anybody. It's a big town."

"All right," Weigand said. "It's a big town. Anybody can stay out of sight for a day or so. The police can't perform miracles. We'd have caught him in the end—if he'd waited. And if the other guy had waited. All we needed was time, Sergeant." Weigand stared out through the windshield at the rain; at the gray light which was just beginning to suggest day. "About a hundred years, Sergeant. Or a thousand. He'd have been dead anyway in a hundred years."

"Well," Mullins said, "you've got him now, Loot. That's something."

"*If* I've got him now," Weigand said. "I've still got him late. Four murders late. If I've got him now, he's done a lot of killing first. Killing his way out of it."

Mullins said nothing. He waited.

"Well," Weigand said, "what are we waiting for, Mullins? Do we think Elliot's going to get up and walk away if we wait long enough? He's not going to walk away."

Mullins started the car and turned it and went the wrong way on the East Drive and cut out by the museum. The red lights flashed a warning through the rain. Behind them there was a siren after they had gone a few blocks. That was the noise they made when removing a man who had been murdered, so he wouldn't clutter up Central Park. A young man who, after being duly warned by the police—warned, in effect, that he would have to look out for himself since the police couldn't promise anything—had gone on his own way and tried to catch a murderer. And had been caught instead.

Weigand stared ahead at the wet street as they went downtown. He thought of Elliot, whom they couldn't catch, but whom somebody else had caught. He had been lying stretched out as if he were asleep, but no one would go to sleep in the slush of Tuesday's snow and the night's rain. He had lain on his side, facing away from the roadway, but not far from it. There had been no effort to hide the body. Presumably a car had stopped for a moment and the body had been rolled out—

rolled out and pushed a little way toward the bushes along the road, but only far enough so that car lights would not pick it up. Not even far enough for that, because the lights of a radio car had picked it up a few minutes after six.

John Elliot had been shot once, at the base of the brain. The slug, from a small-caliber gun, had torn upward into the brain. He hadn't bled much; he had died quickly. About twelve hours before; about an hour, at a guess, after he had talked to Weigand on the telephone. The rain lashing the remaining snow—it was always surprising to find snow still in the park after it had gone everywhere else in the city—had reduced it to a cold slush, and if there had been any marks to tell a story of murder they had been washed into the slush some time after midnight, when the rain began. So now they had four—one, two, three, four. The trail of a man killing his way out of trouble, or trying to. And unless they had him, they were still a long way behind him. Or her.

Did they have him? They could hope so. Weigand thought it over and hoped so. They had got a little out of Alfred Pierson during the night.

It had been a long night and Weigand had slept two hours of it before they wakened him to report that the body of a man, first thought the victim of a mugging, quickly identified as Elliot, had been found in the sodden snow in Central Park. It had also been a long night for Alfred Pierson. Pierson, although nobody had laid a hand on him or threatened to, was not the good-looking, well-dressed, confident man of business he had been the evening before—and that he had remained for several hours. His eyes were red and bloodshot; his black hair fell over his forehead; his clothes looked as if he had been sleeping in them and there were cigarette ashes down the front. Now, presumably, he was still sleeping in them.

Ten minutes after they were back, Weigand ended that. Pierson was brought in again and sat down again and the two tired men faced each other, as they had so long the night before. Pierson didn't say anything; he merely sat and waited, his eyes dull.

"I've just come back from the park," Weigand said. "You know what we found there, Pierson."

It was a statement. Pierson heard it late and you could not tell, from watching him, what it meant. He hesitated before he answered, but his mind was tired and slow from the night.

"What park?" he said. "What are you talking about now?"

"Central Park," Weigand said. "Where you left Elliot. With a bullet in him."

Pierson said he didn't know what Weigand was talking about. He said he thought Weigand had gone crazy.

"Right," Weigand said. "I'll tell you about it, Pierson. Yesterday evening—about six, say—we thought you were in your apartment. But you weren't. You went out the service elevator and met Elliot somewhere and he threatened to turn you in and you killed him. You still thought you could kill your way out of it."

"No," Pierson said. He said it heavily and matter-of-factly, as he had been saying it all night. "I didn't kill anybody. I didn't kill Ann or Miss McCalley or the Pennock woman or anybody.—Not Elliot, if he's been killed."

"You killed Ann because you had been robbing her," Weigand said patiently, as he had been saying, in one way or another, most of the night. "You tried to get her to marry you to cover it up and she laughed at you and said she was going to the police. So you blew up and killed her. With a poker. You hadn't meant to when you went there."

"No," Pierson said, still sulky. "I didn't touch her. She was alive when I left."

"With your cigarette case," Weigand said. "With that famous cigarette case you went back after."

"There wasn't any cigarette case," Pierson said. "I went back to—to talk to her. To explain that she misunderstood the whole thing."

"What thing?" Weigand said.

"About the money," Pierson said. "She thought the same way you do. But it wasn't true."

"Hell," Weigand said. "Quit lying, Pierson."

Pierson said nothing at all.

"So," Weigand said, "you killed Ann Lawrence. And then Frances

McCalley found out about it and you had to kill her, too. I don't know how she found out. Maybe she was there. She was supposed to be there, according to Martinelli."

"There wasn't anybody there," Pierson said. "I didn't kill anybody. I talked to Ann for a few minutes—about fifteen minutes—and went out. I didn't see this Martinelli. I didn't see Miss McCalley."

"Right," Weigand said. "Maybe it wasn't that way. Maybe she wasn't there—the McCalley girl. Maybe she just knew you had been stealing from Miss Lawrence. Or maybe you just thought she knew. And you thought she would tell the police after Ann was killed and that when they knew about the thefts they would find out about the murder. So you decided to kill her."

"No," Pierson said. "No. She didn't know about the—"

He broke off.

"About the money," Weigand finished for him. "But there was something to know about the money. You admit that."

Again it wasn't a question.

"I don't admit a damn thing," Pierson said. "Not a damn thing. About the money or anything else."

Weigand said that, in Pierson's place, he wouldn't admit anything either. He said he would go on whistling in the dark. He said he'd make them prove it. He said Pierson's attitude was very understandable. He said it wasn't going to do Pierson a damned bit of good.

"Because," Weigand said, "we've got you, Pierson. You killed Ann and then the other girl. Mrs. Pennock knew you were at the house; she guessed you had killed Ann; she tried to get money out of you. So you killed her. While she was telephoning."

"Sure," Pierson said, with more life in his voice. "I killed her while I was talking to her on the telephone."

Pierson, even after a night of it, had his wits about him. He saw the catch there.

"I didn't say she was telephoning to you," Weigand said. "She could have been telephoning to—anybody. You followed her and killed her because she had already threatened you. That afternoon."

"She never threatened me," Pierson said. "She didn't have anything on me. You haven't got anything on me. I didn't kill anybody." He looked up for the first time.

"Hell," he said, "even your way it doesn't make sense. Suppose my handling of the Lawrence account could be twisted into something. I don't admit it could, but suppose it could. I stood to go to jail. For a few years. And I had the money. Would I kill anybody to keep out of jail?"

"You didn't plan to kill, the first time," Weigand said. "She laughed at you and you lost your head. After that, it wasn't just going to jail for larceny. After that it was going up for murder."

"I didn't kill anybody," Pierson said. "I can keep on saying it as long as you can take it, Lieutenant. I didn't kill anybody."

Weigand seemed not to have heard him.

"Mrs. Pennock made three," he said. "She had threatened you on the telephone the day Miss Lawrence's body was found. You thought it over and decided to kill her, too. So yesterday you followed her and stabbed her in the telephone booth. That made three."

"Go ahead," Pierson said, wearily. "Go ahead."

"Then you went back to your office," Weigand said, "and found out that we had auditors in. You left early and had a drink on the way and went home. Then Elliot got in touch with you. By telephone, I suppose. You found out that he knew something too—probably, for one thing, he knew about the thefts. Probably Ann had told him. So you made an appointment to meet him somewhere—maybe at his apartment. And you killed him and took his body and left it in the Park and went back to your apartment. You went through the service entrance again and up on the service elevator and after half an hour or so you came out the front and went to dinner. You'd had quite a day. Were you hungry, Pierson?"

Pierson looked at him.

"As a matter of fact," Weigand said, "you weren't hungry. I'll give you that, Pierson. You didn't have much appetite, for a man your size. You had an omelet and ate about half of it. After three drinks."

"You know," Pierson said, "I'll bet you could prove that, Lieutenant. I'll bet that's one thing you can prove. I'll bet you can prove what kind of cocktails I had."

"Manhattans," Weigand said.

"You're marvelous, Lieutenant," Pierson said. "The efficiency of the police. Wonderful. And I suppose you think you can hang me because I had three manhattans, don't you?"

"Right," Weigand said. "I'm glad we amuse you, Pierson. We won't for long."

Pierson looked at him, and when he spoke his voice was not so tired.

"Want to bet on that, Lieutenant?" he said. "Want to bet you won't look funny as hell if you try to hang any of this on me?"

"You bet and I'll bet," Weigand said. "If you lose, I'll see you in the chair." His voice was tired and harsh. He motioned to Mullins, and Mullins turned Pierson over to the guards. Pierson went out looking tired, but he tried to square his shoulders as he went through the door. Mullins looked after him and said he was putting on a good bluff.

"I hope so," Weigand said. "I hope that's it."

Mullins waited for further comment, got none, and finally said it looked all right to him. Weigand smiled faintly. He said that part of it was almost certainly all right.

"After the start," he said, "it's fine. It fits Pierson fine—if he killed Ann Lawrence. It also fits, with a little trimming here and there, anybody else who killed Ann Lawrence."

"Well," Mullins pointed out, "Pierson had a motive. He was there. He could have killed the others—it all fits pretty good, seems to me."

"Right," Weigand said. "Motive, opportunity, means. It fits fine. It also fits Martinelli. Up to last night, around six o'clock, it fitted Elliot. It fits the Harper girl—what's her name."

"Cleo," Mullins said. "Cleo Harper." He paused. "Listen," he said. "Maybe Elliot did kill the others. And then shot himself."

"And then," Weigand pointed out, "swallowed the gun he'd shot himself with."

"Well," Mullins said, "maybe—"

The telephone cut him off. Weigand listened, said, "Right," and looked at Mullins oddly after he had hung up.

"Maybe, as you were about to say, the gun was around somewhere in the snow. And sure enough it was, Mullins. Sunk down in a pile they left when they cleaned the drive. Not too far for Elliot to have thrown it, convulsively, after he shot himself. And, to get it around there, he couldn't have held it normally, so it's an even chance it would have slipped out of his hand. There's even a chance he lived long enough to throw it deliberately. Brain wounds are funny, sometimes."

Mullins thought it over.

"Hell," he said, "we don't get anywhere unless we stick to Pierson. What you say we stick to Pierson, Loot?"

"Right," Weigand said. "If we can, Mullins. Pierson is fine with me—if we can stick to him."

Pamela North thought it over during the night and in the morning told Jerry she hadn't closed her eyes.

"Darling," Jerry said. "Really, darling."

"Well," Pam said, "not for more than a minute or two, or maybe an hour. Because the more I think of it the funnier it seems."

"The more *I* think of it the funnier it seems too," Jerry said, finishing his coffee and holding out his cup. "An hour indeed."

"I don't see," Pam said, filling the cup, "how it is you always know how much *I* sleep. Do you stay awake and watch me, or what? Or do I snore?"

"Well," Jerry said, "you breathe differently. Everyone does. And usually I don't go to sleep until I hear you."

Pam looked at him with interest and said, "Why?"

"I don't honestly know," Jerry said. "It just seems—safer, I guess. And partly it's because if I don't go to sleep until after you do, you won't wake me up by suddenly thinking of something. It just seems to work out better."

"Actually," Pam said, "you usually go to sleep before I do. You go to sleep almost at once, really."

Jerry looked faintly indignant.

"Almost never," he said. "It usually takes me hours. Or half an hour, anyway. I never could just lie down and go to sleep. I know what you mean, but I can't do it."

"I don't mean anything," Pam said. "Except that you do go to sleep almost right away. I think it's lovely, really."

"You think it's bovine," Jerry told her.

Pam denied this. And, anyway, it was more feline than bovine. Cats could, instantly, and nobody ever said cats were bovine. There was a tremendous difference.

"I'll say there is," Jerry said. "Who ever said there wasn't?"

Pam finished her egg and then said she didn't know how they got into this.

"As a matter of fact," she said, "I never know how we get into any of them, do you? I merely said I woke up now and then and wondered about Mr. Beck."

She hadn't, Jerry pointed out, said anything of the kind. She said she had been awake all night and she had not mentioned Mr. Beck.

"Didn't I, dear?" she said. "I thought I did. Because I think he's been stolen. I'm almost sure of it."

"Stolen?" Jerry North repeated, in a strange voice. "Stolen? Mr. Beck? Why—he was right there. Last night. What do you mean, stolen?"

"Just stolen," Mrs. North said. "Kidnapped, if you like it better. I think he's been—" She broke off.

"I'm going to call Bill right away," she said, "because if he has been we ought to do something."

Jerry said he didn't get it. Any of it.

"And furthermore," he said, "I don't see why anything has to be done about it if he has been. I think it would be fine if Mr. Beck were stolen."

"Well," Pam said, "you don't really think that. And I *really* think he's been stolen. That's the difference. So I'm going to call Bill."

"I," Jerry said, "am going to listen to the eight-thirty news. So if you want to telephone, you'd better go into the study."

Pam started and then decided she would listen to the news first. It was eleven-thirty on their dial and eight-thirty on their clock, and time for the latest up-to-the-minute news from the newsroom of the *Daily News,* New York's picture newspaper.

"They certainly get news into it," Pam commented. Jerry said "shush!" and listened. He heard the war news and was about to turn the radio off when the announcer continued:

"Meanwhile," he said, making a looping connective, "right here in New York, the police finally found the long-missing John Elliot, wanted for questioning in connection with the poker-murder of pretty Ann Lawrence in her private house in the exclusive Gramercy Park area. They found him under a hedge in Central Park, shot through the back of the head. The police believe it may have been suicide, but are at a loss to account for the nature of the wound and the absence of the death weapon. And that brings us to the oddity of the day. It seems that Mr. Leo Kennelworth, of the East New York Kennelworths, woke up this morning and—"

The Norths did not discover the oddity which had befallen Mr. Kennelworth, or even how the announcer for the *Daily News* had been reminded of it by the fate of John Elliot. Jerry snapped the radio off automatically. The Norths sat a moment and looked at each other. Then Jerry spoke, and his voice was quiet.

"If you have any theories, Pam," he said. "Any theories at all, no matter how—odd—you'd better call Bill. You'd better call him now."

Pam picked up the telephone and nodded slowly instead of answering. She heard Bill Weigand's tired voice after a moment and her own was as somber as her voice could easily become. She had meant to tell him her theory on the telephone, but when she heard his voice she had another idea. She said she had something to tell him—something important to tell him.

"And you're tired," she said, "and maybe I shouldn't tell it on the telephone anyway. Have you had breakfast?"

"I don't know," Bill said. "I think—I had some coffee around four and some more, I think, a little while ago. I've been—busy, Pam."

"We just heard it," Pam said. "About John Elliot. And I've got an idea. So why don't you come over and have breakfast?"

There was a pause while Bill thought of it, and then sudden decision.

"I don't know any reason," he said. "We're taking Pierson to magistrate's court at ten and I'm going to be there. And after that, the D.A. wants to take it to the Grand Jury immediately. It's—it's that kind of a case. And I talked to Dorian about four and I think I persuaded her I was all right and that she should go back to sleep. So—"

It took him only about ten minutes. Pam waited—and Jerry waited too, and then went to the study and told his office he would be late, and returned and waited again—while Weigand ate hungrily, but abstractedly. When he had finished, Pam thought he looked better, although still very tired.

"Well, Pam?" he said. "What's the theory?"

Pam answered with a question. Was Weigand sure that Pierson was the man they wanted? He hesitated a moment. Then he nodded.

"All things considered," he said. "Yes. That is, I think he's the man. I'll admit it's going to be hard to prove. Because, while he had motive and opportunity, we can't prove he had them exclusively. The defense can—"

"He didn't," Pam said. "Or, if he did, not because of the money. Or, if the money comes into it, not entirely because of the money. Unless he needed the money so badly, to make it good to the Lawrence estate, that he had to steal Mr. Beck."

Bill Weigand looked at Jerry and Jerry shook his head.

"That's what she keeps saying, Bill," Jerry said. "She keeps talking about somebody's having stolen Mr. Beck. I think she means kidnapped."

"I don't care what word you use," Pam said. "I say stolen because I can spell it. And I never know how many p's in kidnapped."

Jerry looked at her and ran the fingers of his right hand through his hair. It was a little thing—but life was made of little things. Particularly as lived with Mrs. North.

"Listen, darling," he said. "I don't want to stop you. But you weren't going to *write* it. I mean—you were just going to *say* it. And you can *say* kidnapped. You just did."

"Of course I can *say* it," Pam said. "But when I can't spell a word, or have to think about how it's spelled, I just don't use it when I'm talking. Not if there's another word just as good, like 'stolen.' It's just a—a feeling. I just *feel* that people ought to say words they can spell."

"But—" Jerry said, and stopped. He thought and tried again. "You mean it's—pretentious, or something?" He said. "To say words you can't spell?"

"Well," Pam said. "It's sort of pretending you can spell them. Or it feels that way to me. Sometimes. Sometimes, of course, it doesn't at all."

Jerry thought it over and said, "Oh."

"As far as I'm concerned," Bill said, "I often feel the same way, for some reason. But I can spell kidnapped. Why do you think somebody has kidnapped Mr. Beck, Pam? Because obviously nobody has. He's still on the radio."

"That's just it," Pam said. "How do you know?"

"Because you can hear him," Jerry said. "If you're not careful. As we did last night, Pam. Don't you remember?"

Pam looked at him as if she thought he was not as bright as usual. She said of course she remembered.

"That," she repeated, "is *it*. How do you know it was Mr. Beck? Because I think it was somebody else *pretending* to be Mr. Beck."

They both looked at her. They looked at her with a kind of surprise and interest and wonderment. Then they looked at each other. Understanding ran between them and by consent Bill Weigand took it up from there. Jerry merely ran his hand rapidly through his hair.

"Listen, Pam," Bill said. "Let's get this straight. You mean that somebody is impersonating Mr. Beck? That the real Beck has been sto—kidnapped, and that the man we hear on the radio is another man altogether pretending to be Dan Beck? Because that's obviously impossible."

"Why?" said Pam. "I do think that. Why is it impossible?"

"Because," Bill began and was baffled momentarily by the multitude of reasons which presented themselves. "I'm tired, Jerry. You tell her."

Jerry paused to get a grip on himself and told her. In the first place, Dan Beck sounded last night just as he always sounded. "Awful." She was imagining things. To start with, she had nothing to start with.

He wasn't, Pam told him, being very clear. But she thought she understood what he was trying to say, and it was a matter of opinion. Suppose, just for argument, that she *had* something to start with. Suppose there *was* something wrong with Beck's talk on the radio the night before. Suppose, just for argument, that it was different.

"How different?" Jerry said, deciding to take it a step at a time. "It was the same voice, wasn't it?"

"I don't know," Pam said. "It didn't sound unlike the same voice. But it was on the radio, remember. They can do it with a mixer, or something. The sound engineers. If the man who was impersonating Mr. Beck had a voice just *something* like his, they could make it sound right enough to fool almost everybody if they were *expecting* it to be Mr. Beck's voice. Because most of the time you hear what you *expect* to hear. Not what you *really* hear."

There was, Jerry had to admit to himself, something in that. But it was, he felt, beside the point. Because even Pam admitted that it sounded like the same voice, if you expected to hear Beck's voice. And that seemed to argue that Pam hadn't expected to hear Beck's voice.

"Really," Pam said, "I didn't notice the voice first. You're right about that. It was only afterward that I realized how it would be about the voice, if it sounded just reasonably like the right voice. Really it was what he said."

Jerry said it sounded like the same sort of thing to him. He said what it sounded like, using the more polite of the several things it sounded like to him.

"Of course," Pam said. "It was the same sort of thing—generally. But it didn't feel like the same thing. It was—a matter of style, I guess. It sounded rougher, and at the same time less—less certain. The other times I've heard it—oh, it swung along. Swang along? Anyway, you felt that it was going very well, even when you hated to admit it was going very well. Confident and—dramatic. And all the sentences the right length. And last night it sounded like an imitation. And then I thought—suppose it is an imitation? Suppose it isn't Mr. Beck at all, but somebody imitating him."

"And then," Jerry said, "you thought somebody had stolen him."
Pam nodded.

"And that somebody was impersonating him," she said. "Nazis. Or Japanese. Don't you see what they could do?"

Jerry looked at Bill Weigand, and now there was doubt in his eyes.

"Come to think of it, Bill," he said, "it wouldn't be a bad trick. It would even be a pretty good trick. It could be made—oh, into a kind of sabotage of minds. Beck has a tremendous following—and a not very bright following. Suppose—suppose you wanted peace, say. Peace of the Nazi kind, of the Jap kind. You could—you could work on them. Subtly, of course. Not all at once. I could do it myself, if I were a Nazi and had the chance. Anybody could do it who knew the tricks. It could be—it could be a tremendous thing, really."

Bill hesitated. He was, Pam decided, thinking it over.

"Suppose you were doing that," she said. "Suppose you were an agent for Germany. And you had it all fixed up—you had somebody to impersonate Beck; you had the people fixed you would have to have fixed. And then suppose, by accident somehow, a girl like Ann Lawrence stumbled on the truth. She knew the real Beck; suppose she saw the substitute Beck—suppose something came up so that they couldn't keep her from seeing him—and knew right away that he wasn't Beck. If you were an agent and found out that she knew, wouldn't you kill her? And if she had told other people—like the McCalley girl, and her servant, and Elliot, as she might, wouldn't you kill them, too? And wouldn't that account for the different weapons and things, and the fact that Mrs. Pennock was killed while she was actually talking to somebody who logically ought to have been the murderer? Because it would have to be a gang and anybody in the gang could be sent out to murder any of them. One of them could kill Mrs. Pennock, for example, while she was talking to another one."

It was a long speech and Pam was almost breathless when she finished. She was also intent and anxious, because the more she outlined it the more she believed it. And Bill had not interrupted her, even by the shaking of a head.

She waited after she had finished and still Bill Weigand did not interrupt. He was thinking about it, she decided, and finding something in it.

He was thinking about it. He was thinking, specifically, of one small odd thing of which Mrs. North knew nothing. He was thinking of a comfortable, middle-aged housekeeper who helped her husband take care of Dan Beck, and of the way, as a detective had left, she had peered surreptitiously after him. It was a tiny, clear picture in his mind, and he had almost forgotten it. And it fitted. It fitted Mrs. North's picture of a gang. Or it fitted another picture, which was—in final outcome at any rate—the same picture. Because, although it was clear that Mrs. North didn't, he doubted the impersonation theory. That would be difficult to bring off. He told her why.

"Impersonation on that scale is story-book stuff," he said. "It isn't possible—or it's so improbable, so involved, that for practical purposes it isn't possible. You could find somebody about Beck's size, probably. Maybe you could find somebody who looked enough like him so that, if you didn't know either of the men very well, you would have difficulty telling which was which. Perhaps you could even find somebody with a voice enough like Beck's to confuse people—on the radio anyway. But none of these similarities, even if you got them all in the same man, would be enough to fool anybody. Not even a little; not even for a minute. Not anybody who knew Beck better than by sight. They'd simply say, 'That isn't Beck.' You could say it looks like Beck and sounds like Beck and anybody who knew him would grant you that and still merely laugh and say, 'But of course it isn't Beck. It isn't even very like Beck.'"

"Well," Pam said, "he could just keep away from people who knew Beck that well, couldn't he? I don't say it would be perfect—really. I said all along it wouldn't be. I said it didn't fool Ann Lawrence."

But Bill Weigand shook his head, and when Pam looked hopefully at Jerry, he shook his head too.

"Beck couldn't, Pam," Jerry said. "That's just it. A recluse—a man who didn't see very many people. But not Beck. For one thing, he broadcasts three times a week. He has to go to a radio studio, with attendants who know him and an announcer who knows him and people in the sound room who know him. All of them would know too well to be fooled. Think of the sound engineers, for example. They must know every intonation of his voice."

"But," Pam said, "I said it would have to be a conspiracy. There would have to be a lot of people in it. I think there were a lot of people in it, not only at the studio but a lot of people in lots of places. Maybe this Mr. Pierson was in it along with a lot of others. Maybe he really did kill Ann—maybe he killed any of them or all of them. But it was because he was in the conspiracy. Maybe stealing Ann's money was part of the conspiracy. Maybe that's how they financed it. Maybe it isn't Nazis, but just people in this country who *think* like Nazis." She paused. "Because," she said, "I do think there are American fascists, even if the newspapers make fun and get indignant. Because there are so many people in this country there would almost have to be every kind of people there were anywhere."

There was a short pause, during which Jerry and Bill Weigand declined the conversational opening provided by Pam's North's concluding venture. Then Bill suggested the other idea. He said that it had come to him as he thought of the little old woman at Beck's—the little woman who looked so motherly and was so evidently spying on him as he left. Of course, he pointed out, she might have been merely innocently curious.

"The other possibility," he said, "is that Beck is really Beck, but that he's under some sort of pressure. I mean, if I believed your theory at all, Pam, I'd believe some such version as that—not the impersonation theory. Suppose Beck was, in some way, really being held prisoner and made to say what these people—the people in your conspiracy, the Axis agents—wanted him to say. Suppose the nice old couple in his apartment are really guards in a way, put there to see that Beck obeys orders. Suppose he knows he'll be killed if he doesn't do what he's told. Or suppose—"

Bill Weigand stopped suddenly and thought what he was saying. It was preposterous, of course, but the further he went into it the more small hints came up to make him think it might not of necessity be preposterous. First the little woman spying; now Beck's past.

"He lived for a good many years abroad," Weigand said. "During the time Hitler was coming up. And it isn't clear just where he lived or what he did. At least it isn't to me. Somehow, in that time, he might have left—hostages. There may be someone over there in Nazi hands—a woman or a child, perhaps—who is being used to keep Beck in line."

Pam shook her head.

"The trouble is," she said, "that there's nothing to all this if it's really Beck. Because the only point to any of it is that I don't think it *is* Beck. So there's no point in saying that it's really Beck acting under duress." She looked at Jerry. "And I can spell duress," she said. She did. "Because if it is, he'd still sound like Beck. And the point is, he doesn't."

They thought of that. Jerry didn't agree, fully. He said that the circumstances might very well alter the way Beck sounded.

"I mean," he said, "if somebody had a gun in my back, I wouldn't sound the way I do now. At least, I shouldn't think anyone would. You'd be nervous and uncertain; you'd probably—I mean in Beck's predicament—be saying things you didn't believe, perhaps even things they had written down for you to say, instead of what you wanted to say. At best, you wouldn't put the same conviction into it."

Pam said it was very logical; she said that all both of them said was very logical. She said that she thought, just the same, that somebody had stolen Beck and that it was an impersonation.

"And after all," she said, "I listened to him. Jerry didn't, really, and you, Bill—you were off arresting Mr. Pierson. I was the one who discovered it wasn't Mr. Beck, really, and it's *my* theory you're both explaining away. Only as far as I'm concerned, it doesn't go away."

"Right," Bill said. "You stick to your theory, Pam. And—just on the chance there's something to it—don't go off on your own and try to prove it. If you get to feeling that you want to, remember Elliot. Just to reassure you, I'll look into it. Right?"

"Well—" Pam said. "If you'll *really* look into it. Not just to humor me, but to find out something. As if you thought there was something to find out. Only I'm not sure you can, because you don't believe it yourself."

Bill didn't like that, and his expression said so. He said he was serious; very serious. Even if she was not really right in her theory, she might run into something if she tried to find out about it by herself.

"Damn it, Pam," Bill said, "it's dangerous."

"It's not dangerous if Pierson is the man," Pam pointed out. "You've got him locked up. If you really believe your own theory, it doesn't matter *what* I do, because there isn't any danger."

Bill Weigand smiled faintly. He stood up.

"All right," he said. "I'm not sure enough about Pierson to risk anybody's life on it. Particularly yours, my dear."

He was rather grave about it. But Jerry seemed confident. He told Bill not to worry.

"Because," he said, "I'll see she doesn't get into any trouble. This time, I'll keep her locked up."

Bill seemed relieved by that, and went on toward the magistrate's court and the arraignment of Alfred Pierson. It was not until he had gone that Pam, very innocently, reminded Jerry that he was going to be on the radio himself that evening—on a book program—and that he couldn't very well be there and still keep an eye on her.

"Unless you mean really lock me up," she said. "And you couldn't do that on account of fire."

Jerry was not as taken aback as Pam expected. He pointed out that he could take her with him. He added that that was precisely what he planned to do.

· 13 ·

Thursday, 10:20 A.M. to 9:35 P.M.

Justice moved briskly through the preliminary stages of the case of the State of New York vs. Alfred Pierson. Pierson was sandwiched between a jostling case, which involved a known pickpocket, and a charge of simple assault. Pierson looked rested. He had managed to get a fresh suit and he sat with an attorney of reputation and presence. The reputation was in some respects a little curious; it was the jaundiced view of the police department that Francis D. Kendall had never knowingly defended an innocent man. Juries, however, rather consistently disagreed with the police department, and most of Mr. Kendall's clients went out, finally, into the free air. They did not, the police felt, notably freshen it.

The preliminary hearing of Mr. Kendall's new client, before Magistrate Barrsmith, was exceedingly brief. Mr. Pierson pleaded not guilty on the short affidavit, signed by Police Lieutenant William Weigand and charging suspicion of homicide. He waived preliminary examination. Magistrate Barrsmith ordered him held without bail for action of the Grand Jury, gave a suspended sentence in the simple assault case, and regarded Franklin Martinelli, held by the police as a material witness. Martinelli remained small and truculent.

The District Attorney's office, represented by an exceptionally downy assistant district attorney, asked that Franklin Martinelli be held in substantial bail as a material witness in the case of the State of New York vs. Alfred Pierson, charged with homicide in connection with the death of one Ann Lawrence.

"The man who was just before your honor," the downy assistant district attorney reminded Magistrate Barrsmith.

"I remember, counselor," the magistrate said testily. "The court is not wholly without intelligence."

"No, sir," the assistant district attorney said. Magistrate Barrsmith regarded him narrowly, apparently considering the answer equivocal.

"Well," Magistrate Barrsmith said. "What do you claim he knows about the case?"

"The State expects, through this witness, to place the defendant Pierson at the scene of the crime," the assistant district attorney told him. "The State considers the evidence which will be given by Mr. Martinelli very material."

"This court," Magistrate Barrsmith said, thinking that if things went on as they were he would really have to see a doctor about his digestion, "does not lightly regard the tendency of the police to regard every citizen, regardless of his rights *as* a citizen and regardless of his presumptive need to make a living, as a mere pawn in the efforts of the police to—"

It came over Magistrate Barrsmith, gloomily, that he did not know precisely where he was going next. This was embarrassing, because the man from the AP local had started to take down what the court did not lightly regard. The other reporters who were covering Pierson's arraignment were not taking it down, but they would get it from the AP man if it was hot enough. Magistrate Barrsmith was unhappily aware that it had cooled off. The AP man, looking a little tired, had stopped taking it down.

Magistrate Barrsmith looked darkly at the downy assistant district attorney.

"You were about to say something, counselor?" he inquired, in icy tones.

The assistant district attorney, who had had no intention of saying anything, and was merely waiting, with rather awed curiosity, to see how the magistrate's sentence came out, jumped.

"No, your honor," he said. "I wasn't going to say anything."

"Then don't interrupt," Magistrate Barrsmith advised, belligerently.

The young representative of the majesty of the State of New York was overcome with a mysterious sense of guilt.

"I'm very sorry, sir," he said.

"Well," the magistrate said, inconclusively. "Where was I?"

His tone did not invite anyone to tell him where he was.

"Oh, yes," he said. "I don't hold with this business—this custom— of the police locking up everybody they think might know something about a crime. At a time when the country needs the hand of every worker if it is to triumph in this vital war against the forces of evil, it is essential that no man's work be interrupted without due cause. What do you claim this boy saw, counselor?"

The counselor looked around at Weigand.

"The defendant going into the house of the deceased," Weigand said. "At about the time set by the Medical Examiner's office for the killing. This man will testify that the defendant Pierson stayed from half to three-quarters of an hour, all of the period being included in the critical time."

"Well," the magistrate said, "what was this man doing there? Have you thought of that, Lieutenant?"

Lieutenant Weigand wished inwardly that Magistrate Barrsmith would do something about his digestion. Or only hold court after lunch, which always seemed to soothe him.

"That question has come up, your honor," Weigand said. "That is one of the reasons we would like to have him held in substantial bail. Your honor will understand that the inquiry is not completed. And this witness is not engaged in essential war work, your honor. His draft board has classified him as 1A."

The magistrate looked sharply at Bill Weigand, who looked back mildly.

"When is this going before the Grand Jury, Lieutenant?" he wanted to know. Weigand looked at the assistant district attorney.

"As soon as these formalities are completed, your honor," the attorney said, unwisely.

"Formalities?" Magistrate Barrsmith repeated. "So you consider this purely a formality, counselor? You regard this court as a pure formality, do you?"

Weigand found himself wishing that the downy young attorney would forget himself and answer "Yes." Merely for the cause of honesty. But the attorney was not that downy.

"No, sir, certainly not," he said. Magistrate Barrsmith seemed mollified.

"Well," he said. "It isn't. And you've wasted enough of its time, counselor. What bail do you suggest?"

"Ten thousand dollars," the attorney said.

Magistrate Barrsmith seemed bored. The reporters seemed bored.

"So ordered," Magistrate Barrsmith said. "Let's get on with it. Next case."

The reporters left with the assistant district attorney, Weigand and Mullins, Pierson and Mr. Kendall, Franklin Martinelli. They had not, Magistrate Barrsmith feared—correctly—taken down anything he said. It was lamentably hard to get in the newspapers from a magistrate's bench, unless you disagreed publicly with Butch. And it was not particularly wise to disagree publicly with Butch.

Justice slowed down somewhat after the magistrate's court. The Grand Jury wanted to hear a good deal of testimony, and did. It heard from the auditors, it heard from Martinelli, it heard from the Medical Examiner's office and from Detective Lieutenant William Weigand and from Deputy Chief Inspector Artemus O'Malley. It adjourned for lunch and consultation, convened and heard from representatives of Estates Incorporated, from Max Silverstone, who went white again when he told how Mrs. Pennock's body had fallen on him. The jury also heard of the death of Frances McCalley and of that of John Elliot.

Built up, with all the issues stated, it made a convincing case, Weigand thought as he listened to the parade of witnesses. If you could get all this before a trial jury—but the trouble was you couldn't. The Grand Jury had wide latitude; the defense did not answer back. Half, anyway, of what the Grand Jury had heard by four o'clock that afternoon, the trial jury would never be allowed to hear. The State could not even try to give the trial jury so full a picture, since it would state its case on the murder of Ann Lawrence. That had been decided at a brief conference before the Grand Jury hearing began. But the State decided, also, that it would take whatever it could get out of the Grand Jury, so as to have something in reserve.

At ten minutes after five, the Grand Jury handed up indictments to Judge Washburn in General Sessions charging Alfred Pierson with the crime of murder in the first degree in connection with the deaths of Ann Lawrence, Frances McCalley, Florence Pennock and John Elliot. It also, in a fifth indictment, charged him with grand larceny on three counts in connection with his manipulation of the estate of Ann Lawrence, deceased, and with second degree forgery. (This last legal anticlimax grew out of certain alterations in records which auditors testified had been corollary to the theft of most of Miss Lawrence's once comforting fortune.)

Judge Washburn issued bench warrants on each indictment and they were duly served on Alfred Pierson, who was already in the new Tombs. Pierson was immediately taken before Judge Washburn and pleaded not guilty, severally, to all indictments. He was remanded to the Tombs, without bail. The Chief Magistrate signed an order dismissing the charge of homicide against Pierson, in view of the superseding indictment. The State of New York was now, formally, ready to proceed. With luck, it might find a gap in the court calendar in about three weeks.

There were few things more tiring than the law, Weigand thought as, with Mullins, he ate a nondescript dinner in a nondescript restaurant at a few minutes after seven. Because whatever Magistrate Barrsmith might like to say in public, this had been a day of pure formality. It had been speeded up, in consideration of the public interest in the case. It had been essential; it all had its vital part in the fair administration of justice. Weigand would not have seen—he would have fought as hard as he could against—any shortcutting of the procedure, because only in the procedure lay protection for the individual. But it had, in fact, been cut and dried.

There had been no reasonable doubt that Pierson would waive preliminary hearing; no possible doubt that Magistrate Barrsmith, in view of the waiver, would order him held without bail. There had not been any actual doubt that the police desire to have Franklin Martinelli kept in storage would be acquiesced in; even less that the Grand Jury, after satisfying itself of a prima facie case, would return indictments. All that was doubtful lay ahead, as it had lain from the start. Could they make the case stick when it came to trial? Nothing else mattered but that.

The rub there was evident.

"We can't show exclusive opportunity," Weigand said. "Or even exclusive motive. The defense can raise a doubt. How about Martinelli? the defense will say. How about Cleo Harper? How about Elliot as murderer and suicide? We're going to need more. A lot more, Sergeant."

"Yeah," Mullins agreed. He drank thin coffee out of a thick cup. "And if Mrs. North gets in with her theory about somebody stealing Mr. Beck—Jeeze!"

Mrs. North wouldn't get in with that theory, Weigand promised himself and Mullins. It was going to be hard enough without that. Mrs. North was not going to get in at all. Not this time. He promised himself that. He promised Mullins that. This time things were going in an orderly fashion.

"Yeah?" Mullins said. "Yeah? You mean it ain't going to be screwy, Loot?"

Absolutely not, Weigand assured Mullins—and himself. Not any screwier than it was, already, at any rate. Mrs. North's preposterous— and away from her he realized just how preposterous—theory of a Nazi plot to kidnap—steal—Dan Beck and substitute a spurious Dan Beck was not going to reach the tender ears of a trial jury. This trial jury was going to hear far too much as it was.

Having made this very clear to Mullins, Weigand was a little embarrassed, on finishing dinner, to explain that he was going to drop in on Dan Beck. Just to check up on a thing or two, he said, vaguely. It might, for example, be helpful to run over Elliot's alibi again, just in case the defense brought Elliot into it as a red herring. It would help if they could, at least, knock that out cold by proving that Elliot could not possibly have killed Ann Lawrence.

Mullins looked at Lieutenant Weigand thoughtfully, and Weigand returned the look with challenge.

"O.K., Loot," Mullins said, after a pause. "I didn't say anything."

In not saying anything, Bill Weigand admitted that evening to Dorian, Sergeant Mullins had shown the restraint proper in a sergeant who does not agree with a lieutenant. But in the things he pointedly had not said, Mullins would have been right. Weigand's second visit to the almost too ample, too restrainedly luxurious, apartment of Dan Beck had been a wild goose chase.

"Or," he added, thinking of Mrs. North, "a wild herring chase. Because there's nothing in Pam's theory. Nothing at all."

He was firm about it; firmer, Dorian thought, than was entirely necessary.

"Of course, Bill," Dorian pointed out, "there doesn't have to be anything in Pam's theories. It isn't a law of nature that there should be. It's just a—a custom."

"There isn't in this," Bill insisted, almost as if she had not agreed with him. "Dan Beck is Dan Beck. Simply that and nothing more, like the primrose. Which after all *was* just a primrose."

"Of course," Dorian agreed. "If you want to look at it that way."

Bill demanded to be told what other way there was, and Dorian said, "Darling! You're tired. It's been an awful day."

"Well," he said, "Beck was very comfortable, anyway. I was just checking on the Elliot alibi, you understand. All very routine. And incidentally, without making much of it, on where he was yesterday afternoon and evening. At this time and that time."

"Mrs. Pennock," Dorian said. "And Mr. Elliot. Yes."

He was, Bill told her, in his apartment, working on his speech for that evening. He was alone, as he always was when he wrote. He had repeated, with that charmingly deprecating air, his account of his idiosyncrasies as a writer. Always resolutely alone, with the door satisfactorily locked; always picking out the words of his "message"—but the

tone had been even more amusedly deprecating at the word—on a
portable typewriter. And always copying the product himself, again on
the portable.

"Because," Bill explained, "he has little tricks that he plays on himself, to guide him in reading. He puts several spaces between words if
he wants to go slow and emphatically. He capitalizes words and under-
lines words, for different purposes, and puts in little asterisks and
things. He says that nobody else could do it the way he wants it done.
He has his own little systems."

Dorian said it sounded reasonable enough to her. Bill agreed that it
did, also, to him. At any rate, that was what Dan Beck had been doing
all the afternoon and evening before—from around two in the afternoon until, at a few minutes before eight, he left the apartment for the
studios of the Trans-Continental System. It wasn't, obviously, much of
an alibi. It wasn't an alibi at all. He could have left any time—he could
have spent the whole afternoon and evening murdering people if he
chose.

"Except," Dorian pointed out, "that he wouldn't have had any script.
And apparently he had a script, because Pam heard it and decided that
he had been stolen because he wasn't like himself."

Bill said that he could, obviously, have written the script in the
morning, if it came to that. Leaving time for an afternoon's killing.

"But," Dorian said, "you think he didn't."

It was a statement, or almost a statement.

"There's no reason in the world to think he did," Bill told her, with
emphasis. "No reason except a crazy notion of Pam North's that he
doesn't seem to be himself on the radio any more. Well, he seemed to
be himself this afternoon, all right."

He had seemed, Bill amplified, to be precisely the Dan Beck of two
days previous—bland and comfortable, not at all like a man who was
dangerous to anybody. His two elderly servants had radiated comfort
and—hominess. The butler had welcomed Bill this time, and had
remembered him politely and taken him almost at once to the big,
sprawling room in which he had seen Beck before. But Beck had not
been awaiting him this time, but had come through another door after

several minutes, with a paper in his hand and his hair disturbed and wearing glasses. These things had made him look less than ever like a danger to society, a man engaged in a perilous impersonation or a man performing in a cage under the threats of implacable keepers. He had looked at Weigand over the tops of his glasses, and his face, which had had a preoccupied expression, took on an expression of concentration and gravity.

"Dreadful about poor John," he said, at once. "Unbelievably dreadful."

The voice was the same thing of beautiful resonance. It was impossible to forget the voice, once having heard it; it was impossible to think of its being successfully impersonated. Dan Beck was Dan Beck; seeing him again, Weigand found his faint suspicions—based, after all, on nothing more tangible than a Pam North hunch—had faded instantly. It was absurd to think of any of the things he and Pam had thought; hard to feel any part of the animus which so clearly moved the police commissioner. Dan Beck was an earnest, comfortable, American man in his middle years; as disarming as a rocking chair on a front porch.

Assuming that Beck referred to the death of John Elliot, Weigand had agreed in its dreadfulness.

"He was a young man," Beck had said, in the tone of a man who was not. "He was brilliant. It is—it is hard to believe. It is horrible to think what is just under the surface of our society, Lieutenant; how close under the surface the animal runs. A young man alone in the park—sudden violence—death. Things like that are frightening."

Weigand had agreed. Murder was always frightening. But this had not been, he pointed out, a simple case of a violent attack, motive robbery. This wasn't a "mugging" case.

"No?" Beck had said, seeming doubtful. He had urged Weigand to sit down, insisted that he have a cocktail. Weigand had had a cocktail, while Beck matched it with milk. "Are you certain of that, Lieutenant?" Beck asked, after they were settled. "Of course, you must have reason to feel that it was not so—simple. So—elemental."

Only, Weigand agreed, that Elliot had been shot, not mugged. Only that it would have been too much of a coincidence. Beck looked at Weigand carefully.

"You don't, I gather," he said, "entertain this suicide theory the newspapers have been hinting about? The theory that he killed Ann Lawrence, and the others, and then himself?"

Weigand let his voice sound surprised. Elliot was, he pointed out, fully cleared of the Lawrence murder by Beck's own story. And the other murders had been part of the Lawrence murder.

"I'm certain I'm right," Beck said. "He couldn't have killed Ann. I've—I've been worrying about it, Lieutenant. If some word of mine led you—the police—to drop all possibility of John's guilt, and so leave him free to go on—and then if he were really not innocent as he seemed to me and all this might have been stopped—I could never forgive myself if that were true, Lieutenant."

Weigand had recognized and admitted the inner doubts which assail men, even when they have no reason to doubt, if tragedy results from something done or left undone. So a railroad towerman, after a wreck, might torture himself with questions. Had he pushed back the proper lever after the freight had taken the siding, leaving the line clear for the hurrying express? He could have sworn he had—but had he? Or had he made some dreadful, now irremediable, mistake?

"But I have thought it over and over," Beck went on, his voice earnest. "I have gone over and over it in my memory. I can't have been mistaken. I don't see how I can have been mistaken. I don't see how Elliot could have killed Ann. I don't see how it would have been possible."

Weigand said that all men had doubts like that.

"Is there any way he could have done it?" Beck insisted. "Any device? Could I have been wrong?"

"I don't see any way," Bill Weigand said. "I think you're worrying yourself needlessly, Mr. Beck."

"But have you tested it?" Beck insisted. "Tested it thoroughly?"

"As thoroughly as was possible," Weigand told him. They had not been able to lay hands on Elliot himself, which had been an evident handicap. But on the story that Mr. Beck himself told, it was impossible to see any way that Elliot could have had time—granting he had had everything else needful—to kill Ann Lawrence.

"I hope you're right," Beck said. "I devoutly hope you're right, Lieutenant. But I'll be frank—it worries me. It still worries me. Because it was I, in the last analysis, who made you believe in his innocence. And if you had thought him guilty you'd have—laid hands on him. Before he could kill these others. I am convinced of that, Lieutenant."

It was possible, Weigand agreed. If they had devoted all their efforts to running down Elliot, if they had been convinced of his guilt instead of three-fourths convinced of his innocence—they might have caught him. But there was no use thinking what they might have done.

"I know," Beck said. "I try not to. But it keeps coming back. Perhaps I was wrong, somehow."

His insistence, while understandable, began to seem excessive.

"You haven't remembered anything, have you, Mr. Beck?" Weigand wanted to know. "Anything that—leaves a loophole? Anything you didn't tell me earlier?"

"No," Beck said. "Nothing, Lieutenant. It is only—only a feeling. There isn't any logic in it. It is a feeling, based on a—a fear. And on knowledge of human fallibility." He smiled. "Including my own," he said. "Most certainly including my own."

Then, Weigand said, he would advise Mr. Beck to forget it. It was partly to learn that, he said, that he had bothered Mr. Beck again. Because, of course, they had to give thought to the possibility that the case had ended in Elliot's suicide. They had to be as sure as they humanly could be that Elliot was a victim, not a murderer who had found his own way out.

"To the best of my belief," Mr. Beck said, "to the best of my knowledge and belief—isn't that how it's said?—Elliot couldn't have killed Ann Lawrence. Unless he was more devious than I can imagine."

"Or than I can," Weigand said, shortly. He wondered, fleetingly, if all this qualification meant, really, that Beck was trying to hedge; that if the police insisted, he would become less certain of the alibi he had given Elliot. The thought passed over Weigand's mind, leaving only the faintest of traces. It was not that, Weigand thought; it was a case of a worrying, over-conscientious mind.

It had taken only a few minutes to get from Beck the fact that Beck had nothing but his word to support his statement that he had been alone in his study working all the previous afternoon and evening. Weigand documented this in a pigeonhole, in which it presumably would languish. It went with the information, gathered earlier, that Franklin Martinelli had been sent on an errand after lunch and had not gone back to the shipping room; that Cleo Harper had left her office early, pleading a bad headache; that Alfred Pierson could have been out and about. The last fact did not go in a pigeonhole. It went in Pierson's record; it was turned over to the District Attorney's office, for action.

Weigand had left after that, he told Dorian, and the motherly woman who helped her husband take care of Mr. Beck had been in the foyer to bow and smile—and not this time to peer after him.

"Why do you suppose she did before?" Dorian wanted to know. Bill shrugged. He supposed, merely curiosity. Lieutenants of detectives, Homicide Bureau, might come a dime a dozen to people of Dorian's experience, and still be a novelty to a motherly, elderly servant.

"They're *not* a dime a dozen to me," Dorian said. "They're—oh, ever so much more valuable. A dime *apiece,* at least."

That, Bill said, was fine of her. That made him feel expensive, and prized. She shied a pillow from the corner of the sofa at him and he carried it back, with the announced intention of making her eat it. There was a short scuffle, of which Dorian's eating the pillow was not the result.

"Well," Dorian said, somewhat later, "how we do carry on. After all this time, too."

Bill smiled at her and lighted a cigarette and gave it to her, and lighted a cigarette for himself.

"And the world," Dorian said. "All full of a number of maladjustments and—things."

She reached out and turned on the radio, just in time to be told by the radio that "this concludes our fifteen minutes of news." It was then, the radio added richly, exactly eight twenty-nine and three quarters. The radio changed voice.

"And now," it said, "as always on Thursday evening over this station, and on affiliated stations from coast to coast, the commentator
with a message—for all of us—Dan Beck. Mr. Beck."

"Good evening, friends," Mr. Beck said. "To all of you—on farms
and in cities, on quiet front porches, in general stores at crossroads, in
modern apartments, in places still gripped by the cold of winter and in
those fortunate communities where spring has already come—my
friends and fellow Americans—to all of you the *best* of evenings. And
now I will tell you what the news of this day has meant to me—"

There was a lusciousness about it; a familiar, poised lusciousness.
There was nothing staccato about Dan Beck; there was not anything
obviously expert. Only a person trained to notice would have noticed
that his breathing through the long opening sentence—a sentence
which varied little from night to night, and then only in deference to the
season—was controlled with almost superhuman perfection. Only an
expert in such matters would have assayed at its correct value the practiced modesty of that last line; the inflection which made of the "me" a
simple, utterly unpretentious individual who, but for the most absurd of
accidents, would have been sitting on one of those very same front
porches of which he spoke so soothingly. A counselor and friend was
Dan Beck, and he would rather have been sitting beside you on the
front porch than doing anything else the world—the world with which
he was, by the same accident, so uniquely familiar—had to offer.

"The same old Beck," Bill Weigand said. "The same ineffable Beck.
What price Pam's theory now, Dorian?"

It was, oddly, a relief to hear Beck; to know, from the first syllable
of his voice, that he was the same Beck he had always been, on each
Tuesday and Wednesday and Thursday of the year; the Beck to whom
even Bill Weigand, before only casually interested and never, in spite
of the commissioner, alarmed, had more or less by chance listened to a
dozen times in perhaps as many weeks. Relaxed, partly by the final
confidence Beck's voice gave him in Beck's evidently unstolen condition, Bill Weigand sank back in his own corner of the broad sofa. Dan
Beck vibrated on.

It puzzled Bill for a moment to realize that Dorian, the cocktail to which she had reverted forgotten, was listening with an odd intentness to Dan Beck. Bill looked at her and started to speak, but she held up a hand to silence him. After an instant, Bill began to listen too.

Because, obscurely, it was Beck and still it wasn't Beck. The practiced voice went on, smoothly, the practiced inflection fell on the indicated words. Nothing tangible was different. But, after a moment, Bill Weigand understood why Dorian was listening with such odd intentness to a voice which usually lulled her into drowsiness. About Dan Beck that evening there was something uneasy, unsure. It was not, after all, the same old Beck. Listening, your attention wandered and you brought it back almost by force; listening, it seemed somehow as if the speaker's attention also wandered. The words were there, and the voice was there, but something under them was missing.

The lack, if they were not imagining it—and when Dorian lifted inquiring eyebrows for assurance, Bill nodded his agreement—was beyond definition. Sometimes it was more evident than at other times, as Dan Beck went on through his fifteen minutes of divulging what the news of that day had meant to him. Sometimes he was surely the old Beck; sometimes he was as surely a new, uncertain Beck. He was, for example, the old Beck at the end, as he had been at the beginning. There was a time halfway between when he was the old Beck, too—the old Beck rolling along. But there were other moments when—well, when it was hard to tell.

He finished, with the peroration which was almost a signature, and Dorian switched off the radio. She looked at her husband and waited. They did not need to say anything, and for a minute—a long minute—neither did. Then Dorian spoke.

"What is it, Bill?" she said. "I know what Pam heard. What was it?"

Bill Weigand shook his head slowly. He was abstracted; deep in thought. And now it was as if the uneasiness which he had heard—or thought he heard—in Dan Beck's voice had been transmitted to his own mind.

"I don't know," he said, finally. "I don't know, Dorian. It's Beck—and it isn't Beck. And that gets us nowhere. I'd swear the voice is Beck's voice, and I heard it only this afternoon—heard it without anything mechanical to get in the way, without any chance of—of any kind of deception. But there's something wrong with it."

"Would we have heard it if Pam hadn't?" Dorian asked, a small doubt in her voice. "Are we merely hearing something we subconsciously expected to hear, Bill? Are we making up—something?"

It was a possibility that they were. The human mind is not reliable. Bill gave her that as a possibility, but he still did not feel satisfied.

"I don't either," Dorian said, answering what he had not said. "I think there's—something. Of course maybe he just had a bad night."

"And," Bill reminded her, "a bad last night. It could be, of course, that he's distracted and upset by what's happened."

But Bill could not quite convince himself that that was it. Dan Beck was a professional—that, whatever else now was lacking, was clear in every intonation of his voice. Professionals are hard to unsettle; professionalism is a hard surface to walk on in the most treacherous quagmire of emotion. Once on the path, professionalism would be an assured guide.

"It's almost as if he didn't believe what he was saying," Dorian said. "Could that be it?"

Bill stood up and began to walk slowly up and down the room. He thought of this suggestion and shook his head over it.

"He said about what he always says," he told her. "The same old—guff. Or dangerous twaddle, or whatever it is. Why would he believe it last week and not tonight? If that's true—well, that would be stronger than almost any other explanation. I'd as soon think he was—stolen."

"Which isn't—" Dorian began. Then he stopped, suddenly. "Bill!" she said. "Could Pam be right, after all?" There was hurried anxiety in her voice. "Because if she is—" Dorian said, and sat looking at Bill, wide-eyed.

"She can't be," Bill told her, but his voice, too, was hurried. "It's—preposterous. And, anyway, Jerry will keep her out—out of anything."

"All of us together never kept her out of anything," Dorian told him. "You know that, Bill. She—when she forgets to be afraid, you can't keep her out of anything. Not even Jerry can. Bill—I'm worried."

Bill stopped walking and looked at her.

"All right, kid," he said. "I'm worried, too. I'm worried without knowing why. I'm worried against everything that makes sense. Because, damn it all, that *was* Beck on the radio. It—had to be Beck. Nobody could get away with anything else."

Dorian looked at him for rather a long time.

"Couldn't they, Bill?" she said. "Are you sure they couldn't?"

Bill wasn't sure. Looking at each other, they both knew it. They knew, too, that they weren't going out, late and lazily as they had planned to do, a day's work done, to dinner at Charles'. Or perhaps at the Lafayette, for a change? Because the day's work wasn't done. Bill argued, briefly, and without too much conviction, that Dorian at least was going out quietly and eat a lazy dinner somewhere, even by herself, and after it come home safely to the apartment. Dorian's answer was to change her housecoat for a gray silk suit and a hat that dipped low over her right eye.

They went first to Dan Beck's apartment at the Hotel André, and Bill wondered what on earth they were going to say to Beck, short of asking him point-blank why he didn't sound as he should on the radio. He needn't, Bill found out, have worried. Dan Beck was not at his apartment. He had not returned from the studio. He was not expected back until late.

It was possible, of course, that he imagined it. But the motherly, elderly woman did not seem motherly when she told them this. There was an odd note in her voice. She spoke as if, suddenly, a need to be polite and ingratiating had ended. She was almost curt, as if it did not matter any more how she sounded to Detective Lieutenant William Weigand of the Homicide Squad. Lieutenant Weigand had an odd, and further unsettling, conviction as they left that the motherly little woman was laughing at them, and laughing with something very like malevolence.

· 14 ·

Thursday, 10:59 p.m. to 11:31 p.m.

From where he sat at the head of a long table, set with individual microphones instead of plates, Jerry North could look across a long room and up at a kind of mezzanine at the other end. The mezzanine was fronted with heavy glass, so that parties on conducted tours could walk into it and look down on broadcasting and walk out again without adding their sounds to the captive sounds below. But now there was no touring party; there was Pamela North, who smiled and nodded reassurance to Jerry, and there were two men from Jerry's office and several other people who were friends of the several authors on the Book Forum. Thus, Jerry thought, proving that after all authors had friends.

Behind Jerry's back, in the control room—walled by glass from the studio, like the mezzanine opposite it—the sound engineer lifted his hand. The announcer, standing at his own microphone—and within Jerry's range of vision—stiffened just perceptibly. The hand went down quickly and the announcer spoke.

"This evening, as every Thursday evening at this hour," the announcer said, bending close to the microphone as if about to caress it and, seemingly, whispering in its ear—"This evening we bring you another session of the Book Forum—a half hour during which authors, critics and publishers meet, informally, to take you with them into the world of books."

The announcer's voice acquired a special hush, as of reverence, when he spoke of the world of books. Mr. North felt slightly ill, but remembered that hundreds of thousands of people probably were listening, and that some of them—perhaps a good many of them—might buy Humphrey Creighton's *Beyond Yesterday*. Jerry North looked at Creighton, perspiring briskly at the other end of the table. Not if they saw Creighton, Jerry thought morosely. But fortunately they couldn't; possibly the war's only benefit was that it had postponed television.

"—Humphrey Creighton," the announcer continued, "author of that vivid novel"—the announcer hesitated and stared with apparent disbelief at his notes—*Beyond Yesterday*. The announcer looked anxiously at Mr. North, who nodded. The announcer looked relieved, but still puzzled. Probably, Jerry North thought, they should have changed the title after all. It was one of those books they might have called anything. "And last but—"

Jerry waited, with a kind of fixed hopelessness. Sure enough—

"—not least, Mr. Gerald North, the proud publisher of Mr. Creighton's best-selling book, and tonight's guest host on the Book Forum, brought to you as a public service feature by the Transcontinental Broadcasting System over its member and affiliated stations from coast to coast. Mr. North!"

Jerry jumped slightly and the announcer, turning from the microphone, pointed a commanding finger at him. Jerry looked down at his introductory speech—the speech which he had carefully prepared the day before to start the Book Forum on its thoughtful, but nevertheless entirely impromptu, way and began to read. He was a little surprised, as he had been each time fate brought him before a studio microphone, to discover just how unfrightening it was. Called upon to speak before an audience, Mr. North clutched at the nearest fixed object and trembled violently, at least until he was well under way. Confronted by a microphone, before which so many insisted that they became blue with mike-fright, Mr. North was calm and undisturbed. Probably, he had sometimes thought, this was because he did not really believe in radio—not deeply and personally. He simply did not believe that, when he talked into an object which—on this occasion particularly—looked like a cage for a very small bird, anything further happened. He did not believe that his voice went mysteriously out into an alien world and was heard by thousands of alien people, ten of whom, made visible, would have constituted an audience and a menace. He knew that his voice was going out and that it could, if they chose, be heard by thousands. He merely did not believe it.

He talked easily, finished the page, and read the paragraph on the page following which threw the ball—rather neatly Mr. North thought—at Humphrey Creighton. Mr. Creighton saw it coming and a wild look came into his eyes. Mr. Creighton, it appeared, was one of those who really believed in radio. Mr. Creighton made a small, stifled sound, cleared his throat—which made the announcer, whose throat never needed clearing—glare at him—and started over. Mr. North thought that Mr. Creighton looked, and sounded, very funny and looked up toward the mezzanine which held Mrs. North to see if she shared his amusement. She was listening, presumably, to the broadcast, picked up on the studio receiver. Mr. North looked casually, then he looked intently. Then his look became fixed, and somewhat glassy. Because Mrs. North was not there. Mrs. North had quietly left the world of books. She had gone out into another world—and it came over Mr. North, clammily, that he had never actually persuaded her to promise that she would stay in the glass-enclosed coop in which he had left her. If she had promised, she would have stayed. But somehow she had avoided promising.

Mr. North half-started up. Everybody glared at him: the announcer, Mr. Creighton, two other authors of rival firms—brought in to show that this was really the world of books, in which commercial rivalry was unheard of—and one rather tired-looking reviewer, who had thought Mr. Creighton's *Beyond Yesterday* a colossal bore in the first place and was trying to recall why he had consented to appear on the Book Forum. (Not that it wasn't reasonably good advertising, of course.) All of these faces, which were extremely varied faces under usual circumstances, confronted Mr. North with a single expression of shocked horror. "Don't you know," the faces said, in pantomime, "don't you know we're ON THE AIR?"

Mr. North sat down again, but his thoughts were elsewhere. It wasn't funny any more. It was agonizing. Desperately he wanted to be out of there; frantically he twisted to look at the clock behind him. Eleven-four. Twenty-six minutes to go. And in twenty-six minutes Mrs. North could do anything. There was no trouble in the world that Mrs. North, on the trail of a murderer, couldn't get into in twenty-six minutes.

In his office, Bill Weigand cradled the telephone. Dorian, sitting opposite, had no need to ask. Mr. Beck still had not come in. Bill shook his head and took up the telephone and spun the dial. He waited; he waited longer than there was any sense in waiting. He cradled the receiver.

"Still," he said. "Where the hell are they?"

"Try to remember," Dorian urged. "You don't forget things."

That was fine to say. It wasn't true. He had forgotten something that Jerry North had said as he left the North apartment early in the evening. Or was it the day before, or the day before that? Something that had seemed incompatible with something else—something about Jerry's keeping Pam locked up, which didn't fit because this was the night that Jerry was going to do something he thought ridiculous and had mentioned amusingly. But Bill couldn't, for the life of him, remember what it was.

And now he wanted desperately to remember, because he wanted to be sure that Pam North was locked up, and not pursuing that theory of hers. Because, driving down to the Homicide Squad headquarters from the fruitless visit to the Hotel André, Bill had suddenly seen another solution of the whole affair—seen it sharply and frighteningly, and with a disturbing conviction of its truth. If it was true—if it really fitted as it seemed to fit—Pam North was walking, in that gay way of hers, into a danger of which she had, even now, no real understanding whatever.

Pamela North, pleased that she had not promised anything, but hopeful that Jerry would be too absorbed to look for her in the mezzanine booth, went quietly out and down some carpeted stairs. There would, at any rate, be no harm in making a telephone call. She asked a uniformed attendant if there were public telephones and was directed across a wide lobby, off which corridors ran in several directions. The corridors were dimly lighted and there were red spots along them. Pam found a telephone booth—fitted with a very special kind of telephone, evidently the New York Telephone Company's fraternal tribute to the Transcontinental Broadcasting System—and dialed the Hotel André. The Hotel André would ring Mr. Beck's apartment, and did.

Mrs. North waited, summoning her resources—and a little wondering what she would say when she got Mr. Beck. A male voice answered, with a formal tenderness.

"Is—is Mr. Beck at home?" Pam said.

Mr. Beck was not at home, the voice said. It was not certain when Mr. Beck was expected. But any message—?

"No message," Mrs. North said.

She came out of the booth. So after all she was not going to break the promise she hadn't made; she was really going to sit in the glass coop and be a citizen of the world of books. She made way abstractedly for a small, broad man who was hurrying down one of the corridors—and looking, Pam thought suddenly, like the rabbit in the Tenniel illustrations of *Alice in Wonderland*. He went down the corridor and, half way down it, disappeared under one of the red spots. The red spots, apparently, marked doors. Pam started back toward the information desk.

A small boy in an absurd uniform, with a pill-box cap, was standing in the middle of the lobby staring after the man who looked like the Tenniel rabbit. His eyes were round and excited. When Mrs. North came up to him he had to share the experience.

"Gee, lady," he said. "You know who that was?"

"No," Pam said. Since this seemed unduly final, she smiled to complete it.

"Gee," the boy said. "That was Mr. Beck. You know—Mr. Dan Beck? My old man says he's the greatest—"

But Pam was not listening. She stopped suddenly. She stared down the corridor. Mr. Beck must have gone in under the third red light which marked a door of some kind. Perhaps she could find him if she hurried.

She hurried. The little boy stared after her.

"Gee, lady," he said, in an awed whisper. "You hadn't ought to bother Mr. Beck. Not *now.*"

There was nothing to do but to wait and keep trying. Dorian thought they might as well wait at home, but she realized her husband's uneasy impatience, and did not suggest it. But she did, idly, snap on a small radio on the window sill, and switch from the police calls on which it was set to the broadcast band, and turn the dial at random.

"—and how do you answer that, Mr. North?" the radio inquired, conversationally.

"I don't know that it needs answering," Jerry North's voice said. "I'm not sure it doesn't, essentially, answer itself."

Jerry North did not sound as if he cared much. He sounded as if he were thinking of something else.

Bill Weigand was on his feet by then, and Dorian's slim fingers had twitched off the radio. Bill remembered all of it, and cursed himself for forgetting. This was the night of Jerry's broadcast. Which meant that he and Pam would be at the Transcontinental's towering building on Madison Avenue. Bill moved, and Dorian, not asking needless questions, moved with him. But in the car she had reassurance.

"Anyway," she said, "Beck won't be there, if that's what you're afraid of, Bill. He's through for the night. Don't you remember—we heard him."

"He does a repeat later," Bill said. He opened the Buick up, with its red lights flashing a warning. He let the siren growl gently at intersections. "For the West Coast." He whirled the car recklessly east through Twenty-eighth. "If he gets the chance—" Weigand went around a bus and Dorian decided she had better not talk, because if he was going to drive like this he needed all his concentration. She wondered why Beck might not get a chance to do his repeat broadcast, but decided that there would be a better time to bring it up. If they lived.

● ● ●

Pamela North went through a door under the red sign, which said: "Keep Out. Rehearsal." All the red signs said that, but the first room she had entered, timidly, had been empty. Nobody was rehearsing anything, and it was not where Mr. Beck had gone. So now Pam entered with more assurance.

She went down a short corridor and opened another door. She walked into a small studio—much smaller than the one in which Jerry was broadcasting. Mr. Beck was in it, sitting at a small table on which there were two microphones. The floor was of some substance which deadened sound, but Pam must have made some noise because Dan Beck looked up. He looked up with irritation.

"Well?" he said. He had a wonderful voice, but it was not suave as Pam had expected. "Well, what do you want? I got the others out of here because I wanted to be by myself. Just"—he looked up at the clock—"just eighteen minutes by myself. Before I go on. Now what do you want?"

"I—" Pam began.

"Anyway," he said. "This is the standby studio. You ought to know that, if you work here. You ought to know nobody's allowed in the standby studio except the announcer and the engineer. Even I'm not allowed in here, under the rules."

That made the rules tremendous. Even rules which should have barred Dan Beck from somewhere, and had understandably failed to bar him, were tremendous rules. Even trying to bar Dan Beck from anywhere was a tremendous thing. That, somehow, was all in the voice.

"Well," Pam said, "where are they?"

"I told them to get out," Beck said, succinctly. "Now I'm telling you to get out. My God, girl—don't you know who I am?"

"Yes," Pam told him. "You're Mr. Beck. Or you say you're Mr. Beck."

"Then you ought to know—" Beck began. He stopped suddenly and looked at Mrs. North. "What do you mean by that?" he demanded. The voice was anything but suave now. "Who says I'm not Beck?"

"Nobody," Pam said. "Everybody says you *are* Mr. Beck. You say you are—everybody says you are. Are you?"

She had not meant it to go this way at all. She had meant it to be subtle, indirect.

"Look," Dan Beck said. "Are you crazy? Do you work here?"

"No," Pam said. "I don't work here. I came to see you. I saw you going down the corridor like a Tenniel ra—I saw you going down the corridor. And I wanted to see you so I just came."

Beck stood up. He was not really an imposing figure, but still he was formidable. It suddenly occurred to Pam North that he was very formidable, with the two of them alone in the small studio.

"But if I'm disturbing you, I can come back," she said, and began to back toward the door. "I'll come back later. Some time. With Bill and—"

Dan Beck moved fast for a man with short legs. He moved, it seemed to Pam, with a kind of scuttling motion. He was around the table and beside her. He put a hand on her arm. It was a strong hand.

"Wait a minute," he said. "Wait just a minute. Who are *you?*"

"Mrs. North," Pam said. "Pamela North. I'll go now."

She moved, but the hand tightened.

"Who's this—Bill?" he said.

Pam hesitated a moment. But it would be better if he knew that she was a friend of Bill's.

"Lieutenant Weigand," she said. "He's a—"

"Yes," Beck said. "I know who he is. And he sent you here. To ask if I'm really Beck?"

"No." Pam said. "That is—yes. He's—he's right outside."

Beck pushed her out of the way and was at the door. He turned a catch which took the place of a key.

"We'll keep him outside," he said. He turned and looked at Mrs. North. "All right," he said. "What do you want, Mrs. North? I'm Dan Beck. What do you want?"

He did not look like a rabbit any longer. Certainly he did not sound like a rabbit. Pam tried to keep her voice light and steady.

"Nothing," she said. "Nothing at all—if you're really Mr. Beck. And not just a—just a voice."

She was not, after she had said it, clear why she had said it just that way. Perhaps, she eventually thought, she had had, subconsciously, a glimpse of the way things really were; perhaps her subconscious had chosen the words for her. But, then, she was not prepared for the effect upon Dan Beck of what she said.

He stood for a moment staring at her, measuringly. His eyes seemed to grow smaller and his brows came together; although for a moment he did not move, there was still a kind of thrusting forward of his short, compact body. Without actually moving his feet, he came nearer. He came nearer threateningly.

"So," he said. "You did guess. Or was it Weigand who guessed?"

"I don't know," she said. "Both of us. It was—it was obvious, Mr. Beck. If you want me to go on calling you Beck?"

He looked a little puzzled.

"What would you call me?" he said. "I'm Beck—I'm still Beck. What would you call me?"

It was hard to understand what he was getting at. He seemed to make an admission; now he seemed to withdraw it. But Pam decided she must not show that she did not understand.

"Jones," she said. "Smith. Anything." She met his threat steadily. "Because, whatever you say, you're not Beck. Not really. I knew that last night. I ought to have known it all the time, probably."

The last was bluff. She could think of no reason she should have known it all the time.

"All the time?" he repeated. "But—but Elliot was alive until yesterday. And I didn't run out until yesterday. We kept ahead, you know."

He was talking less to her than to himself, Pam North thought. She was authentically puzzling him; somehow they were talking at cross-purposes. But there was no lessening of the menace he presented—his face set hard with the brows drawn together, his body a little forward on his short legs. He was grotesque, as he stood there, Pam thought. Grotesque—and dangerous. And she was alone with him in a room with a locked door behind her.

She tried to speak lightly, and it was harder, because now she realized fully her danger. Because whatever was obscure and unclear in the situation, the situation still was dangerous. Pam began to move backward, slowly, toward the door which had let her in.

"You couldn't have known before," Beck went on, explaining it to himself. "Not from the broadcast. Because we kept ahead, you see. As a margin of safety. In case Elliot was ill some day, or couldn't—" He broke off and looked at her and saw her backing away. Then he smiled. It was an ordinary smile, doing ordinary things to lips and cheeks. And it was horrible. It was horrible because it was ordinary. It was horrible because Beck was a squat little man, almost grotesque, and smiling— and moving toward her to kill her. Because that's what he's doing, Pam thought. That's what he's doing!

"But you know now, don't you, Mrs. North," he said, and he gave up any pretense that he was not moving toward her. "And they sent you to—what would you say, Mrs. North? Probably you know the words too, Mrs. North. Like Elliot. Elliot knew a lot of words, Mrs. North. He died just the same."

"I don't know!" Pam said, and now her voice went up a little. "I don't know what you're talking about. I just thought you weren't Mr. Beck— that you were only pretending to be Mr. Beck. That somebody had kidnapped the real Mr. Beck. But I think you are Mr. Beck." She was almost against the door, now. Her fingers were reaching up behind her for the catch on the door. "Truly, I think you're Mr. Beck," she insisted.

He did not answer. Instead he lunged toward her, his hands up and the fingers spread out. They came at the level of her throat. Pam North screamed. More quickly than she would have thought she ever could, she leaped to the side. She half-jumped, half-ran, past Dan Beck. One of his hands caught the shoulder of her dress and the silk tore and she went on, the dress falling from her shoulder.

But there was no place to go. He was between her and the door. Then at the other end of the room, at one side, she saw another door and ran toward it. Behind her she heard Beck laughing. He was laughing and running and still trying to talk.

"You thought you'd fool me, didn't you?" he said. But the words did not come evenly, as in a sentence. They came jerkily. "Thought I wouldn't know you knew about Johnny. Cute little Johnny, with all the pretty words . . . "

Pam reached the door and clutched it open. It opened on a passage which ended in a blank wall. But at her right was another door. There was no place else to go, so she went through the door, although she knew it was leading her into a trap. It led her into the control room. There was a slanting table with a chair behind it, and another chair, and on the walls some sort of electrical equipment in cupboards. There was no other door.

The door had opened inward and Pam tried to shut it behind her. But Beck had reached it, and he was heavier, and the door opened against her easily. It seemed terrifyingly easy for Beck to force the door.

Before he could reach out and grab her, Pam leaped back into the control room. She hit the chair and it clattered, dully, on the floor. She pressed back against the slanting table, covered with switch keys, which it had fronted. Pam put her hands behind her against the table and faced Dan Beck. Beck stopped hurrying and came in and closed the door. He was smiling again—the same horribly ordinary smile.

"But you didn't fool me, Mrs. North," he said. "So I can't let you go, can I? Because you'd try to stop me, Mrs. North—you'd try to end all I'm doing. I know you would, Mrs. North—like the others. Like Ann. She didn't know it was so important—so much more important than she was. It's more important than you are, Mrs. North."

He had stopped and that was more frightening than anything else. Because it meant he was sure. So sure that he no longer had to hurry.

It was as if he had read her mind.

"Twelve minutes still, you know," he said, as if he were making conversation. "Then, of course, I have to go on again. I have to talk to the people." He stopped and looked at her. "*My* people, you know," he said. "Not Elliot's people. *My* people. I was the one who talked to them. Elliot only helped. The ideas were all my ideas."

Pam got it then, although still she did not fully understand it.

"But Elliot wrote what you said," she told Beck. "It wasn't really you who said those things. You were just—just an actor. All the time you were just an actor."

A strange grimace came over his face.

"That's what Ann said," he told Pam. "Just before she died Ann said that—that I was just an actor. I hadn't been sure what I would do to her before. Not really sure. It wasn't important either way, but I'm not sure I would have killed her if she hadn't said that. It—it annoyed me, I'm afraid."

It came over Pam North then that Dan Beck was mad. Not mad in an ordinary sense. Not mad in his logic. Only mad in his premises. She started to scream, but almost before Beck laughed she realized the futility of a scream.

"Perfectly soundproof, Mrs. North," Beck told her, and now he was smiling again in quite an ordinary fashion, as he moved forward to kill her. "Control rooms have to be, you know. They're made to be. The walls will keep sound in—any sound."

Keep sound in, Pam thought. Keep sound in. But it wasn't that—really. It was all to let sound out. It was all a cunning, skillful way of trapping sound and then letting it out. Letting it go everywhere. And the control room was where you let it out. You—

Faster than she thought, Pam moved. Her fingers groped behind her. There had been a switch larger than the others somewhere on the panel. Perhaps it was the switch which let sound out. Trying not to move her body, groping desperately, she sought the large switch with her fingers. Fumbling frantically, she felt other switches move under her fingers. Maybe that was wrong; maybe it was all wrong and hopeless. But nothing could be more hopeless for anything she did now than what she had already done had made it. She found the large switch and it moved under her fingers.

Now she could scream. She screamed. Beck laughed.

"Very effective, Mrs. North," he said. "Very effective. And nobody can hear you. I can hear you, but it doesn't mean anything to me. Ann screamed too, you know—Ann started to scream. It's too bad we aren't on the air, Mrs. North, so that everybody could hear such an effective scream. If we were on the air, now—and out at the microphone. Instead of in here where nobody can hear you."

That was it, Pam realized, and knew what she had to do. The sounds were let loose from the control room. But they had to begin in the studio. She had to—

In one movement she stooped, grabbed the light chair and threw it. She was stronger than she had dreamed she could be. But she was not strong enough, and not quick enough. Beck's hands flew up in front of his face and the chair banged into them. He held it there. But he was surprised and staggered slightly and now Pam North moved as she had never moved before.

In master control the sound engineer saw the light flash from the standby studio. It was unexpected; it meant that somewhere in the world all hell had broken loose. It meant that, without warning, a news bulletin had come through of such vital importance that no other program mattered. His hand reached automatically for a switch and threw it. But instead of a bulletin there was silence from the standby studio. The engineer's fingers moved another switch. In Studio 3C a panel on the wall lighted up dimly. It said: "On the Air."

In Studio 3A, Humphrey Creighton opened his mouth. He was now about to tell how it occurred to him to write *Beyond Yesterday*. He had his extemporaneous remarks on this subject so well in mind that he hardly needed to look at the paper on which he had them well typed. In the guest booth of Studio 3A Mr. Creighton's agent leaned forward with a slight enhancement of interest, approaching a receptive ear to the radio receiver. He hoped old Humpty-Dumpty would knock them dead with this one. Old Humpty-Dumpty hadn't been so damned hot so far, but you couldn't tell.

Pam North got to the door before Dan Beck could let go the chair. She was almost through it before he grabbed for her and got the collar of her dress. It parted. Thank God, Pam thought, running, they make them out of old movie films or something—thank God they come apart. She went out into the studio, and as she ran, panting, she began to scream again.

• • •

"I was sitting under a tree at my little place in the country," Humphrey Creighton said, with the casual air of a man who also has big places in the country, and can sit under half a dozen trees when he likes. "When suddenly—"

Suddenly was the word for it.

"Help," Pam North's voice said, rising in crescendo. "Help. Help everybody. Dan Beck's trying to kill me. Dan Beck's trying to kill me—just like he killed the others. Help. Oh—help!"

It was afterwards estimated that at least half a million book lovers, from coast to coast, had been about to hear about Mr. Creighton under the tree. There was a little group of them in an apartment in Kansas City; they met every Thursday evening to loiter in the world of books. In Memphis, the Book Forum was reaching an even larger group, composed of the ladies of the Forward Club—and four of their husbands—over loud speakers. In Jersey City, there was a small, scattered but devoted audience and Schenectady contributed, on an estimate, more than five hundred. (It was snowing heavily in Schenectady.) Milwaukee, Louisville, Keokuk, Iowa, Wilkes-Barre, New Orleans and St. Paul had each its quota of listeners, and all of them thought something odd must have happened. It was, they agreed in talking it over, a very funny thing for Mr. Creighton to say at just that point. About Mr. Beck, too.

Half a dozen receivers were open in the Transcontinental Building, including one near the reception desk, at which Bill and Dorian Weigand had just stopped. That was why Bill Weigand, with half a dozen attendants following him, was first to reach the standby studio. It was fortunate, as it turned out, that it could always be opened from outside, in case of emergency, by pressing a concealed button. It was fortunate that one of the attendants knew where the button was.

Pam North was on one side of the table, her hands grasping it, leaning forward—and yelling toward the microphone. Dan Beck was in a somewhat similar position on the other side, and he was swearing with a kind of horrible anger in his voice. He had just started to move around the table when the door opened. He whirled to face it and then, without pausing, he charged at Bill Weigand. Nobody ever knew what he had planned to do. What he did was crumple to the floor when Weigand's fist caught him.

Pam still stood behind the table, her tattered dress hanging in strings from her shoulders. She continued, with a kind of terrified, mad insistence, to shout into the microphone.

But the great radio audience was no longer hearing her. The engineer at master control, after some seconds of horrified astonishment, had hurriedly pulled more levers. Probably if he had thought of it, he would have returned the Book Forum to the air. But it was no time for thought. Desperately, the engineer at master control cut in on a band from Los Angeles. It was playing "Oh, What a Beautiful Morning." The engineer in master control sighed in relief and slumped in his chair.

Dorian's arms were around Pam North, who trembled convulsively in them. Dorian was saying, "It's all right, dear, Bill got him," when Jerry North, white-faced, burst into the room. In his excitement, he embraced both Pam and Dorian. Dorian smiled up at him and slipped from his arms. He folded them around Pam very tightly. "It's all right, dear," he said. "It's all right, kid. Bill got him," Jerry paused. "You were wonderful, kid," he said. "And your slip shows." Jerry thought of this for a moment. "At the top," he said. He thought again. "Not that it matters," he assured her.

Pam clung to Jerry. She was shaking in his arms, and crying, and laughing a little.

"He wasn't stolen at all, Jerry," she said. "He wasn't ever stolen. I was all wrong. He was just—just an actor. He didn't even know the words, Jerry. He was just—he was just Elliot's Charlie McCarthy. Isn't that funny, Jerry? And he killed all those people because he was just somebody else's dummy, and so people wouldn't know. Isn't that funny, Jerry?"

Jerry held her very closely. When he spoke his voice was low and quiet.

"No dear," he said. "It isn't very funny, Pam. Not very funny."

• 15 •

FRIDAY, 6:30 P.M. AND THEREAFTER

BILL WEIGAND came late to the Norths and looked tired and there was a kind of hush while Jerry North measured gin and vermouth, three and one. The ice clattered in the mixer; Jerry poured and twisted lemon peel and Bill drank. Bill said something which sounded like "unh!" in a tone of great contentment. The Norths and Dorian looked at him and he smiled faintly and shook his head.

"No," he said. "He didn't come through. He's going to make it hard for us." Bill looked at Pam. "It's too bad," he said, "that you didn't persuade him to confess over the radio, Pam. There was a recorder on, and that would have made things very nice. Very nice indeed."

"Well," Pam said, "I was busy. He was trying to choke me. Or something. In case you didn't notice."

That, Bill Weigand admitted, would help. Efforts to choke people before witnesses were not well thought of by the Police Department. But a confession to the murders of Ann Lawrence, Frances McCalley, Florence Pennock and John Elliot would have been better.

"Neater," Pam agreed. "I can see that. Do you have to have it?"

Bill shrugged. He said he hoped not. He said that, on the whole, he thought not. But it would be, at best, a case of intimations—a case made up of small details, each suggesting one thing; none proving, if the jury chose to be literal, anything. Even now, Bill told them, it would be easier to convict Alfred Pierson. Even now, the case against him was simpler and more direct; more understandable.

"Only," Pam pointed out, "Pierson didn't kill anybody. And Mr. Beck did." She considered this. "Which ought to make a difference," she pointed out.

Bill smiled a little and said it probably would. In the end. The end wasn't yet; there were still the minutiae of evidence to be amassed. But now—and this was the way it usually happened—they knew where to look.

"Like," he said, "at Beck's old scripts, enough of which we've found. All written on Elliot's typewriter. Like the story Beck's servants will tell, once we persuade them it would be a good idea to tell. They've told part of it already—they've told that Elliot used to come every day; that he was always with Beck during the time that Beck was supposed to be writing his broadcasts. And they'll tell, because they know, that Beck did go out the night that Ann was killed, instead of staying innocently at home. They won't be able to tell where he went, but it will give him something to explain—and the jury something to guess about."

"Were they in on it?" Pam wanted to know. "The servants, I mean. The nice old couple?"

The couple was older than it was nice, Weigand said. Were they in on it? That would be hard to say; they wouldn't be charged with anything, if they talked up properly. They were not in on the murder; it was not even certain that they knew about it. They were in on Beck's ramp, to the extent of knowing about it. But that was not criminal. There was, he pointed out, nothing criminal in hiring a ghost. If there were, half the public speakers—

He broke off and corrected himself.

"More than half," he said. "There's no law against it."

He paused again, thinking it over. He said that that was what made it so odd. There was no law, there was not even custom, against a man having his speeches written. And that was all Beck had done—unless you went below the surface. And that was what it was going to be difficult to make a jury understand. That was all Beck had done, except to kill four people to prevent a fact coming out which, in the case of another man, would be no more than a pinprick to vanity. The fact that Beck—the great Beck—was only a voice.

You could begin to see how it was, Weigand said, when you talked to Beck. Because in a way, when you talked to him, it turned out that Beck was mad.

Pam nodded.

"He's crazy," she said. "It's—it's frightening. I never met one before— a—a leader. If that's what he is. A man trying to be God. And believing it."

A megalomaniac, Bill Weigand said. Probably actually on the border-line—that mystic, blurred line which lay, perhaps, between what was called insanity and what wasn't. A mania shared by most of history's vil-lains, and by not a few of its saints. A mania which became most danger-ous, perhaps, when it distorted a mind which was not essentially a very good mind. Like Hitler's. Like Nero's. Like Dan Beck's. The compar-isons were not absurd. Beck was probably as efficient an agent of retro-gression, and of terrorism, as Hitler. The danger from Beck had remained, so far, chiefly potential. But there was no reason to think that, given the right time and place, he might not have been as devastating as Hitler—as good a figurehead for tyranny. His mind was as good; if any-thing, he was slightly more coherent, a little more plausible. And he had the same delusions. He saw himself as a man on horseback.

"Not, I think solely for what he could make out of it," Bill amplified. "It isn't as simple as that. Unless you broaden the term—make it mean what he could *be* out of it. He isn't insincere, any more than any mad-man is insincere. Probably he would argue—although not very well since he killed Elliot—that he is really heading, or preparing to head, a great movement to make people happy. But the arguments would be merely window-dressing. Because what made his ideas great, to him— what would have made any idea great—was that he represented it. He was what was tremendous. The greatness lay in him. And I suppose he thought of himself—thinks of himself—as somehow sacred. To stand in his way is—oh, I don't know. Standing in the way of Man, or some-thing."

"Did you," Jerry wanted to know, "get all that out of talking with him today?"

Bill Weigand started and then grinned.

"Right," he said. "It's pure interpretation, based partly on what has to be true. Because he admitted to Pam that he murdered Ann Lawrence, and that was why he murdered her. There wasn't any other reason." Bill turned to Pam. "Incidentally, Pam," he said, "you'll have to testify to that. It will be admissible. And you'll have to stand a lot of cross-examination and—and slurs."

"All right," Pam said, equably. "I don't think people ought to kill people." She thought this over. "I never did," she added. "And you're right about the way Beck feels about things, Bill. You make it very clear."

Or, Bill qualified, very turgid. But that, or enough of that to go on with, was what the jury would have to understand. Because once they understood that, the rest would be simple. They would still have to use their imaginations, but they would have something for imagination to stand on. They would have to make the assumptions which followed logically—the assumptions to which the State would point.

Ann Lawrence had been telling Elliot that he had to give something up. They could prove that from Mrs. Pennock's statements, which were part of an informal record—admissible, they could hope, on the testimony of members of the police force who had heard her make them. What the jury would have to believe was that Ann was telling Elliot he had to give up writing for Beck. The State could suggest—would suggest—the reasons she must have had. She thought the work Elliot was doing, cynically, was a dangerous and anti-social kind of work. They could prove without much trouble that she had strong views about things like that. She thought, the State would further suggest, that Elliot ought to be doing his own work—that, even if not a "wrong" thing, writing all Beck's speeches for him—writing for Beck everything attributed to Beck—was an unwise thing for Elliot to do. Unwise from the point of view of his own future. The State would suggest that Elliot had come up against a choice between Ann—who could give him not only love but the money and more than the money he made from

Beck—and Beck himself. Fighting for Elliot, Ann probably threatened to tell what she knew of the Elliot-Beck collaboration, exposing Beck.

"Which," Weigand said, "would have ruined Beck if it had been believed. Because Beck, to his followers, wasn't just a man who said things on the radio. He was the Great Man. And he couldn't be just part of a great man—just the voice of a great man. Which was what he really was. Elliot, and the scripts we have show it, was more than a ghost. Elliot was the brains of the whole affair. Probably that knowledge, as much as the money, kept him at it. Elliot had power of his own—and loved it. That's why, even when he began to suspect Beck, he didn't come to us, but tried to work it out on his own. He wouldn't stand for murder, and that in the end killed him. But he would stand for a good deal to keep the Elliot-Beck game going. It was a game he enjoyed. He wasn't, evidently, very scrupulous."

The night of Ann's murder Elliot, as they would try to reconstruct it for the jury, had listened to the girl and been to a degree swayed. Probably he was easily swayed—and if he was, Beck knew it. Beck was shrewd. Probably the girl's effort to get Elliot away from Beck had been going on for some time, and recently intensifying. After he had left the girl, Elliot had called Beck. (This was assumption, but it fitted.) He had indicated that he was thinking of calling the collaboration off. And Beck went at once to Ann's house for a showdown.

He did not, Weigand thought, go with the explicit intention of killing her. Probably he hoped to persuade her. But if he did he failed. And if he failed, his whole megalomaniac world-structure fell apart. Perhaps the last straw was when she threatened to expose him. And then—

"Well," Weigand said, "then she was an obstacle and invited—well, invited the thunderbolt. It fell."

That was the first murder. The second—the murder of Frances McCalley—they could only guess about. (But Beck would not be on trial for it.) During her conversation with Beck, Ann undoubtedly let fall something which revealed that she was not the only one who knew that Beck was really only a voice with Elliot's mind directing it. She let it out that Frances McCalley knew too. And after killing Ann, Beck realized that this knowledge in Frances McCalley's mind would, if she was allowed to reveal it, be a signpost pointing directly at his guilt. So he had to kill her. So he did kill her.

Mrs. Pennock was killed because she had seen Beck come to the house after Elliot had left. But she had also seen Pierson there—Pierson had gone there between Elliot's departure and Beck's arrival. Mrs. Pennock wasn't sure that Ann had not been dead when Beck arrived—she wasn't sure whether Pierson or Beck had killed the girl. (She knew Elliot hadn't; Elliot was a shield set up to protect the other two men to keep them safe for blackmail.) So she had tried to blackmail them both. And there Pierson would come in. Already, twisting this way and that to get out of his own trap, he had hinted that he would admit that Mrs. Pennock had been talking to him when she was killed. He might even, Weigand thought, say that he had heard Mrs. Pennock speak to Beck before Beck killed her.

"And if he does," Bill said, "I think he'll be lying. To save his own skin. Which it won't—he's going up for larceny, whatever he does." He smiled slightly. "Of course," he admitted, "the length of time he goes up for may—but you wouldn't want to hear about that."

"No," Jerry said gravely. "We couldn't bear to."

Elliot probably suspected Beck from the first; presumably he had gone to the considerable trouble of escaping because he wanted to get to Beck and find out. Probably Beck talked Elliot out of the idea—or almost out of the idea—for a time. And he gave Elliot the alibi, which was at the same time an alibi for Beck. It was easy to half-persuade Elliot of Beck's innocence, because Elliot wanted to believe him innocent. He wanted to keep the collaboration going. But that half persuasion became a good deal less than half when Elliot heard of Frances McCalley's death. Here were the two people who were linked, chiefly, through him—and the two who knew he was more than half the great Beck. It must have become pretty clear to Elliot then, and it must have become clearer the more he thought about it. Until—

"Until he went to Beck again," Pam said. "And accused him. And then Beck got violent again. And killed him. Because by that time there wasn't any choice, even if he did lay the golden eggs. Because you have to kill even that kind of a goose if it can—can—What can geese do, anyway?"

"Hiss at you," Dorian said. "Fly at your eyes. I don't know."

This one, Bill pointed out, could send Beck to the electric chair.

Bill Weigand discovered, with faint surprise, that his cocktail glass was full again. He noted, with pleasure, that he had neglected to keep any sort of count. He put the cocktail where it belonged.

"And so, I think, can we," he added. "With a little here and a little there, and the right kind of hints and things." He looked at his empty glass reflectively, holding it not quite out, but so that a really ardent host might think of it as being out. Jerry North obliged.

"I hope we can," he said. "It will please the commissioner very much. The commissioner doesn't like Mr. Beck."

Pam considered this. She thought of Beck on the other side of a very frail table, and of what she had seen in Beck's eyes.

"Do you know," she said, "I think the commissioner and I will get on fine. When we meet, of course. He seems to dislike the most—the most unlikeable people. And Mr. Beck was, wasn't he?"

It was interesting, Bill Weigand thought, to notice that Pam North used the past tense in speaking of Mr. Beck. Now if the jury could be brought to see with Pam North's eyes. He thought this over and sighed. There would have, he decided, to be an easier way than that.